# THE HOUSE OF W

D1284269

# THE HOUSE OF WHACKS
# MATTHEW BRANTON

BLOOMSBURY

First published 1999

This paperback edition published 1999

Copyright © 1999 by Matthew Branton

The moral rights of the author have been asserted

Bloomsbury Publishing Plc, 38 Soho Square, London W1V 5DF

A CIP catalogue record for this book is available from the British Library

Extract from *Alzheimer's Rhetoric* by Wayne Burrows, reprinted by permission of the author. From *Marginalia*, Peterloo Press, 1999.

ISBN 0 7475 4415 8

10 9 8 7 6 5 4 3 2 1

Typeset by Hewer Text Ltd, Edinburgh
Printed in Great Britain by Clays Limited, St Ives plc.

The dying seek out narrative . . .
they connect anecdotes, marshal photographs
and letters, reminisce . . . as if only by
telling their story can they find
their end

— Isadore van Doren,
*Why We Die*


Get in late
Get out early

— screenwriters' maxim

Chicago, 1950

# MCML

*The sun came up over the sea and washed Manhattan clean; pushing inland, tinting pinks and golds into the billowing white clouds above New Jersey smokestacks, sweeping light across Pennsylvania, Ohio, flowing up the seaward side of hills and pooling in the valleys beyond. A platinum tide raced across the prairie, submerging in an hour tracts of tallgrass that would take a truck whole days to transverse, the scenery unrelieved in its monotony all the while. There was no pause in the headlong rush westward: but slip out of the slipstream, in the race across the flatlands, fall behind; and see blur coalesce into detail, watch the horizon quiver out into a flat line; see the glass and towers of a mythical city rise up by the lake, shining back clear and radiant glory to the sky.*

*The sun came up over Chicago, and burst over the crowded city. Through stained glass in Oak Park and paper-mended window in the Loop, into the boudoirs of bankers' wives and the garrets of newsboys, heliographing back from the windows of the Tribune Tower and Hull House orphanage alike, it shed its equal ray everywhere. It found a window, the basement window of a tatty warehouse downtown, where the achromatic glare of a dozen arc-lights pushed it back. Undeterred, it ascended the walls, brimmed over at first floor windows – into an office lined with file cabinets, a storeroom stacked high with stuffed buff envelopes, a post-room with a battered franking machine on a palimpsest-patina'd worktop. It pushed under doors and into corridors, down a ramshackle flight of stairs to the bright room, crept up behind the thousand-watt bulbs and found . . .*

My child,
if we were planning
to harm you, do you think
we'd be lurking here
beside the path
in the very dark-
est part of
the forest?
– Kenneth Patchen, *But Even So*

The rope was too tight around Susan's ankle, but she couldn't do anything about it. Her hands were tied above her head, and the gag in her mouth kept her quieter than a mistress at a funeral. She scowled as best she could down at Alice; but Alice, crouched at Susan's feet, was making a big show of finishing off, drawing her lips back from her teeth as she tugged at the knots.

'Enough,' grunted Earl from behind the camera, making them both look up. He straightened and pushed a hand into the small of his back, exhaled in a *sheesh*; then swiped his forearm across his eyebrows and bent back over the tripod. 'Move it along, huh?'

Alice teetered over to the bench by the loading-bay doors, and selected another length of the silky white rope; then sashayed back, heels clocking on the unfinished cement, before kneeling again beside Susan's free ankle. Susan *mmmf!*'d against the red rubber ball-gag, but Alice didn't look up. Soon it was quiet enough to hear the shutter of the Rolleiflex slide open before snapping back, interspersed with Alice's little grunts of exertion as she wound the rope hard around first Susan's ankle, and then the thick wood of the A-frame.

It was Susan's first shoot, and she didn't know if it needed to be so tight. Maybe Alice was cinching it hard on purpose? Susan wondered what she might have done to offend her. She'd certainly gone out of her way not to: even though Alice was a ditz, she was, for the present, the extent of Susan's world. Susan and Alice had buddied up when they were chorus girls in summer stock, touring Massachusetts last July; Alice had done this last winter, and at the start of October it'd seemed like easy money. Susan'd had six months in New York last winter, waitressing off Broadway and trying out for *Streetcars* and *Seagulls* in Brooklyn back rooms, and it'd been lousy; Alice's plan seemed a much better way to get through to spring season. Susan had figured she'd do maybe a few shoots a month, spend the rest of the time reading parts and getting them off straight. She'd started already; had been on a Ben Hecht jag all week – *The Twentieth Century* and *Design for Living* – but her lousy hostel room was next to the can; the walls were made of Kleenex and spit, and the girl across the hall was an actress too so she was home all damn day, took a leak every half hour like she was trying to drill a hole through the water. Drove Susan crazy. And since she hadn't had so much as a sniff at an audition since summer stock ended, it was all the more important that this stuff for Earl kept on the rails.

So it was unthinkable that Alice – the only person she knew in this city, the one who got her this job, the one who maybe knew the people who could stamp her visa into the future, the one she put so much *work* into last summer, for God's sake – could be mad at her. Susan smiled sweetly down, but Alice bared her teeth back in a grin full of malice, her makeup hard-faced and trashy, her garters cutting deep into the white flesh over her hips as she crouched to do Susan's other ankle. However disconcerting this was for Susan, it was perfect for the camera, as it clicked and whirred – *Good*, Earl grunted, but always a moment too late, too slow with distraction to catch something as it happened, so you were never quite sure whether what you were doing now was good, or whether it was before you moved, or maybe before you moved the time before that. It was all too weird.

But even the basics had been mystifying. Susan had known they

5

were going to be posing for the kind of mail-order stuff that you don't open at the breakfast table, but she'd thought it would be tits and ass – sweater-girl poses, bending over in tight shorts, maybe some art shots with the clothes off and the lights down. When she'd changed into the lingerie Earl had provided and gone down to find a basement with a torture-rack in the middle and a table to one side covered with whips and what the hey, she'd balked, demanded what the hell kind of set-up this was. Earl had barked round his cigar at Alice.

'Ya bring me anudder princess? I toleya, I don' want no princess. *Christ*,' and he'd turned away.

'It's okay, Earl,' Alice droned, her voice at least an octave lower than Susan knew it. 'She's just nervous is all.' *What's with you,* she'd hissed sideways at Susan, who just widened her eyes. *They're just for show,* she went on, pretending to adjust Susan's brassiere strap for her. *Skin don't get past the censor, and no one buys plain underwear shots. That stuff's just to make it more interesting. I'm not really gonna whup yuh, c'mon.*

So Susan had shrugged her shoulders and submitted. Now, Alice cinched the last rope tight and tottered back behind the camera to fetch the blindfold. Susan was glad of it – the gag she could've lived without, but she was starting to get a headache from the lights. She wished Earl would maybe play the radio or something – it was kind of boring, especially when he stopped to fix the light levels – but it was giving her time to think: thoughts that weren't necessarily about strategy, and in time when she needn't feel guilty she wasn't doing something more remunerative than just thinking. She could kind of drift away, the way she used to when she sat for life classes at college. It'd paid her tuition but she'd hated it – bunch of rich girls, daughters of movie actors and atomic scientists and cough syrup tycoons, frowning over sketchpads at Susan toga'd up like Isadora Duncan. Here she was again, but until the actressing panned out, what could she do? She was beautiful. She couldn't go work in an

6

office because she ruined everyone's day. Men, though generally flushed with success by the post-war-effort profusion of women at work – where they could get at them all day – nevertheless shied away from her. It was her beauty: there was no conduit for it between her and them, so it stayed locked up in her face and body, where it represented, to those sorry-looking weekday wolves, only distance, unlikeliness, and failure.

It was even worse with nice guys, the kind she wouldn't have minded some attention from, the ones who didn't go out of their way to bother women like her. Some guy'd come in to work, thinking that maybe, okay, things weren't going too great but at least he could switch off a few hours and get through to another five o'clock, when bang! There she was. And then he had to think about how he was never going to be in her league – and he was right, not even out of charity, buster – but it loused up everything. It ruined his day and it ruined hers. Nice guys thought she was out of their league: it was only jerks who had the blind self-assurance to try it on. The nice guys, the ones she could see trying not to look at her because it'd only make them feel hopeless . . . so office work was out. Nursing was pretty much the same way – she didn't want to think about old women, let alone touch them – and as for teaching school, it seemed she was allergic to chalkdust as well as children. She was drop-dead but she'd dropped out of college; there wasn't much she was going to be allowed to be successful at, so if she didn't find Him that was pretty much it. Her jury was still out on whether it was better to pass this up than persevere, but here she was anyway, wintering in Chicago.

It wasn't going to work, she could tell. It wasn't going to come to any good because it was just like any other first day on a lousy job. There was even a load of dumb jargon to confuse a new girl. Once Earl had been satisfied that she was, in fact, enough of a professional to get on with it, he'd grunted *Okay – Alice, bottom – new girl, you're the top*. Susan had been as bemused by this order as by

7

her first view of the props, but Alice had immediately launched into some dumb story about her armpits – how she had a rash from the cold and couldn't shave them too close – and since the bottom was going to spend most of the session with her wrists tied above her head, she'd have to be the top. Susan deduced from this that *top* was tyer, *bottom* was tied. Earl, complaining that since he'd only borrowed the chainfall and pulleys for a couple of days, and there was no way he'd get another blonde at short notice, appeared not to have any choice but to agree; so Susan had stepped up to the rack. But as she did so, Alice had sotto voce'd *can you believe I only ever get to be understudy*? And Susan'd had to laugh at her cheek – it was obviously easier to be the butch than the bitch, and Susan would've gotten out of it if she'd thought of it.

But if this was going to be typical first day, Susan resolved, then let it. Besides, college had taught her that whoever you buddied up with in Freshers' Week was the one you spent the rest of your time avoiding. So the hell with Alice, she decided. Alice could kiss her pucker. Susan could do this, like most things, better than her. She'd get on the right side of this Earl guy and see where it might lead her. A guy into this sort of shit would have all kinds of connections. She'd dropped her chin forward so that her bangs hung over the blindfold, but now, as Earl muttered *head back,* she offered her throat to the lights, shaking out her hair reflexively before the cords of the ball-gag were tied tourniquet-tight around it. Earl snapped off a few, then Susan heard him crack the camera open, and a slithery whirr as he wound back the film. Alice lit a cigarette, and the scent of the smoke seemed doubly fragrant now Susan was blind: a symphony of mellow richness. She figured that those Madison Avenue guys were wasting their time. She ought to've told them: forget the soft-focus lovers being winsome under the trees; just go to the cinema, tie up the audience, blindfold them, then puff a few passing clouds their way. They'd be gasping. The corset and six-inch heels were strictly optional.

'Okay, let's go. And get that damn smoke out of the frame.'

Earl's accent was thick Bronx – he said his own name like it was something that drains out of a sump. Susan didn't know how he'd wound up in Chicago and she didn't anticipate finding out. When she'd showed up earlier, for example, he'd just grunted when she asked him how he was doing, but she figured that his surliness might have an upside. When Susan had auditioned he just had her strip to her underwear while he smoked up some stinky old cigar – he'd barely even looked at her. Easiest audition she ever did. Best money too.

The camera was snapping again, so she redoubled her efforts, tossing her head back, breathing heavily, straining the sinews in her exposed throat, then letting her head fall forward in exhaustion, drawing hard on the ties. The camera stopped.

'Hey, give it a rest, huh?' barked Earl. 'I don't want that stuff. It's corny. Look like, I dunno like you're tryna stop yourself from laughing.' The whirrs and snaps resumed.

Huh! Corny? This from a guy who drove up that morning in a two-and-a-half-ton candy-pink space rocket, with chrome tits on the front and astro-blasters in back? Sheesh. But suddenly Susan started to feel weird. That mountebanked sexual exertion seemed to have done something to her. Alice was stroking what felt like a cat-o'-nine tails along her legs and – this was the strangest thing – it was kind of cool. It felt so unusual through the nylon, then up, over the tops of her stockings, the raw strips of leather teasing the smooth flesh of her thighs. She had to admit, this wasn't so bad: she guessed the average stenographer didn't get to have someone play with her as part of her job description – she started to let herself go with it. The way she was tied, star-shaped, pushed her chest out to relieve the strain on her shoulders, and maybe it was something to do with being blindfolded, but she was acutely alert to her breasts inside their stiff satin bombshell cups, the pressure at her waist where the corset cinched her, the electric sheen of nylon on her

9

legs, and the coarse tightness at her wrists and ankles from the ropes. It was hot in this basement – the furnace for the whole warehouse was just through the wall – but she didn't need to be able to see to know she'd got chickenflesh all over. She was suddenly aware of the warm air around her, brushing every tiny hair on her body this way and that with eddying thermals, sending a thousand sweet signals to her breasts, now full and firm and straining against the material, and she was thinking, hmmm . . .

When the loading-bay doors crashed open, and the fat growl of a V8 engine swelled the room.

# Il Miglior Fabbro

'. . . Everything you're hearing now
May soon enough be all you know.'
  – Wayne Burrows, *Alzheimer's Rhetoric*

'Chicago is the one city that is America.'
                – Frank Lloyd Wright

## THIS AIN'T KANSAS

*It took a moment for Dorothy to accept that nothing had happened. She'd felt the seatbelt and head-grip disengage, and had opened her eyes as the visor lifted. But when her focus kicked in, she saw that the wall-mounted instruction plaque was still in Flemish: this confirmed it, and she exhaled in irritation. This was Transmit, not Receive. This wasn't Kansas; this was still Belgium.*

*She'd suspected something was wrong from the start. The ReTran method was supposedly transparent to the user, a fact that had figured prominently in ReTran's ultimately successful pitch for the post-Europe franchise. The processes used by all ReTran's competitors involved total short-term sedation, as a precaution against a palette of psycho-traumatic side-effects; ReTran's unique selling proposition had been that the consciousness of travelers remained unaltered during the instantaneous transfer from port-to-port.*

*This had won the game with the card-swiping caste, who didn't have the time or inclination to be put under – sleeping in suits was, for most of them, a boring reminder of the infamous old red-eye between*

Stockholm and Seoul, the last route where intermittent warzones had prevented ultrasonic flight. So ReTran had won, and their slogan – ReTran: you won't know you're there – had passed into the popular consciousness of the nineteen-nineties.

But a hundred million women soon found otherwise; if you ReTranned during your period, you got cramps once you were ReComposed. Most female travelers took a pain-damper before, but no one was keen to talk about it, and ReTran kept their slogan. Dorothy, however, was two days into her cycle, and had felt nothing at all. She knew something was up.

Misfunction did not occur in her life. Things worked, and worked well, automatically and how they were designed to. She'd never heard of anything like this. Of course, there were stories; some ReTran operative was supposed to have used the system to dispose of . . . a corpse? Contraband? She couldn't remember. He'd pushed it into the Transmit pod, then closed all Receive ports worldwide, so whatever it was had been Dematerialized and never Re-. But, until now, Dorothy had never believed the system could be anything other than infallible. Those dumb stories only had currency amongst the Losers – the cardless, the canceled, the conspiracy-theorists. Which was no currency at all.

The pod began to open. Someone was going to get debited for this. She was on a schedule, and time was money. She brushed her irritation aside, and thought litigation until deactivation was complete; then swung her legs out of the pod, straightened up, and strode imperiously over to the door of the Suite. It didn't respond to her body heat; neither did it check or reject her aura. It just stayed shut, and Dorothy huffed her exasperation. She had never done that before, it occurred to her; huffed, or had reason to. Whatever. She set her briefcase down on the carpet – eighties' revival, oyster-gray with plum highlights – and dialed her attorney.

She was still engaged with the AutoSue, outlining her draft estimates of lost income and reputation, when the screen by the door *flipped on. A ReTran executive seated behind a desk that was larger than Dorothy's waited patiently for her to finish her conversation. Dorothy took her time about it. When she was good and ready, she turned and made eye-contact.*

*'Good morning, Mrs Gale,' said the executive, evenly.*

*'Get me out of here,' barked Dorothy. 'What's going on? Why aren't I in Kansas?'*

*'You are in Kansas. You left the ReTran facility at Kansas City Hub ninety-four seconds ago and took a Jolt cab uptown.' The ReTran suit smiled, efficiently.*

*'Excuse me?'*

*'You are in Kansas. You've been rematerialized at your destination, but not dematerialized here. It happens very rarely, but we have contingency measures in place.' The suit smiled her smile again. 'We will simply perform a whiteout in four minutes.'*

*'Whiteout?'*

*'Yes. Obviously we need to terminate you.'*

'Terminate *me?*' *Dorothy's jaw dropped.*

*'There's no cause for alarm, Mrs Gale. It's a perfectly routine procedure. An operative will be with you directly. Thankyou for choosing ReTran.' The screen went dead.*

Did he know? I peered at him over the top of the typescript, but he was sunk in a back issue from 1936. This was crazy; there was no way he could've found out. But I swear, I was flipping out all the time those days: finding out you had six months to live could send a person a little flaky, it seemed. I cleared my throat, tossed the sheaf of double-space onto my desk, and said,

'So she's got three minutes to get out of Dodge?'

'Uh-huh.'

'Then find the replicant and kill her?'

'Yeah, kind of.' Buddy shrugged his skinny shoulders, and his terrible coat skewed even further off his frame. 'I thought I'd, you

13

know, do some stuff like, where the double makes it hard for her. Takes over her job and apartment and money and stuff, so she can't use her credit-ID to pay for anything. So she can't get around. She has to go underground, kinda.' He had six inches of shirt-cuff on one side and the coat-sleeve over his knuckles on the other. I didn't have to look to know that there were maybe two unbroken buttons, tops, under his tie. I said,

'So the replicant's defending herself without knowing why she's doing it?'

'Uh-huh.'

You could tell Buddy wrote fantasy fiction because he'd only got two versions of the same woman. If he did realism, he'd have needed at least five. But maybe this was just me. I said,

'She's married?'

'Sure.'

'So the final scene could be the husband choosing between the replicant and her?'

He nodded.

'It's good.' It really was. 'There's all kinds of stuff you can do with it. You think about making it full-length?'

'I could, I guess.'

I went to say something else and stopped. He looked like he was going to cry, and I couldn't blame him. I was the only one he ever worked for, and telling him he was toast had been terrible. I'd colored right up to my jaw. I could force the flush out of my face, but the rest of me had been burning up.

'Buddy, I'm not firing you. I'm firing Isadore. You know that, don't you?'

This was the hardest thing I ever did. But it was the end of the line. There was more red ink in the books than in the whole gory run of *The Slasher* series, high on the shelf behind him.

'What's going to happen to him?'

'The will to live is to do with purpose. Take one away and you

14

can say so long to the other. Isadore's going to die, Buddy. He's old.' Shit, I was old – as old as the century, and lucky to have seen it halfway. I shook out a Gitanes, tapped it tight – for luck, you hadn't needed to do that with cigarettes for ten years now – and fired it up.

'I'll miss him,' he said.

'So will I.' And I would. We went back a long way.

Isadore van Doren was a prolific and distinguished writer of undistinguished stories. Lurid literature and weird tales. The kind you pick up for a few cents from the magazine rack at the drugstore. The kind whose four-color cover cost more than the inside to produce.

Nickel a shot, a quarter the lot. I had a fantasy, when I was a kid, that if half of America dummied up a nickel I'd never have to slave away at something I hated: I could use all my time doing something good, something fine, something that would pay back the nickel a hundred times over. I was in the real world now, but I'd managed to swing it, so far. Isadore van Doren was twelve guys, and he let them do what they did because half of America was ready to ante up five cents for Mr van Doren to get them through a bus journey, a week of lunch hours, or a night alone someplace lonely.

I pulled focus from the middle-distance to the dice on my desk and, absurdly, got the urge to do that crazy thing again, first time in twenty years. Roll a one, you have to sit next to a solitary guy on the train home; two, you have to wink at the short-order cook when you buy your lunch; three, take off your underwear until you get home; four, go to a bar alone; five, let the first guy who wants to buy you a drink do it; six, go back to his room with him. It's important, what you keep on your desk: Dickens had a pair of dueling frogs, Flaubert had a stuffed macaw, Lawrence a photo of his mother in her girdle; I had a pair of dice in a shotglass, and a picture snipped from the obituary pages that I thought ought to look like Isadore.

Isadore van Doren was a house name, a portable by-line that my guys used so they didn't have to use their own. They couldn't, because like movie stars getting married, they did what they cared about under their own names. The stuff they did as Isadore paid the rent; the stuff they did under their own names was what they wanted, some day, to be taken seriously for. I was like, not holding my breath in most cases, but they had to do it: no one canonizes a priest who spent his youth getting picked up in cathouses. So it was Isadore for the flophouse, real names for the church, should any of them ever dupe their way into a dog-collar.

But you never can tell. I'd wanted to be the priest once, but it turned out I was the Madame. It didn't bother me. All I wanted to do was get away from before, and that's what I'd done. It hadn't been a breeze, but I never thought it would be. I'd seen places fold before, and I'd started new stuff from scratch. I could probably have done it again, but there wasn't any point. It was almost a relief, not to have to worry about what I was going to do next. Whatever. I wasn't the problem here.

'Are you scared, Buddy?'

He looked out the window so he didn't have to look me in the eye.

'You shouldn't be. You know everything about this stuff.' He didn't look so convinced. 'Sure you do. C'mon. Give me a time-travel paradox.'

He trotted it out on automatic, like I knew he would. 'If you go into the past you can't do anything that might jeopardize your being born. If you go into the future you can't visit your own grave. You can't find out when or how you die.'

And I nearly blew it and told him there. *I already have, buddy. I know when and I know how.* But I didn't. It didn't help that I was old enough to be his mother. I felt that way about all of them, and damn anyone who said, if you were a guy, you wouldn't think like that and it wouldn't get in the way. I had responsibilities here. I'd known Buddy – he'd worked for me – for nine years, since he was fourteen, when he mailed me his first Isadore on feint-ruled pages torn from an exercise book. 'The Crystal Case' – nine years. Jesus.

'Y'see? You know this stuff backwards. You can work anywhere you want. You'll be okay.'

'But I don't know anywhere else.'

'Buddy, you'll be okay. You're a writer.'

'Only because my parents wanted me to be. I wanted to be an astronaut.'

His parents, as far as I could gather, never wanted him to be anything, including alive. But this meeting was supposed to be business, and it was starting to get sloppy. I brusqued it up.

'Meantime you ought to send an outline of this to Dirkham House. They could put it in *Horrorshow* or *Black Masque* for sure. You'd have to pitch it lower, though.'

Dirkham House was the reason I had to do this. One of the reasons, anyway. If I was the camel, then Dirkham was the straw, growing plump and heavy, and giving my back the gladeye. None of the others got this, which surprised me. I'd seen all my guys in the last couple of days – I'd done this scene with every writer who was Isadore – and they'd all assumed it was TV that was forcing us out. I guessed it was because TV was kind of obvious, kind of new, and kind of even trashier than we were. They looked down on it, thought it was hooey. The irony no one was getting was that the guys doing trash for TV learned to do serious work first; in the same way that Picasso learned to paint like a camera before he started horsing around. I knew this because I knew them – the TV guys – used to work with them, back west, two decades before. My guys learned trash first, and they were brilliant at it, and that ought to've been good enough – it had been for fifteen years, all the time there were just little outfits like mine. But now I was being squeezed out by new divisions of the big guys, who thought trash was just trash and made *real* trash.

17

'I'm serious,' I said. 'Write a pitch tonight and mail it off in the morning.'

'I'll think about it.'

'Of course, they don't pay a lot.'

'That's okay, I don't earn a lot.' He smiled then, from beneath his skewy fringe of ratty hair, crying out for a cut in the way that only a small boy's ought to.

'Buddy, we can't go out like this,' I said. 'Think about the party, huh? It won't be the same if you don't come.'

I was having a farewell dinner for Isadore a week later, for all the Isadores still in town. Most of my writers were coming, but Buddy had got a little weird when I first asked him: either because these people were his gods, his oracles and his elders, and he didn't want to see them made flesh; or, more probably, because he didn't want to see what he was going to end up like. 'Call me?'

He flipped his eyes to the floor, half-nodded, and it was only then that it occurred to him he had to leave now. This was always a tough moment for him – God knew how he spent the rest of his time, but I suspected that my office, that ramshackle room above a carny goods wholesaler, was the only place he ever got to feeling like a real person. He gave me an awkward kiss – European style, but he'd never been any good at it – and left.

And, god, I wanted to go with him. When you've spent half your life in Hollywood, some habits are hard to shake off. If a guy and a broad are in a room and the guy leaves, then the camera follows him. You don't stick with the broad. This office – gray aluminum cabinets and cheap deal desk, my life in index cards stacked around me – might've been somewhere to start but it was no place to stay. If it was twenty years before, when I would've been putting this into one of my scripts, the camera would've tracked Buddy out into the street, and off into the story beyond. Maybe it could've paused a moment, caught me framed in yellow-white at the window, above the line of dripping plastic pennants strung across the Supreme Novelty Co. sign (*Party Favors, Magic Tricks and Carnival Goods*) that marked the first floor; but then it'd be back to a tracking shot at street level: he sidesteps a bum, turns up his collar, hunches into it as he passes a hooker; dissolve to his cold-water walk-up, where he slumps at the typewriter, gives up, goes back out into the night; drinks too much, gets mixed up with a chorus girl, drinks some more, starts going to hell; takes bad money on the street, knocks the girl up, her brother comes looking for him – you know how it goes. But you don't stay with the broad in the office. If I figured at all in the rest I'd just be there to warn him, to try and hold him back from the danger that's coming – maybe I'd even get to be in the final scene. But I'm here now and I'm not going away. You're sticking with me.

The growling saloon rolled to a halt behind Susan, stopped inside the frame; and Earl, dumb with shock, thumbed the button involuntarily a couple more times, freezing the tableau forever. She'd get to see the pictures in a week or so's time, and it wouldn't be lost on her how the car fit the monochrome motif perfectly: ropes the color of the silk inside a chestnut shell in sharp relief against the sable sheen of her nylons and opera gloves; her raven hair, and the arc-lights sucking the color from her skin like a kid with a Popsicle; the whitewashed, unfinished walls behind her; and the gleaming, inscrutable car. It was a symphony in monochrome. If he hadn't known it might get him whacked, Susan bet Earl would've included the prints in the four-dollar set out of sheer aesthetic appreciation.

Three doors *chunk*ed open – three doors *chunk*ed shut. There were footsteps, flat and clunky, but Susan didn't know how many. She heard Alice back up behind her, then swish a robe off a chair and clatter swiftly offstage.

'Well, well, well,' drawled a voice full of molasses and tobacco. 'Looky here, looky here.' He was off to one side, but Susan couldn't tell how far away he was. She pulled uselessly on the ropes.

'Can it,' said another. 'Leave her.' They walked around to in front of her – she guessed there were three of them now – then they stopped. 'You know who we are, Earl? We're associates of your business partner, Mr Giotto. You do remember your business partner, don't you?'

'Whaddaya want?' Earl sounded as frantic as Susan felt.

'No need to take on, Earl. Mr Giotto values your business. We're here to make you a little proposition. Why don't you conduct us to your office?'

She didn't know if anyone'd pulled a piece on him or what, but he went without arguing, and the door to the stairs closed behind them. She'd thought about making mumf-ing sounds against the gag, but she didn't want to draw too much attention to herself. She didn't know where the hell *that* had come from from a minute ago, but she kind of suspected there was an unmistakable rosy-red flush across her face and bosom. She'd been glad of the ropes then – being unable to bring her thighs together denied focus to whatever the hell it was she was feeling, which seemed to make it more intense – but now they were back to being awkward again. Her thighs were quivering from the tension of standing, legs apart, in six-inch heels for half an hour, and her shoulders had begun to ache like hell. She also needed to pee pretty soon. She jerked her wrists in frustration, and the chains above the pulleys whipped and jangled.

'Miss?' Oh sweet jesus. 'Excuse me?' It was coming from the car! 'Miss? Are you okay?'

'Mmmmf!' She tried to make it sound as angry as possible. 'Rrrrrr-mmf! Mffff!'

The door opened and shut, and he came over behind her, unbuckled the ball-gag. She spat it out, and he got some on his hand.

'Hurrrr! Wha' hell -,' her lips had gone dead, and she pressed them together like she was distributing lipstick to get the blood back. 'Who the hell are you? And get this damn blindfold off me.' She tossed her head angrily, and his hands found the ties at the back. 'What were you doing back there?'

'Preparing to join my associates.' He sounded like he was trying hard not to laugh. The blindfold fell away, and Susan reflexively slit her eyes against the light. This new pain irritated her even more.

'The hell you were! What were you, whacking off . . .' She regretted it as soon as it was out of her mouth. This guy was, after all, some kind of wiseguy even if he was only the lawyer or something; and she was, it occurred to her, tied up, alone, and wearing exceptionally talented underwear. If she screamed, who was going to come? His three friends upstairs? He didn't need to whack off at all.

'I'm sorry,' he said. 'I thought you were a mannequin. It was only when I saw you move . . .'

Then he stepped into her field of vision, and Susan couldn't believe what the Lord had finally sent her. No way was this a lawyer. This must be that Giotto guy they were talking about. But young! Twenty-eight tops. She thought the boss guys were always, like, godfathers, grandfathers, whatever. She scowled at him.

'So what *were* you doing? And say, you going to untie me, or just gawk at me all day?'

He stepped back behind her and worked on the knots at her wrists, contriving to do it with the once-in-a-lifetime delicacy of a prom-date helping his girl on with her wrap. When he was done he brought a chair from somewhere in back and Susan sat down, massaging her biceps. He knelt to do her ankles and she swatted his hand away.

'*I* can do that.' That came out too sharp, but she just remembered she was still in her underwear. He stood aside and considerately glanced away, so she took the opportunity to check him out. Sober but sharp Italian suit, crisp white shirt with French cuffs, tan hands without any rings. Rich black hair that looked as though it was trimmed everyday, nice teeth, mouth with just the right squinny to it, offset by a flawless jaw and eyes that'd looked long and often at the sky and the ocean. This was kind of a shock. Susan had been dry for so long that, paradoxically, she'd lost her taste for water from the faucet – it was fresh from the spring or nothing – and to find it here, in front of her, was almost too much.

22

She'd been thinking about this just lately, mostly because it'd been so long. It wasn't like she believed all that horse's-ass stuff about Mr Right, but it must've happened to someone occasionally. Her girlfriend in New York had a baby last fall, and she said it was the strangest thing, waiting for it to be born – waiting to see the face that's going to be at the front of your mind for the next twenty years. The face that's going to drive you crazy the rest of your life, every moment it's out of your sight, wondering if it's warm enough, if it's safe, if it has enough to eat. Falling in love – really, in love – must be like that. This is the face you elect to be the last thing you see; these are the hands you'll be holding when you die. Trouble is, you never know, and most of the time you're kidding yourself. This is the point of dating. If you really like somebody, you'd be making disgraceful suggestions and interfering with their clothing there and then. Dating is like, I don't really want you but I'm hoping you'll grow on me.

But Susan didn't want to date this guy. She pulled the last rope through, then coolly slung one leg over the other.

'Well?'

'Well what?' He looked perplexed.

'What are you doing here?' Totally hardball. 'I'm working, you know. You've interrupted my work.'

'Oh. I'm sorry.' He knitted his brows, dropped down an octave. 'Your – uh – *boss* is going to be a little while here. Listen, why don't I take you somewhere. For breakfast? You want to . . . would you like to have a cup of coffee with me?'

'Sure.' She stood up, walked over to the car. He didn't follow. She stopped, smoldered over her shoulder at him like Betty Grable, but he looked pained.

'Uh, miss?' he said. 'Don't you want to put a dress on?'

He drove out of the South Side, to a diner on the lower edge of the Loop. As they got out of the car, an El train dropped cinders from

23

above, making them both skip to the door with their heads bowed as though they were caught in a rainstorm straight off the lake. Inside, Susan ordered Greek toast and jelly, eggs over easy, sausage and coffee; he took New York steak, hash browns, double eggs and sausage, glass of half-and-half, with coffee and toast on the side. Big eater, but then he was built solid, Susan noted. No lunk, though; he was only a little taller than her, but she could've climbed him like a tree.

He was quiet while they waited, lighting cigarettes and pouring icewater; and when the coffee came, he stirred in the smallest pinch of sugar and sipped at it. He was so casual he could almost've been bored. Meantime Susan was in overdrive.

This was now straight in the top ten of the most propitious mornings of her life, ever. She couldn't believe what the Lord had seen fit to send her. She was just getting through the day, putting up with the usual work crap, maybe thinking about the laundry and whether she'd get time to drop by the Stop&Shop when she was out of there, and then bang! He'd loused up her day. And probably the rest of her life.

This was suddenly so right. She'd known the real world wasn't for her. She was going to meet some guy? Marry him? What for? A war-bride bungalow? Painting by numbers? Restaurants only on anniversaries? Peeling back the foil from god's bounty every night in front of an 8″ Motorola? The hell with it all. If she'd been that type girl, she'd never have worked for Earl to start with.

She didn't know where to begin. Whatever. He was cute – she may as well start there, she decided. Besides, she couldn't help kidding him a little.

'So tell me, *Signor* Giotto, have you killed a lot of people?'

'Not yet.' He smiled; Susan gave him an eyebrow. 'Besides my name's not Giotto. I'm Ben Kahane.' He smiled with his eyes this time, and extended a hand across the table.

But Susan was like, what a gyp. She knew it. This guy was just a damn lawyer or something. Small-time. He wasn't even Italian. Ben Kahane – what the hell kind of name is that?

'What the hell kind of name is that?'

'Polish-Irish.'

Cool. This coulda been the biggest break of her life, and she was stuck here with some gimp when the action was back at the House of Whacks. With Earl and Alice, neither of whom knew shit from Shinola. Suave.

'What were they doing back there?'

'Some business.'

'Nothing to do with you, right?'

'Everything to do with me.' He lit a cigarette, offered her one. She refused, even though she wouldn't've minded one.

'So why have you brought me here?'

'To talk business.'

'To get me out of the way.'

'On the contrary. You don't need to be there, and neither do I. Our time is better spent elsewhere.'

'So who were those other guys?'

'They work for me. They know what to do.'

Susan took a sip of coffee while she considered this.

'So why've you brought me here?'

'To learn about your business.'

'Right. So you're going to pump me and dump me in the river.'

'I don't dump anyone in the river.'

'You get someone else to do it for you, right?'

He blew a smoke ring. 'You watch too many movies.'

'So what do you do?'

'Whatever I need to.'

This was getting her nowhere. He wasn't going to tell her, which only made it all the more urgent that she found out: if he was a nobody, he would've been shooting it off like he was a hotshot.

Her guess was that he, or whoever he worked for, wanted a piece of Earl's mail-order action. Susan knew there must've been a lot of money going through the place because she'd seen the piles of buff wrappers waiting to go out. Alice had, anyway. Roomfuls. And Earl paid pretty good too, it had to be said.

All this guy wanted to know was how much she got, and how far she was prepared to go. It occurred to Susan that he thought she was just some doll-faced hick from the sticks, down on her luck and fallen into this. He didn't need to be here with her at all. He hadn't needed to get out of the car. He could've just let the dumb doozy hang, and enjoyed the view.

The food came, and they both started in on it.

'So, tell me,' he said, chewing, 'do you have a day job you have to get to? I mean, you work pretty early.'

'We don't always. It was just something I was trying out,' she said. 'Blacks and whites. Skin and silk, white rope and black velvet. White wall and dark window. Blonde Alice and – well, me.' She shrugged. 'When the sun was right up, we were going to turn it round. Reverse the image. Black out the walls, Alice on the rack. You see?'

'*You* were trying out? So you have some say in what happens?'

She snorted, but didn't overdo it. 'I'll say. You haven't done your research, fella. I art-direct the shoots. I'm the art director. '

'*You* control it?'

'Yeah, maybe I do. I had a trainin' in North Carolina. You got a problem with that?' She held his eyes, level across the table a moment. He held it back, just long enough, then dropped to his plate, sliced off steak.

'No, I think it's good.'

'You better.' Maybe she was overdoing it. Lighten up. 'Us broads have made all kinds of advances since the war, y'know. We're not all typists, buster. We got out of the kitchen and we're not going back. Not like your business at all.'

'Well, no offense, but you don't know my business.'

'None taken, but you don't know mine either.'

'But I'm trying to. Tell me, how'd you meet Earl?'

She spread jelly on toast so she didn't have to look him in the eye.

'I know him from way back.'

'From Los Angeles?' He pronounced the 'g' hard. But Earl in LA? Susan brazened it out.

'He never talks about that.'

'So you were what, an actress?'

Earl was in Hollywood? 'Maybe.'

'I thought so. Didn't I see you in *Miss Julie* onetime? Upstate somewhere?'

Susan was like, I wish. 'You don't have to do this,' she said. She needed to signal to him that she was available. 'If you want to know about my work, I can tell you. If you want to know what I do after work, I can tell you that too.'

As soon as she said it, she was worried she'd overdone it. It occurred to her that maybe she shouldn't be worrying about whether he knew she wasn't out of his league, but about whether she was in his, however beautiful she was. This was the first time she'd ever had to think that, she realized with a start. He was the biggest-league guy she'd ever met. But Ben had conceded the point, pausing in his breakfast a moment.

'I guess Earl will go back to movies again, when this thing blows over,' he said. 'McCarthy's had his head already. He won't be tolerated forever. We ought to have seen him coming.'

'What's it to you?'

'That's what I do. You know who I work for.'

'I'm not stupid.' This was finally getting somewhere. 'I didn't need to see what happened earlier to know you're not a . . . civilian. Because neither am I. I wouldn't do what I do if I was. You mind if I smoke?' He was not done eating yet.

'Go ahead,' he said, sawing at some sausage. 'So tell me about it.'

She settled her shoulders back into the seat. It occurred to her how much she'd rather be telling him about her working day as a fashion assistant on *Mademoiselle*, but she sat on it fast. If she was that girl, then she wouldn't be here. So whatever. Hardball time, as ever.

'We take sex and we square it. We cube it. You take a picture of a beautiful girl in her underwear – so what? But you tie that girl up, and you've tripled the stake.'

'It doesn't disgust you?'

'What doesn't?'

'The guys who buy this stuff.' He crossed his fork to his right hand, stabbed at some eggs, gestured disgustedly with them. 'Fat old guys sweating it up in their shorts in the basement. While their wives watch *Kraft Television Theater* upstairs.'

'It's the wives watching television that have the problem. The only thing that disgusts me is people who spend their lives with the lights off. Like I said, civilians.' She stared back at him coolly, let smoke drift out of her mouth, and narrowed her eyes at him through the tendrils. 'Now tell me what you do. Really. I'm tired of this.'

'How old are you?'

'Twenty-five.'

'You're kidding. No way you're thirty.'

'No, I really am twenty-five.'

'C'mon, you're an actress. If you were twenty-five, you'd say you were twenty.'

She crushed out her cigarette, chuffed smoke irritably above the table. 'Why should I? I went to college. I'm not going to pretend it never happened. It was hard to get there and it was hard to stay.'

'Which one?'

'Smith.'

'You went to *Smith*?' He put his fork down.

'On a scholarship. But then I thought I was knocked up, so I got

28

married and it was withdrawn. Like, whatever I was wo...
before disappeared the moment I was married. Whatever. So
turns out I'm not, and two months later the guy gets his draft and I
never see him again.' She looked at him flatly. She didn't need to be
telling him this. 'Why, is it such a surprise I was at Smith?'

'Kind of. We must have gone to the same dances. I was at Yale
when you were there.'

'You were at *Yale*? Then how the hell did you wind up in the
Outfit?'

It was out of her mouth before she realized how loud she said it.
Thankfully the restaurant was empty except for an old guy with a
cup of coffee, and the frycook was staring out the window, making
buzzy noises with his harelip to the samba music on the radio.

Ben laughed, and dashed a handful of silver across the table.

'C'mon. We oughta do this someplace a little less public.'

He drove her back to the House of Whacks, barely saying a word.
His goons weren't anywhere to be seen as he pulled up in back of
the lot.

'Look, I have things to do now, but we oughta talk. You wanna
have dinner with me?'

Susan shrugged. 'Okay.'

'The Bismarck, say? Tuesday?'

'Sure.'

The rolling doors to the loading bay commenced to clank up,
revealing Howdy and Doody behind them. The gangsters moved
toward the car then stopped, raising their eyebrows first at Susan,
then at each other, then at Ben. This was too gimpy. It was like
getting caught with a guy by his friends on a church picnic. Susan
stepped out of the car, swinging her purse, sashayed past them into
the warehouse. She didn't look back.

When Buddy was gone I waited for Dan, perched on the window-sill, peering into the night. Outside, it was typical Chicago January: rain only a shade from snow, and as black as the sky it fell from. It'd been like that since Thanksgiving, and it was driving me crazy. If you were only in Chicago July and January, you'd find it difficult to believe it was the same city. It could get so cold that you could see why people weren't meant to live at this latitude. I hated winter here when I was a kid, but it was a thousand times worse four decades later. I went to the hook by the door for my overcoat, then resumed my position at the window.

Danny was five minutes late, and I was itching to get out of there. I ought to've arranged to meet him somewhere else, but his call – the week before, when I was in the middle of calling everyone else – had caught me off balance. He said he needed to see me soon, and it wasn't anything he wanted to talk about on the phone; this was pretty much the same spiel I'd been giving to all the others, and it had been weird having it come back at me. I'd scribbled him in at the end of the schedule and, when I put the phone down, had reflected that this was probably the best place for him. I knew that however relieved I'd be by that point, that would also be the time when I'd be feeling like I was on my own the worst.

Danny had known me longer than anyone; knowing me best, maybe he'd even be able to tell me if I was crazy or not. At any rate, there was a chance that whatever he wanted to tell me would be something that'd take the sting out of what I had to tell him. Now, sitting in the window, I was clutching at both. I wanted him to come and tell me what to do.

I could barely see anything below. I turned back a moment, tapped out another Gitanes and considered Carmen, the dancer, the gypsy, the smoky blue shadow on the pack; then I touched the tip to flame, inhaled, and placed the perfect white paper cylinder in the ashtray. It was tough to wait. I'd been seeing my guys back to back since ten that morning, and I just wanted it to be over. I'd sacked people before – I had one job where I didn't ever do much else – but never so many at once. Henry Ford had written off thousands of lives in one afternoon, twenty-one years before, then mounted machineguns at the factory gates in case anyone didn't want to take it. The only difference was that I was more subtle.

My eye fell on a cutting I'd tacked to the wall years back, when I first moved in to that office. It was from a calendar, the kind printers send out at the holidays for goodwill: I'd cut a motto from it to pin up, imagining that it might have some different effect on me everyday than the bare wall behind it, but it had become the kind of thing your eye passes over a dozen times a day without seeing. *You have to take full responsibility for who you are, accept the obligation to make something of yourself, and believe that success or failure is largely of your own creation*, it said. I wouldn't be needing it anymore. I tore it down, balled it up, and tossed it in the basket.

Then I opened my purse and took out the doctor's letter; softening at the folds even then, smelling of lipstick and Coty powder and leather, like the kind of worn Kleenex I used to keep in my purse twenty years ago, to spit on and wipe smuts from Nicky's infant face. The letter was my weapon, my gun at the gates; it was my abdication of responsibility clause, my insurance. It wasn't the thing that broke it to me – that had been a process, not an event, as my chest gradually got worse and sleep became something other people did – and neither was it the first or last piece of evidence.

But it was something to carry round with me, to touch when I felt like it was just something I dreamt, when I got to feeling, unconsciously, like I could've just drifted and ignored it. I opened it out once more, flipped through the pages, running my eyes over the tabulated figures, the percentages, checks and blanks again, as if I needed more evidence of that new franchise on my body. Then I put it in my bag, and was just about to give up on Danny and pick up the dice, when an elevated train rumbling past made me look up again, and there he was, crossing the street below, then vanishing out of my sight-line, and clumping up the stairs below me.

Danny had worked for me longer than any of my extant crew, and as he came through the door it struck me that in the same way dogs start to look like their owners after a while, he was looking more and more like the random picture of Isadore that'd been on my desk for the last decade. He went to take off his hat, but I put the strap of my purse over my shoulder. I couldn't do this without a drink.

'Let's go to Schlagl's,' I said.

It turned out we had something to celebrate, in an ass-backwards kind of way.

'I'm going back West,' he said, after we clinked our shotglasses and sipped at the calorific liquor within. 'Gonna hang up my galoshes and get me a suntan. Shit, gimme ten years and I'll be one of those oven-baked old guys playing chess on the boardwalk at Venice Beach.'

We were in a banquette by the bar. Schlagl's was my usual place. It was an old literary hangout, and people used to come and gush over its idiosyncrasies – the silver dollars embedded in the floor of the bar-room, the row of vermouth bottles lined up in the window, casting shafts of yellow light for you to pass your martini glass through (Dex, the bartender, figured that was as much vermouth as anyone ought to want in a martini) – but I'd spent so much time

32

there since I came back to Chicago after the last war ended that it was just where I went now.

'You're kidding,' I said, incredulous. 'You sold a script?'

'Maybe in the next world,' he said. 'But this'll do fine for this one. Script supervision on a twenty-two parter.'

'A serial?' I wasn't following.

'TV,' he said. 'Crazy, huh?'

I couldn't have been more wrong-footed. Suddenly I felt like I was a hundred years old.

'That's great,' I said. 'Really it is. Way to go.' I'd almost have preferred it if he'd told me he had cancer too. I reached into my purse for my cigarettes.

'Getting my own office, the works,' he said, like he was trying hard to keep a lid on his own disbelief. 'Pool of a dozen writers. *Midnight Mask* – hour-long creepshows, start in the fall.'

'Crazy,' I said. 'Hey, let's get some champagne over here.' He grinned his assent, and turned to wave to Dex.

But champagne was the last thing I wanted. I didn't know what to say to him. TV had come so late in my career that it was the kind of thing that could make a person think about retiring. I was still having a hard time dealing with the fact that it hadn't gone belly-up straightaway. But most of all, I couldn't believe that Danny was going west again. He raised his glass.

'I'm sorry,' he said.

'Forget about it,' I said. 'It's high time someone held you to a steady job, you shiftless bastard. Now get that hooch inside you before I have to tell you what it costs.' He toasted me with his glass and took a swig – a little too enthusiastically, because he sat back, blinking from the fizz.

'Wooh,' he said, pulling out a handkerchief and mopping at his eyes. 'Lost the knack for it. How long's it been since we drank champagne together?'

'Too long, buddy,' I said, and brimmed his glass again.

'No, I can tell you,' he said, almost disbelievingly, gazing at the stem of his glass as he rolled it between his thumb and forefinger. 'You remember that place I met you and Walt at out in Santa Monica?' He looked up. 'Shit, must've been twenty years ago. Where my date got a bad oyster and tossed her cookies in the cab home?'

'She said she didn't like the Taittinger because it tickled her nose,' I said drily. Danny used to have terrible taste in dates, back when he was young enough to get any.

'But shit, you know when that was?' he persisted, looking wonderingly over at me. And then all of a sudden I did.

'I'll be damned,' I said. He was talking about when we'd gone out, twenty years before, to celebrate my doing the very same thing he was about to – when I gave up writing and picked up whichever trail had led me here. He'd been such a part of that back then, and ever since, that it was almost inconceivable I could carry on without him now. But then I remembered that I didn't have to, that it was over now; and the relief was mixed with regret so bad that, for a moment, I almost asked him to take me with him.

Because we used to be out West together. Not, like, together – I married Walt – but he was the only person I knew when I got there, and the only person I cared much for till I left.

He'd been one of my brother's buddies, when we were kids here in Chicago – one of the guys you gape at in awe, when you're fifteen and they're a couple years older. Laurie's gang drank corn liquor out of silver flasks, drove jalopies too fast, never danced with the same girl twice, and rarely seemed to be out of stiff collars and studs. Then they all joined up to go fight the war, and Danny was the only one who came back.

He'd dropped in to see my parents when it was over, to tell my mother lies about how Laurie died while my father stood to attention behind her chair. On his way back up the garden path, I jumped off the swing and collared him. I couldn't stand home anymore – I was almost eighteen then, and crazy for the world beyond the banking families of Chicago – and I had a notion that, since Laurie had been the son least likely to follow the family business, one of his friends might know a way out.

I wasn't wrong. The movies had started in Chicago, when we'd both been in diapers, and had only moved to LA when they got big enough to need year-round production. One of Danny's uncles had got into distribution in the nickelodeon days – he'd owned a bunch of drugstores on the North Side – and was out there already. Danny'd had a scenarist's job waiting for him, and he scribbled down an address for me on the back of his warrant card. It wasn't much longer till I was old enough to knock on his door.

So I started out as an actress, working for Danny's uncle, but got sick of how dumb the stuff he made me do was, and sold my first script for three hundred bucks just before my twentieth birthday. It was really easy, but then you should've seen the kind of crap we did before. It was like, you got a title card, and then you acted out what was on it; then there was another title card, and you acted out what was on that. It just occurred to me that, with so many cards, it was difficult to build to any climax other than the obvious ones if you had to explain everything along the way. I figured you could trust an audience to think a little, and if you did, then you could move on from chases and cliffhangers to something a little more interesting. So the way I started was, if I wanted to show a woman going shopping for a new hat, rather than have a scene of dialog with her husband and three title cards to make it plain just precisely what she was doing, I could simply show the tattered ribbon round her old hat, and cut straight away to the shop. It really was that simple, but no one thought of it before. I sold four more scripts in a month, and threw away my return ticket to Chicago.

I dumped the actressing, got a contract writing full-time for Famous Players-Lasky, and hung in there when it became Paramount in twenty-seven. It was a good time to be a writer, an even better time to be a woman. We were at the centre of the industry. People went to movies to see the women as well as the men – guys don't go to a movie to see what the hero's wearing – but there was a feeling everywhere that men couldn't write women; the guys who ran things figured that what women wanted from a heroine was somehow mysterious, something only another woman could know, was kind of the idea, however dumb it sounds. So we were brought in to do revisions on guys' work, uncredited at first, and I swear, we had to carry script-binders round with plain covers, so no poor guy would feel insulted that the tyranny of women was being exercised over his creation. It was a wonderful feeling, to know that you were doing all the real work undercover, but it didn't last long. We'd gotten the vote in 1920, and that was just the tip of the iceberg. Hayseed America was scared silly about what us career women were up to, and it needed reassuring. So us gal writers got glommed into glamorpusses: shoveled, yelping, into tailored suits, rhinestone glasses and lipstick; given original opinions regarding the sanctity of the family and of married love; photographed for as many publicity handouts as the stars, and generally exhibited as being nimsier than your Sunday school teacher down-home.

But it was a fine time to wear a brassière. There were cities, there were apartments, there were typewriters and there were paychecks. And that was just the civilians. We were someplace no woman had been before, and we had to make it up as we went along. Danny, though his uncle was soon out of business and his own career reeked, had stopped me from getting too full of it.

We used to meet up once a month and talk shop, get blasted. Now, drinking champagne and shooting the breeze about the future felt just like it used to.

'So I guess this is the end of the line,' Danny was saying. 'It's a tough call, but sometimes you gotta bail out. Leave you slackers to sink or swim without me. You know? I carried you all for too long, and it was wrong of me. I've gotta let you see if you can't find your own feet. I've gotta learn to let you go.'

'Fuck you,' I said. 'You're just one less asshole I gotta spoonfeed.'

But he'd never been the one I had to worry about. I'd come back to Chicago five years before, after my boy died in the war, but Danny had been there since the turn of the forties. However much he'd never had what it took to hold his head above the mob as a writer, he'd always been good at talking; he knew what to say in meetings, and had got a series of short-contract drama department jobs on radio stations. He'd continued to knock out the odd piece for me, but more to satisfy the vanity that he could still kick it than because he needed the money; the last couple of years he'd been doing, sporadically, the graveyard shift *Midnight Macabre* on WLZR, and it paid so well he'd even bought a car.

'So we're not going to be graced with anymore of your half-assed ramblings?' I said, but suddenly he looked like he was through with kidding.

'Shoulda given it up long ago.' He took one of my cigarettes and tipped back in his chair. 'I just wanted to say thanks, Misty. It's meant a lot not to shut down that part of me. But TV's what I've been waiting for. It's going to be enough to keep all of me occupied. Finally. It's time, now. Just like it was for you.'

I didn't know what to say to that. He was talking about the Crash, which was when everything changed. Its biggest effect out in LA should've just been the downturn in box-office as the Depression bit, but, in the kind of way you can never expect, there was more. It had hit much worse back East, where the newspapers took it in the tush along with everyone else, so they generated a flood of lit young men westward. This was at the time when everyone in Hollywood was getting antsy about what we were going to be allowed to get away with – the Hay's Office was only a couple of years away – so they were given the keys to the kingdom on a velvet cushion. The idea was that they were 'genuine' literary talent, that the studios could show off: talent that had proved itself elsewhere, rather than just us hard-boiled hacks who knew nothing but Hollywood. Of course, we had to keep a lid on the little assholes – the new writers' building they put up over at Fox had 'One picture is worth a thousand words' on a plaque over the door – and I can still remember Scott Fitzgerald getting taken off *The Redheaded Woman* in '31, because he didn't know the difference between laughing at and laughing with.

While it had meant Danny was out of a job almost immediately – he wasn't up to the competition – it was the best thing that ever happened to me. After almost a decade of it, I'd started getting weird about writing. It wasn't anything to do with the talkies making me obsolete, or anything dumb like that: dialog still needed strong images to make it work, so my training on the silents was still the best. And it wasn't even the work, which was mostly corpse rouging – rubbing the life back into some moribund story that had spent so much time in smoky offices it had gone blue from lack of oxygen. It was more that I couldn't go on having to sit down in front of a blank piece of paper every morning, knowing I'd have to fill it and a dozen more like it from nowhere before lunch. I couldn't stand the feeling that someday nothing was going to come. Some morning just like any other, and the white sheet would just get whiter all day. Plus I was going through a bad patch with Walt. He was working at Sovereign by then, which was just the kind of joint to prove the truth that writers ranked somewhere between the publicists and the hairdressers. By the time scripts got to Sovereign, they were quite literally falling out of their binders from having been read and tossed aside by almost everyone else in town.

Walt once said that the writers at Sovereign were the women of the film industry, but soon after he said it there were a thousand real women in Hollywood: women who'd been journalists, copy-writers, but were sick of the jibes already; screenwriting was a more grownup place, where you could get treated like you had a head on your shoulders. But this wasn't sisterhood, this was competition, and suddenly I was like, the hell with it. I didn't need it. The women just off the bus did: to work where they were taken half-seriously was relatively restful to them, but I'd had that all along. I always hated to see other people hustle, and suddenly I didn't want to do it myself anymore. The woman who'd been able to pierce production guys with a fanatical eye and tell them, practically foaming at the mouth, what a demonic hundred-percenter she was – all the time knowing she's the fifth broad through his office in half an hour – didn't get out of bed with me one morning, and I never quite found her again.

At the same time there were suddenly ten thousand guy writers in that town, and only a hundred pictures a year. So I moved to the reading department, and was getting fifty original stories a week. 'Original' just meant unsolicited – if you wrote original stories, it was because no one would give you a job. So out of fifty stories a week, maybe a dozen a year would get optioned, and I thought, what's wrong with all the rest? The truth was, very little, except that they weren't right for the studio that particular week. So I started picking out the most obvious ones, getting the writers to rework them into magazine fiction; they were desperate for money, for the most part, and jumped at it, Danny included. It was ironic because their story ideas came from magazines – from features, interviews, pictures, headlines – and all I was doing was selling them right back, though further down the market. I got to know about printing, production, distribution; and pretty soon I'd left the studio and was putting two issues of *The Dark Hour* a month onto the drugstore racks. There hadn't been too many highs since, but neither were there lows. My home life aside, I'd been on an even keel for the first time ever.

Until now. I stuck a dancer in my mouth, talked around the stub. 'So, you gonna need any writers in Hollywood, bigshot?' I was asking more out of politeness than any lame hope for my boys. But Danny was staying serious.

'Out of my hands,' he said regretfully, but I think he was glad he didn't have to say that I hadn't anyone good enough to chance his arm on. 'Network picks 'em. I'm not in a position to kick against it yet. A couple of seasons, and who knows . . .'

It wouldn't be my problem by then anyway. Suddenly I wanted to get out of there. In the opposite booth there was a college boy keen to impress on his date what a slick sonofabitch he was for choosing this place, and eyeing us like we were a couple of tourists. I knew if we stuck around he'd start talking too loud about how everyone who'd made Schlagl's a slick joint to be seen in wasn't half the writer he intended to be. I'd wanted to tell Danny everything, and now this wasn't the place.

'Listen, you wanna come back to me?' I asked him, pushing away my wine. 'We can pick up some pizza, play a few records, huh? Whaddaya say? I never had you round in five years. You oughta see it before you go.'

'Whatever you say,' he said, so I called to Dex for the check.

In the cab back to mine we talked about who was still out West, while the pizza burned our chilled fingers through its greaseproof paper. There weren't as many as you'd think. As he paid off the driver, I told him how much he was looking like Isadore these days.

'You can't trust your eyes in this town,' he said, getting Marlowe on me for a moment. It was a good fix to an awkward moment. Suddenly I was thankful he didn't tell me what I was looking like lately.

My apartment was deliberately furnished to make me want to go to work. If I'd made it too comfortable when I moved here I would've done nothing but mope around the place, so I bought lousy furniture: wardrobes and chests of drawers that tell you to go outdoors, the kind of armchairs you get for visitors in hospital – the sort no one wants to sit in too long. It was physically difficult to

40

spend too much free time there, but this meant it wasn't so hot for entertaining guests.

'Here, gimme that. I'll stick it in the oven a second.' He'd been unwrapping his pizza – a garbage slice, the variety with whatever's lying around in the kitchen on it that the Italians call capricciosa – and preparing to wolf it straight out of the paper. 'We can take it up to the conservatory so it doesn't stink up the place.'

'Conservatory' was kind of pushing it, but I never knew what else to call it. Once it had just been the roof of the porch, running all the way along the front of the house; then I guess someone put a balcony-rail on it, noticed how bad the weather sucks here and enclosed it with a roof of its own and clapboard walls, but huge, waist-to-ceiling windows running all the way around. There was a long wooden bench, meant for plants, that I used to work on. The sun would bleach a book yellow in a morning, but it gave me plenty of room to spread out layouts and stuff.

'Here,' I tossed him a box of kitchen matches. 'Make yourself useful and light the lamps in there, huh? They warm it up a little.'

He caught the matches and clumped upstairs. The lamps were meant for plants, but since I spent most of my time at home sat in there, I used them for myself. The kerosene fumes could make you light-headed, but it was a good place to drink my coffee in the morning, watch the weak winter sun rise over the low gables and fall on blistered clapboards painted powder-blue, primrose and white. I put the slices on china plates, stuck a bottle of Kentucky under my arm and followed him up.

'Y'know what this reminds me of?' He was already tipped back in a straight-backed chair at the bench, the lamps lit in a line underneath it to trap the heat. He'd picked up a writer's cat-like instinct for the warmest spot in a room, if nothing else. I put down the plates, pulled up a chair, but since he was only halfway down his cigarette, I poured us out some whiskey. He gestured at the skyline with the glass I handed him.

41

'Just like that old office, huh?' It took me a moment to work out which one, but when I did, I saw what he meant. I'd never noticed it before. Around the turn of the thirties my office was right in the middle of the studio lot, looking out on the back of Frontier Gulch's strutted plywood mainstreet; now the roofs and gables of Belmont, silhouetted against the glow of the streetlamps, could've been the same thing. Maybe that was why this neighborhood, rather than the towers of downtown, felt more like my Chicago.

Danny crushed out his Camel and put down his glass. 'Whaddaya say? You think that skyline's an echo from back when that street was still paved with dirt? Or did they build the movie frontier towns to look as if what's here now grew out of them?' He picked up a slice of pizza and chewed ruminatively.

'That's the killer, with backstory,' I said. 'It's easy to make the past fit whatever you want.' It seemed as good a time as any, so I told him about shutting down *The Dark Hour*.

'There's nothing a grand would do?' he said. 'I got a little salted away.'

'Naw. You're sweet to say it, but it's just gonna prolong the agony. You know the way things are getting now. I can't compete anymore.'

He put down his pizza. 'But c'mon, Misty. This isn't like you. Why don'tcha step it up a little instead? Crank up the distribution?' He pulled a dancer out of my pack on the bench and lit it. 'C'mon, you gotta be crazy. Everything's saying this is the time to turn it up, not turn it in. There's so much money floating around you could surf on greenbacks from Boston to Big Sur.'

I picked off an oily chunk of zucchini, teasing out quivering strands of melted cheese before I changed my mind and put it back down again. 'There isn't time,' I said.

'Sure there is,' Danny remonstrated. 'Whatcha gonna do, retire? I tellya. I know a couple of guys who shill the horror list for Dell –

always tryna get us to plug the books on the show. You oughta talk to 'em about taking *The Dark Hour* on.'

I could've cast the net wider years ago, but I didn't. After I came back here, I never wanted to be any more successful than would take care of the needs of the present. It was no use thinking about what I could have done. Like I said, that's the killer thing with backstory. So I told him about the cancer too, mostly to get him off my back.

'Whoa,' he said when I was done, and took a big swallow of the sipping whiskey. 'Wooh.'

I poured one myself, sipped at it. Now I was on a roll, it seemed questionable whether just going back a long way with Danny was reason enough for me to expect him to be able to tell me what to do. Maybe he'd become one of the few constants in my life out of default rather than anything else, just because he'd followed me around. Even the things I associated with him – my brother, my marriage, my time in LA – probably only seemed like they were so important because he'd always been there to remind me about them. I almost went so far as to express this to him, to relieve his embarrassment. The world without me wouldn't be so different to him, it seemed suddenly.

'What're you gonna do?' he said, eventually.

'Whatever I have to.' I shrugged.

'You gonna stay here?'

'Sure.' I loved it there. I'd loved LA – the heat, the canyons, the streets of mock-Tudors for writers, mock-Spanish for industry – and then I loved New York – the clamor, the exaggeration, everyone teetering high above the street. But I loved this city most: burned to the ground before I was born, then built again for the new century – built low and long as the prairie, built low like children are, so there's not so far to fall. This place was the reason plantation slaves used to look north when they put down their sacks at the end of the day; this had been their promised land, and I'd

43

always expected it to be mine. When Walt asked me if I missed it, I used to say that when I was old enough to make peace with where I came from, then I'd go back; and so I had come back, when there was nowhere else to go.

'You told Walt?' Danny asked.

'What's it to him?' I said, a little too sharply, but I meant it. I'd married Walt when I'd been West eight years. I was tight when I proposed to him, and if he'd been a gentleman he would've forgotten about it; but he manoeuvred us both into a judge's office, mouthing the words while we gazed at each other with eyes as clear and innocent as a couple of Florida real estate dealers.

'He'd want to know, Misty,' Danny said. 'C'mon. He was your husband ten years.'

We only dragged it out so long so that Nicky, our son, would be old enough to take the separation, or at least to understand it. If he'd been any other kid we would've had to wait another five, but he wasn't.

'He hasn't been for almost twenty,' I said, matter-of-factly. 'I've picked up a heap of other responsibilities since then. If I gotta worry about anything now, it's them, not Walt.'

'You're not gonna tell him at all?' he said.

I was beginning to think he was sticking on that point to avoid talking about anything more scary, and my irritation at myself for blurting it out made me react even harsher. 'I'll write him a letter, get my accountant to send it on after,' I said.

'You know how long you got?' He poured me out some more whiskey.

'Six months, eight months,' I said carelessly, and picked up the glass. He poured himself one too.

'Misty, that's a lot to carry on one back.'

'I'll manage.' I swallowed back my redeye, reached for the bottle again. Danny was tipped back in his chair, looking out at the skyline. We drank in silence for a moment.

'One of my uncles had a farm out in Ohio when I was growing up,' he said out of the quiet, his voice pitched low. 'Used to go stay there in the summer – get a sunburn, ride the horses. My aunt died when I was four and his kids all moved away, but my uncle wasn't the kind to retire. He was always coming up with new schemes, and one year he got the idea to breed pedigree collies. He bought Thomas Parke D'Invilliers II at the county fair for a hundred and fifty bucks, and from what the guy said there was a dynasty of dollar-dogs waiting in his sacs.' He blew out smoke and crushed his cigarette. 'I swear, Tom was the sweetest dog you ever saw – loyal, playful, cute as all-get-out. But he was kind of a tease. Bitches got trucked in from far and wide, but all Tom wanted to do was fool around. You shoulda seen this one bitch, I mean she meant business. Her jiveass owner drove her two counties to get it on and she knew it. She gave Tom the gladeye soon as she saw him – fluttering her lashes, mincing around him, twitching her little butt upside his head. He just wanted to play. My uncle went crazy.' He snorted at the memory. 'Sure, there was no way he could sell Tom back to the guy with the magic beans, so he started working on him – made the dog take cold baths and sleep outside to toughen him up, played jazz on the radio when they brought on the bitches, mixed Spanish fly into his doggy chunks. Then he lost the farm when the bank foreclosed his mortgage. He shot the dog out in an open field, let the rest go to hell or the neighbors, and moved to the city. A year later he had a stroke in his apartment, couldn't get off the floor. He took four days to starve to death. Ripped his nails out on the linoleum. I think he was tryna drag himself to the cooker so he could bang on the oven door. Kicker was, there were people twenty feet away, who would've heard a dog bark.'

'Meaning?' I said. He always had a thousand dumb stories.

'Whatever you want,' he shrugged. 'I guess the older you get, the tougher it is to go it alone. Maybe you have to swallow your pride and take what you need where you can get it. Loyalty can come to mean a lot.'

He was right, of course. I was quiet for a moment. Then,

'I'm having a lunch for all the guys next week,' I said. 'Wanna come?'

He looked taken aback. 'Maybe it's best if I pass,' he said after awhile. 'I don't wanna be rubbing it in. I mean, I guess they're maybe all out of a job now.'

I'm sure he didn't mean it that way but it bit. 'That's partly it,' I said. 'I want to tell them an idea I had – something that oughta look out for them when I can't.

'You worrying about them?' he said, incredulously. 'Fuck 'em. Like you said, you spoonfed them long enough.'

'That's my point,' I said. 'If I hadn't I might not be leaving 'em so high and dry now.' I knew how dorky it sounded even as I said it.

'You're kidding. You think they'd worry after you if they all got a fat deal apiece tomorrow? I tellya, I didn't when I got this contract.'

'Sure you did,' I said, kidding him along, anxious to change the subject. 'You thought, how's she gonna get along without my drivelings?'

'I'm serious, sweetheart.'

'So'm I. I owe these guys. I've kept them where they are.'

'You gotta be crazy,' he said. 'You can take this however you want, because I sure haven't made any Rockefeller out of myself: what the christ do I know about anything. But the only thing I ever learned that's been any use is that you've got to leave home sometime. Same way you have to let go of other stuff as you get older. You can't spread your loyalty over a whole bunch of people forever. You've gotta narrow it down or it gets stretched out of shape, and then it's not good for anything.'

I looked insolently back at him.

'I'm serious. You can't go on forever like you owe a dozen

46

people. It's what growing up means. You have to find just one, Misty.'

'Then come here,' I said. It wasn't fair of me; but like any guy, he could forget what he just said in a moment. After a while I led him back into the house.

Alice knocked on Susan's door about two hours after Ben dropped her back. She knew Alice would urgently need to gab about the morning's events and so she'd gone back to bed while she waited, planning how best to extract whatever juice Alice might be able to yield in the hope that it might give her some background on Ben – she wasn't about to take his story as the only available testimony if she could help it. So she'd left the door unbolted and, when the knock came, called *it's open!* Sure enough, Alice stalked in.

'I swear, that sonbitch Earl gonna pay for my new dress,' she said, bunching her fists on her hips and launching into Susan like it was her fault. 'My good new rayon, and it's down in that damp old basement all day! I swear, I'm never workin' for that lowlife sleazeball no more. I'm gonna send him a note sayin' he can send the dress to the laundry and bring it to me with my money. And then he can put his thumb up his butt and snap some pictures of that, the dirty lyin' shitbird, 'cos I ain't workin' that type place no more, I tellya. I do'need this type crap right now. They use me understudyin' this time, next time I'm in the chorus for sure. I'm tellinya 'cos it's the truth.' She paused, to catch her breath. 'Say, you got a cigarette? How'd you get back?'

'Over in my purse,' said Susan, sitting up as Alice took a Lucky from the pack and started to rummage around on the chiffonier for a match. 'So, c'mon. Tell me what happened.'

'I'm tellinya, I didn't see nuthin,' Alice said over her shoulder. 'Those guys bust in, I just grab my coat and get. I'm scared, okay? I even leave my good dress. Seven bucks! An' prolly lyin' in some grease puddle. Wheredja *keep* the damn matches? I'm still shakin' so bad . . .'

'Hey c'mon,' said Susan. 'I'm not takin' on. Been me, I woulda just run too. I'da done just the same as you. Here,' she held out the book of Lucifers from her bedside table. 'Come and sit awhile.'

'You're not mad?' Alice said, warily accepting the matchbook.

'Sure I'm not,' said Susan. She wanted some background. 'I just didn't see anything and I'm intrigued. It's gotten me all intrigued.'

'Well I did see a little,' Alice said slowly, like it was just coming back to her as she sat down. 'I was just gonna get, y'know? I mean, I ran up the stairs in just my coat over my underwear and all, but I figure, those guys aren't gonna steal my dress – I mean, that's not what they came for.' She blew out smoke, shaking out the match. 'I figure, y'know, I can come back'n get it tomorrow, or have Earl send it on with my money. But then I open the door to the street and it's icemelt freezing back onto the sidewalk – I try walking on it but those heels just skid across, and I'm gonna ruin my chance at the chorus if I bust up my ankle or something. My street-shoes're still down by the China screen in the studio so I figure, maybe they'll go in the office or something and I can go down and get my shoes – yeah, and untie you. So I just went in that post-room and put my ear by the crack of the door. You got an ashtray? Oh, that's nice. Wheredja . . . ?'

'Slipped it in my purse at 21,' said Susan, 'go on.'

'Yeah anyways,' said Alice, who'd never been. 'After awhile I heard them come up the stairs and go in Earl's office. I wait a couple minutes case they come back out, but when they don't I go back down in my stocking feet, but you weren't there. I didn't know to call the cops or who. But first I figure I just oughta get home, y'know? So I get my shoes, but then I'm thinking, well, maybe this means no more money for us two, so at least I wanta know why. So I creep back up to the office door, duck down by the frame, tryta listen. But all I can get is Earl mumbling, something sharp from one of the other guys every now and then, a lot of banging file cabinets and stuff. So I split.' She squashed out the butt. 'But then I get home and I'm thinking maybe we oughta do something. Tell somebody. I dono who. And then I'm thinkin, maybe you dint get out. Maybe they kidnap you away. So I come over to check before I do anything.' She did big Alice-eyes, and nodded.

'Sweet of you,' said Susan. 'Say, throw me one of those cigarettes, would you?' Alice got up, took one too, and lit them both. 'So whaddya think?' Susan said, and narrowed her eyes against the smoke.

'I think maybe Earl's into something else,' said Alice, propping her butt on Susan's chiffonier. 'Maybe he got greedy. Maybe they killed him already.' She gestured like an actress with her cigarette. 'You think we ought to call the cops, get them over there?'

This was not in the gameplan. 'Alice, you're crazy. You know what we do . . . well, it's not illegal, not exactly, but it's not the kind of thing we need the whole world to know about. You want to explain it to some cop? They'd finger you for a hooker soon as look at you. You wouldn't be able to go out for cigarettes without some dumb old boy with a badge giving you a number.'

'Hey, I'm not the only one who does it. You were there too,' Alice said. She sounded about twelve. 'And anyways, where the hell'd you get to? When I came back down you were gone. Don't tell me you untied yourself 'cos I won't believe you. I tied you good. I was a Girl Scout of America.'

Susan didn't know whether she was kidding about this. 'There was another guy, in the car,' she said, regretting she had to tell her even that much. 'He let me go.'

'The driver?'

'Whoever.'

'I wish I could think.' Alice bit on a knuckle, gnawed at it. 'I bet Earl took money from them. To start up this business. I bet he's

50

finished paying them, but those guys never want it to be over. I bet that's it.'

'Why would Earl have needed money to start this thing?'

'Well, when he got on the blacklist . . .'

'Earl was on the *blacklist*? You mean McCarthy?' What did Ben say? Alice stared dumbly back. 'Earl was in *Holly*wood?'

'Sure. I toleja.'

'Alice . . . ,' Susan started, but didn't bother going on. When she'd first told her about this job, last fall, Susan asked her where this guy Earl came from, how he ended up in this crazy business. Alice'd just shrugged and started talking about some lunk in her acting class who was turning it on with her. Susan swore, this girl made Lucy look focused.

'I mean, Earl wasn't one of the Hollywood *Ten* or anything, but he had to go the same time. So did a whole bunch of people. Dintcha read about it in *Variety*?'

Susan didn't. This all went down in '47, the year she got married and kicked out of college. If someone had told her she'd be actressing in three years she'd have laughed in their face. She didn't even know what *Variety* was then. 'Sure, I remember,' she said.

'He was a script editor or something. One of the old guys, been there forever. Since the Thirties, anyways. I toleja.' Alice started picking at a thread on her hem.

'I remember. Look, so you didn't hear anything?'

'That's what was so weird.' Susan had got her attention again. Alice Toschiem, Girl Detective. 'You'd think there'd be tough-guy stuff, and calling each other lousy punks and everything. But they were real quiet, real . . . like guys who've been sat in a bar all afternoon. Talking about the sports, and too tired of each other to even argue.'

'So what do you think?'

'I say they were making him an offer he couldn't refuse. He owes

51

them money or something and, now he can't pay, they want him to do them some favors. Or else, they want a piece of his action. You know how much he makes?'

Susan shook her head.

'Well all those file cabinets in his office are just guys he mails the pictures to. The whole office. This girl who did some shoots with me last winter, she looked one time, and they're all just guys' addresses, lists of what they've bought. In forty-eight states. Ugh,' she shuddered. 'I get so I don't want to go out on the street some days, like there's some guy who's just been looking at pictures of me and then wham! There I am along the counter at the diner. You never think about that? Some guy might be hitting on you 'cos he recognizes you?'

Actually Susan didn't. She was pretty sure it wasn't her face they were looking at in the pictures.

'Best just to think about the money, Alice,' she said.

'But this could be like, some guy in my hometown. The guy who kept the drugstore! I swear, someday I'm going to get into that office and look under the name of every guy I've ever known.'

'If you find one of them you oughta send him a letter saying, I know. I know all about you, buddy. And if you don't want your mother to, you better mail me some slick.'

Alice sniggered, came and sat on the bed. 'We could clean up.' She lay back, her spine arched over Susan's legs, stretched her arms over her head.

'Alice, what's the Bismarck?'

'It's that big old joint on Congress and State.'

'Some guy's taking me to dinner there Tuesday.'

'You're kidding.' She turned her head.

'No, really. Why, is it terrible?'

'As if. It's the swellest place in town.' She considered this a moment. 'Except maybe the Blackstone. I went there New Year's, with Mitch. Who's taking you to the Bismarck?' Alice tried to sound like she wasn't so interested.

52

But Susan was wishing she'd never mentioned it. She'd probably said too much already, and Alice wasn't the kind to play her cards close to her chest. Or anyone else's, for that matter. Oh, the hell with her. 'The guy who untied me?' she said tentatively.

Alice sat bolt upright, her mouth hanging open. 'You're crazy! You know who those guys are? Dintcha see *The Scarface*?'

'He wasn't like that.'

'Sure he wasn't. He'll get you put twenty feet under the second he's tired of you. This is Chicago. You don't mess with those guys.'

'I liked him.'

'Huh. He's only the driver. You said so yourself.'

'What's it to you?'

'*I* gave my number to one of the guys who was with Earl.'

'Oh, Alice.' She really was hopeless. Susan laughed, and she joined in. 'Where are you going? What's his name?'

'Joey Volante.' Alice said it like a cartoon chef, making a circle of her thumb and forefinger and shaking it in the air for emphasis. Susan giggled.

'We'll wind up a couple of molls. You'll see. Razors in our evening bags; .22s under our garters.'

'Baking files into cakes.'

'Stashing diamonds in diapers.'

And so on. By the time Susan got rid of her it was pushing one, so she went out to the drugstore for a Swiss cheese sandwich and a malted. She meant to have a quiet think, but some guy who was, incredibly, just her type was giving her the old eye over the top of the book he was reading – *Erik Dorn* by Ben Hecht, which ordinarily would have had Susan almost sitting in his lap – but today was different. She already had a date, and it was typical. The only other times she saw guys reading Ben Hecht books, they were either as old as the man himself, or else had the same figure. This guy looked like she always pictured the guy in *The Laughing Man*. It was almost like, all the really good guys had some bulletin board somewhere, where they posted up details of their newest discovery and suddenly, after three years of man-drought (or jerk-glut, depending on how you looked at it) she'd got guys she actually wanted for a change falling over themselves to catch her eye. There must've been a hundred of them out there, dusting off their tuxes, setting their square jaws as they made with the witch-hazel, scrabbling at the radio dial to find WKRP-DreamGuy and catch the latest bulletin: *We interrupt this program to bring you a progress report – she's at the drug on Jackson and State, and we can confirm that an operative is in position. Latest reports indicate, however, that a no-good car salesman with a history of insincerity and emotional callousness is headed for the vacant seat beside her. There's no time to lose, fellas! Get there now!* Susan managed a half-smile at the guy as she got up to leave, but it was no good. She went home and went to bed for the afternoon, feeling lousy.

Next morning she got a message from Earl, telling her to come back and finish the shoot that noon. Susan thought she'd heard the last of him, but she turned up and did it, and he was like nothing ever happened. So was Alice, her ruined dress notwithstanding. She was out of there by two and he even paid her, peeling off twenties from a roll of bills as big as his fist, asking her if she could do a girl-fight session end of the week. She said sure. But she was like, the talent scouts from the Discretion Allstars were never going to be asking Earl to sign on the dotted line. The talent scouts from Sing Sing, however . . .

Alice was right. He'd got a big chunk of change from those guys, maybe with more to come, and Susan had no idea why. It bothered the hell out of her, but she'd got other things to do.

First, she went to Carson, Pirie, Scott and blew thirty bucks on a note-perfect Dior knockoff, so heavily boned and thick with petti-coats that it stood up by itself on the changing-room floor when she took it off. This was the most she ever spent on an outfit, even for a date with destiny, but it didn't make her feel like it should. Susan was thinking, maybe she should've brought Alice – she was all pumped about her date, they coulda done that gal-thing. Alice loved all that, but Susan'd tried to stay out of that summer-stuff, the same as when she was in New York. Made her dizzy to look at: everyone with a dozen dates at once, Madison Avenue guys, UN translators, copy-chasers at Time-Life, all just marking time while they concocted the final novel or stageplay or free-verse memoir; going to openings, first-night parties, new restaurants, Yale Gamma Psi dances at Delmonico's – the whole dizzy round. Susan kind of planned to stay away from that. Aside from the three loving weeks of her marriage, she was doing okay so far. That stuff was for Alice, not her. She wasn't going to know what she wanted again until she found it.

She walked the couple of blocks over to Michigan, swinging her purse as she clipped along the sidewalk and up the Art Institute steps. She checked her shopping in an empty foyer, and felt the familiar rush of privilege at being there when no one else was. Last winter in Manhattan she'd spent a lot of time at the Met, midweek, when she'd had whole rooms to herself; it was just the same in Chicago. Having had no one to talk to in either city, these places were somewhere she could talk to herself without feeling like a crazy woman. She started around the rooms, and time passed somewhere else.

Presently she stopped, as she always did, in front of Van Hennessen's *Judith*. Susan wished she had her body – buff and powerful, wiry and fly. She didn't want to be weak. Weak people gave in to the temptation to deny themselves pleasure; and Ben made her feel like a barfly on election day, just thinking about him. There was nothing she could do about this – this *ache*. He made her think about all the stuff that she didn't dare expect anymore, but couldn't help hoping might happen anyway. He made her think about giving up too early. She was twenty-five, and however hard she'd tried to sit it out, she figured it might be time to take one last dance, while she still knew the steps.

The Contesse de la Choire was reposed forever on a sofa, in white, with a book in her hand; in 1789, just before the shit hit. It was like the prints of her tied up just before Ben arrived – she couldn't wait to see them, and hugged herself at the thought. He'd pretended to have seen her in plays to flatter her, and it made her dizzy to think about it. Usually she only realized this kind of thing later. Years after the event she'd think, my god, he was coming on to me. But this was happening now, and she knew he hadn't got anyone. However much of a highroller he might be, he had that too-quick smile of someone who suspects that less successful people are having a better time and getting laid a lot more often than him.

But she knew she was being crazy. Ben and his buddies were still gangsters, even if every last one of them went to Yale. They wanted Alices, not her. She knew she should never have got mixed up in any of this to begin with. It wasn't her. Most people feel kind of like impostors at work, as though someone's about to denounce them any second, but they ought to try stripping down to their under-wear and having another girl pretend to spank you with a hairbrush for money, when you know you're better educated than the President's wife – or the President himself, for that matter. She didn't know where she went wrong; or rather she did, but it didn't help. Trying to be an actress had been insane, but she'd done it for the same reasons that poor hick guys wear shoulderpads and helmets through college instead of eyeglasses and frowns. When all anyone sees is your body not your brain, then that's your ticket out.

It made no difference that Ben was what he was. If it was easy then it was the wrong guy – Susan was beginning to suspect this was how you told the difference. The guy you meet at a wedding with a nice smile and a great job is the wrong guy. The laughter-lined Adonis who teaches your acting class is the wrong guy. The right guy is an insurance salesman, when you're married to a creep you can't stand the sight of. You're the Big Man's wife, and he's a footsoldier charged with taking care of you. That was how you knew. When it was the last way you imagined, and it could cost you everything that you had, then it was the right guy. She slipped out into the night.

She'd never been to the Central Library before but she'd seen it. No one who can read ought to be able to look at a library without hunger, and this one could make a person feel like they never ate – the Narnia lamps on wrought-iron stems suspending spheres of light in the gloom along Congress, the green eagle scowling at the sky above State Street. Susan checked her shopping, went straight to the reference section, and got the bound volumes of *Variety* for '47. It didn't take long to find what she was looking for and she went back to the counter for a Guild directory, cross-referenced the two. Earl Schulmann, cinematographer. Worked with Selznick! At RKO, followed him to MGM in '33, and into independents through the thirties and during the war. If he'd stayed at a studio he might have rode it out, but his name was right there, on the B-list of the blacklist. This was useless information on its own, but it was a start. She checked her bags back, went home, thought. Next morning she went to the Chamber of Commerce, paid half a dollar for a search on incorporations in '48 under Schulmann. By mid-afternoon she knew that Earl ran Picture Star Network, a movie-star portrait mail-order outfit in Chicago from three falls ago. The House of Whacks was incorporated in 1949. Obviously, once the machinery was in place, it became clear where the real money was, and Earl capitalized. She didn't blame him, poor schmuck. He must have worked all his life, too caught up in the present to think about the future; then, just at the point where he started wondering about how he was going to live when he was too old to do anything else, they pulled the plug on him. She'd have done the same, if she'd been smart enough to think of it.

Whichever. She felt prepared now. Ben couldn't throw her any curveballs she wasn't going to see coming. There was still a night

57

and a day to go before she saw him, but, in the same way that people seem to get rid of their income however much they make, Susan filled her time regardless of however little she had to do. Before she knew, it was tomorrow night and she was late, checking her eyes for the last time, running down to the street and cabbing it uptown to the Bismarck.

Where it all went to hell in a handcart. Ben didn't show up.

If Susan'd had the money she'd have gone into the dining room and eaten alone, but she stayed at the bar, feeling suddenly certain that her shoes and her costume jewelry were broadcasting to whoever was listening that her new dress represented most of the dough she had in the world. A half-hour after the appointed time she'd had enough, and the bartender was looking at her like she was a hooker. Not, Susan suspected, that he disapproved especially, but more that he would've expected to have taken his cut up front. It could only be a matter of time before one of the real girls showed up and demanded to know what Susan was doing, working her patch. She was thinking she could use one of those neat black holes that cartoon characters disappear into, the kind that roll up when not in use and can easily be stored in an evening bag. Maybe Sears Roebuck did them? Anything to avoid running the gauntlet of bitches in banquettes, with furs and rocks and husbands, that stood between her and the door.

But she didn't want to give up just yet. It was clear that he wasn't going to show, but he wouldn't have suggested this if he didn't want it. Maybe it was something beyond his control, and he was as pissed about it as she was, she thought. Either way, he didn't know her number or where she lived, and though he evidently had ways of finding out when she was working, the House of Whacks was not the kind of place you sent roses with apologetic cards to. Susan got an idea, and waved the barkeep over.

'Bring me the city directory, and a telephone.'

He gave her a look like she just asked for the head of John the Baptist with a side order of sauerkraut, but he brought it anyway. Her plan, for the benefit of the rubberneckers with foxes around their shoulders and doorknobs on their knuckles, was to pretend to look someone up, call them, and loudly arrange a change of plan, as though with a business associate. She could be a reporter, say, and her date a Senator. But while she was pretending to flip through the book, she came to K without meaning to, and there he was – Kahane, B, 2461 N. Michigan. What the hell kind of gangster had their number listed? She didn't believe this shit. She dialed the number of her rooming house instead, and told the mystified girl who answered that she quite understood, and that she'd reschedule the interview with Senator King for tomorrow morning at his office. Then she laid a buck on the bar and sashayed the hell out. She was just about to wave a cab over when some knucklehead in a shiny suit stepped out in front of her.

'Miss de Souza?'

Jesus. 'What's it to you?'

'Mr Kahane sends his apologies. He's been held up. He asked me to take you home.' He extended an arm to his car, at the curb.

'Well I don't want to go. You take me to him.'

'He tole me to take you home.'

'You hear me, palooka? I don't want to go. You damn well take me to him.' What she did next was probably dumb, in front of a swanky hotel and all, but what the hey. Susan pulled the pearl-handled Derringer out of her purse – a wedding present, and the one good thing that came out of her marriage – and he immediately disarmed her, twisting her arm round and thumping her into his embrace, but this was just what she wanted. He stuck the little gun in his coat pocket, threw her into his car, then got in and drove. When he pulled up outside her place, he opened the door for her, then took her weapon from his pocket, emptied the chamber and held it out to her.

'Here's your piece, miss. You oughta take more care of it.' He looked pretty pleased with himself, smirking down at her, so she pulled his .38 out from under her thighs.

'And here's yours.' It was worth it just to watch his eyes get round. 'Likewise, asshole. Now fuck off.'

She held the Smith & Wesson on him until he was back in the car, down the street and turning on to Dearborn. Then she ran down to State, ditched the weapon in a trash can and hailed a cab to North Michigan.

Susan had the guy pull up outside. Ben's apartment turned out to be above a funeral parlor – no doubt the one with the famous double-deck coffins – and the play of steamy blue light against the upstairs windows suggested that the jerk was home and watching TV. She gave the driver a buck, told him to wait a moment, and slipped across the street and up the cast-iron stairs. Outside his door she took a second to compose herself, to work on the great vengeance and furious anger she was about to lay upon him, when it occurred to her that there was no sound coming from inside. So he watched television with the sound off? Maybe he couldn't concentrate on more than one sensory input at a time, the retard. She was just about to hammer the hell out of the door when the phone rang inside and got snatched up instantly, like someone was sitting next to it, waiting. She couldn't make out what was said, but it sounded like the kind of thing that might preface his imminent emergence – in which case she didn't need to be discovered hanging around in the corridor like she was too scared to knock. She did a fade back up the corridor, away from the stairs.

Sure enough, his door flew open and he burst out, shrugging his coat on behind him and taking the stairs two at a time. Susan followed as fast as she could in her heels, and made the street just as he was pulling away in a brand-new Cadillac. She ran over to her

60

cab, still pluming great clouds of exhaust into the cold night air, and told the guy to tail the Caddy.

'He's my husband. Cheating on me,' she extemporized. But the driver'd seen it all before and slumped low in his seat as he shifted through uptown traffic like he was on a rail, like he was being towed on a forty-yard cable by the Cadillac. They tailed out through the North Side, through Roscoe Village, past the city limits. Susan was wondering where the hell this was going, hoping to God he wasn't headed up to, jesus, Waukegan or somewhere; she'd only got enough dollars for another twenty miles or so, and then no way of getting back. But ten minutes on, in the middle of nowhere, the Cadillac turned off the highway into the trees, and the twin cones of its headlamps strobed and flickered back through the trunks as it pushed along an old logging road into the woods. Susan had the guy go on a hundred yards then pull over.

She got out and went round to the window, realizing how insane this looked, as if any philanderer would be conducting sex-trysts in the woods on a night so cold that if you spat, it'd clink when it hit the ground.

'Must be some hot dame he's got in there,' the guy said as she paid him off. She told him to go fuck himself, and regretted it instantly as he squealed away. She got down beside a bush at the roadside until she was sure Ben hadn't come back to see what the noise was, then, shivering furiously already, walked the verge back to the dirt road, the steel tips of her heels skidding over the frozen ground. She hesitated a moment before she headed on in – what was going on in there might probably be something she didn't need to see – but it occurred to her that she'd die of exposure if she stayed out in this much longer, and the light in the woods represented her only real chance of a ride back to the city now. And besides, she was more Alice than Alice was: Susan was never the kind of girl who could resist a rabbit hole. She'd always suspected that quality of life is determined not by its length but by the measures you take to shorten it: hence booze, staying out all night, driving poorly maintained vehicles too fast and wanting to have sex with people you just met. So she headed into the woods, toward the light from the now-quiet Cadillac.

She didn't hear anything until she got real close. She was already off the track and pushing as quietly as she could through low branches; she'd lost her wrap a hundred yards back and thorns tore into the meat of her arms and shoulders. Her skin was frozen so it didn't hurt, but the thought of not being able to work for a couple of weeks until the scratches faded just made her more pissed. She was really going to give it to him, she didn't care who he was – no one jerked her around, *no one* stood her up, and no one made her hike across twenty miles of arctic tundra just so she could give them a piece of her mind. What the hell was she doing creeping around anyway? She pushed her way back to the track and marched briskly toward the circle of light from the headlamps, twenty yards ahead.

Then she heard someone puking. She rounded a tree and there it was, in a clearing, a tableau frozen in two sets of headlamps – a couple of guys leaning on an Oldsmobile; Ben, doubled over, wiping the back of his hand across his mouth; and behind him, a pile of frozen earth, with a muddy skeleton and a decomposing corpse next to it.

This was like something out of a movie, but one that wouldn't get past the censors for twenty years yet. For a moment, Susan'd forgotten the cold. She watched Ben get to his feet and turn toward the Olds, nightmarishly silhouetted against the glare of the head-lamp bulbs.

'Why in hell didn't you stop digging?'

'We were here to dig up some guy,' said one of the goons. 'That's what you tole us. No girl. Some *guy*. So we find a girl, we carry on.'

'But we call it in, y'know, in case you want we bring her back too,' put in the other. They exchanged a look of honest puzzlement between them.

'So, what – you want we put her back?' said the first one.

'No, asshole,' barked Ben. 'Fill in the hole, put the Guinea in your trunk and get the fuck out of here. I'm calling the cops.'

The goon looked incredulous. 'Say what?'

'You heard,' said Ben. 'I'm calling the police. This is a real person. This is nothing to do with us.'

'You crazy?'

'No, I'm your boss. You do as I say.'

The goons pointed out that they'd messed the corpse up pretty bad with their picks.

'And you'll mess things up even worse if you don't get the fuck away from here. *Now*. And pick up those damn cigarette butts. Jesus.'

The goons went to work, and he sat in his car and watched them, the heater audibly running. Susan would've given anything to be there with him – her flesh had turned to blue ivory all over – but she knew she didn't dare show herself while the goons were still there. There'd have to be another corpse if she did. But if no one else saw her, he wouldn't lose face. Thank christ, they worked fast – it wasn't the night to slack, even if the boss hadn't been watching – and they slung slabs of soil into the hole with abandon, bundled up the bones in a tarp and were out of there within five minutes.

Ben, meanwhile, had watched them impassively from behind the wheel, and only when they'd gone did he get out of the car and walk over to the cadaver. He knelt a moment, then stood and looked away. Susan hesitated before doing it, but if he got back in the car and drove off she'd die there anyway. She stepped out into the clearing.

His eyes went round as silver dollars. He muttered something, stepped back involuntarily.

'Hi,' she said. She'd meant, even up to ten minutes ago, to really let go on him, but now she couldn't. The girl was still on the dirt.

'Jesus,' he moaned, and Susan got that ground-opening-up feeling of having gone too far; like when she went down on some Ivy League guy first semester at Smith, and when she went back into the party five minutes after him so as not to be too obvious, she knew that everyone else knew, and that she was finished there already. But Ben was taking off his jacket and putting it round her shoulders. He stepped back and looked hard at her. 'How long have you been here?' She couldn't say anything. 'It doesn't matter. But, jesus fucking christ, Susan. I should get you taken care of, you know that?'

She couldn't do much but look back at him. If she looked anywhere else she'd see the girl on the ground again, see the thick blonde hair fallen over her wilted face. Ben was still gaping at her in disbelief.

'*How?*' he said, finally.

'I went to your apartment and you were just leaving . . .'

'You went to my *apart*ment? How d'you know where I live?'

'It's in the phone book,' she sniffed.

'I'm in the *phone book*?' His face could've been a commercial for Aghast.

'Uh-huh.' Susan'd had enough now. It was probably the cold, but she felt like she was going to cry. 'Look, what did you expect me to do? You stood me up. I hate that.'

He exhaled heavily, composed himself. 'Okay, whatever. I didn't have your number. I'm sorry. Okay?'

'Okay.' Her voice was thin and high, and wavered from trying to stop her teeth chattering. She couldn't feel any of her body now.

'So what, you go to my apartment, and then you Peter Pan me all the way out here?'

'Peter Pan you?'

'Like sewing on a shadow. You know.'

64

'Oh, okay. I guess.' She thought for a moment. 'Look, you can do what you like with me after, but will you let me sit in the car and put the heater on? I think I'm dying here.'

'Let's just get out of here. Jesus,' he said, and that was that.

So she spent her first night at his apartment. He drove back to the city, stopping at a payphone to notify the police, but when he came back to the car he could see she was still blue, even in the orange glow from the sodium lamps on the lot of the truckstop. So he took her back, wrapped her up in a quilt, put some brandy inside her and put her to bed. Then he got in beside, still in his suit, and let his body warmth envelop her. She slept till twelve the next day, and when she woke up, he was gone.

Across town, a mile and a half downtown, our cab pulled up outside Schlagl's.

'You think they came?' I peered at the restaurant while Danny paid off the driver.

'Sure they did,' he said, opening my door. 'Bet none of the cheap bastards ate for a week. You think you're going home with change from a hundred then I've got some real estate in Florida you really oughta see.' I snickered, but he put his hand on my arm. 'You know I think you're crazy, don't you?'

'You oughta be sure that I am,' I said. 'I printed your lousy crap for twenty years, didn't I? C'mon. You coming in, or what?'

'Sure. But I gotta get on a plane at four,' he said.

'Plane, huh? Slick,' I said. But I knew what he meant.

'So I guess we oughta say so long now.'

'Sure.' I wasn't up to faking the kidding anymore, and put my arms around him, there on the sidewalk. Our heavy coats gave the embrace a clumsy, cartoonish quality.

'I'm gonna see Walt out there,' he said. My face was crushed into the lapel of his topcoat, but I could hear well enough. 'It's gonna happen, of course it is. If he asks how you're doing, whaddaya want me to say?'

I pulled away. 'Tell him I'm not gonna see him again,' I said, then grinned as a line came to me. 'Tell him I'll leave him my hope chest. Now, c'mon.' I dragged him inside.

Danny was right. Five minutes later and it was like a freeloaders' convention in there. My crew liked their shore-leave.

66

'Atomic bombs are just a diversion.'

'Really, Vincent.' I smiled indulgently at him, across a table crowded with other writer sonsabitches, folded my arms on the white cloth, hoisted an eyebrow like I really wanted to hear. But what I really wanted to do was sit back and listen, and think about if it wasn't for me, none of this would've been happening here. Without me, these guys wouldn't've been able to do what they did. They'd be stuck in the world with the rest of the dorks, going round and round like lab rats on wheels, never pushing themselves, never moving on. I'd given them a break – for twenty years, some of them. If one of them did something good someday, then it would all be justified, but it kind of was anyway. I'd loused almost everything else up in my life except this, and I loved it.

'Think about it, chrissakes,' Vincent was saying. 'They're just to get your eye off the ball. They're not gonna land those suckers on cities like we think. It'll be much scarier than that. Why take out just one city, when you can mess with a whole continent? Nuh-huh,' he snapped his fingers, 'they're into tidal wave initiation, hurricane manipulation, ice-cap liquefaction, seismic activation – imagine it. Do what we want or we'll blow so much volcano smoke into the atmosphere that you won't have a summer for three years. That's how you really piss people off. Three years of Chicago February – sheesh.'

Some of these tigers had real editors at real outfits, but they were the kinds of gimp-joint that'd splash out on lunch for a writer maybe once in five years. Even the most gregarious of my guys got away from his desk about as frequently as elephants get it on. I bet they got so they'd go for lunch with McCarthy, if it was his shout. They were all there. The only empty seat was the Banquo's chair we kept for Isadore, for the real writer, for the one who never showed up: the cold martini in the sweating glass, the cigar unlit in the ashtray beside his place setting – sacred offerings of wine and fire to propitiate the sudden, the savage Mr van Doren.

'Maps are outdated,' Joe Lucca around on my right was telling Danny. 'We oughta be drawing them up on the side. The physical world is changing; old maps are from when geography mattered. New maps should be about other things, with enough levels to make them complex, like the world is now. You could have one for telephone and telegraph networks; one for broadcast reaches – where does ABC cover? Where's CBS? And another for corporations and their catchment areas: if you live here, here and here, your food supply is going to be controlled by these guys, and these guys over here control your broadcasting and newspapers, and this other bunch of guys lend you your money. You see? Geography is getting to be kind of beside the point.'

They'd all dug out tuxes, which surprised me. These were one-room, one-suitcase guys. They'd have made good hitmen – rootless. I knew a couple of them in LA, a few in Manhattan, and the rest kind of drifted in. I'd come back to Chicago, any other reason aside, because it was the hub of the railway – *The Dark Hour* was always printed here because it's a good center for distribution. And they kind of followed. I seemed to attract that kind of guy. I dreaded to think the kind of places they lived in – the cold water, the mattresses, the roaches – and I thanked god I'd never been far gone enough to go home with any of them.

I was even worried that some of them wouldn't come – that I'd be piling it on too much, or that they wouldn't want to see each other. Writers can be funny, even successful ones. When I was at Paramount, twenty years before, the writers used to eat at tables depending on their politics; over at the Warner Bros commissary, they sat in groups according to their income. But then, I was always weird about throwing parties. You need to be good value to everyone around you, was the way I was brought up; you must be certain of being good and deserving, and you need to maintain friendships, and service them. Thirty-two (jesus) years before, when I left Chicago for LA, I got rid of my parents for the weekend and

68

gave one for all my debby friends and their preppy dates, even though I was probably never gonna see them again. I made my own dress and all the food, hung the ribbons myself. I sat for six hours on my own, feeling like a plum, until this one Mayflower asshole turned up, drunk, and told me they all thought I was a whore for going off to work in the movies when I wasn't even married. He didn't seem to mind doing me over the deli spread, however, whore or not.

But this didn't feel how it usually did when things were coming to an end, like whenever someone left me – when you know that you have to go back out there, into the spin, just when you'd got used to being still, or close to it, at the eye of the storm that is you. When aside from thinking about the new velocity you have to spin back up to, you've got everything – songs on the radio, valentines displays, lovers dawdling in the street, arms draped around each other on the last elevated train home – to remind you that once you were happy and now you're further from that than you're going to be for a long while. But that was stupid, crazytalk. No one was leaving anyone here. This was, rather, when you know that the end and everything that follows it is coming, and no one's going to help you stave it off except you.

Which is when you get to think, jesus, why do I let myself get into these things? You go into them so gaily, you give your heart away so gaily, but you forget how truly weird everyone else is. Someday you say something you don't really feel, and it hits some undreamed-of nerve and takes root, growing until it's become almost your defining quality and accumulating around it all the other stuff your lover doesn't like about you. And then, there you go again. If you could remember pain, exactly how bad it feels, you'd never do anything again for fear of it. When I was having Nicky, one of the damn nurses said that I might be in agony now, but I'd forget it as soon as it was over: I'd only remember it if I went through it again. I never did, but that's beside the point. This was nothing like anything else. This was something I did, and it was up to me whether I let it finish here or if I was going to make it into another beginning.

Because these were my guys. Outside, these were men who'd find themselves bemusedly opening Xmas cards in February, wondering who the hell they were from and why they'd been on their desks so long. Thank fuck I used the phone to invite them.

'You hear that movies are finished?' said Quent on my left and tipped back a shotglass of Wild Turkey.

'People have been saying that since the talkies,' pointed out George next to me.

'No, I mean, movies have finished. They're not going to make any more. Hollywood has ended.'

'Yeah?' George leaned back in his chair.

'Sure. Started with a comedy over at Paramount. Someone said, hey, doesn't the premise here rest on her thinking a rich guy is a sonofabitch when it's actually the poor guy who's a heel? 'Cos we did that one already.'

'It's true,' said Buddy, picking it up. 'I heard Jack Warner on the news this morning.' He did a mogul-voice. ' "We're very, ah, *grateful* for all the hours the fans have spent watching, but we feel we've taken the medium as far as it can go. Anything more would just become a tired rehash of old ideas, and we'd like the movies to be remembered as something bigger than that." '

Jack Ketch dumped down his Scotch-rocks and picked up Isadore's cigar. 'Celluloid was a nice enough medium while it lasted, but we knew in our hearts we could never compete with Broadway. Who were we kidding?' The stogie waggling between his teeth. 'We knew all along there's no substitute for the old-time magic of the real theater experience. I'm just glad we quit while we were ahead.' He put the cigar back in the ashtray.

I used to hate this Von Trapp kind of crap but this is why I called them all together rather than seeing them individually – when they were doing this they weren't guys who were thinking about how the hell they were going to pay the rent next month, or how they were going to live when they got too arthritic to type. These little circle jerks were all they had.

'Where are the stars gonna go?' I asked.

'Back to their old careers as waiters and waitresses,' said LeRoy LaVerne Smith. It bounced across the table to Larry Boyl. 'And sitting at the counter of Schwab's.'

This job just paid the rent, so they weren't like Writers with Writers – each was more like a vacationing college-kid sitting down with the other waitresses, or the guys from the road gang. This was how I wanted them.

We almost always came here. It suited me – another old wreck creaking under the weight of a half-forgotten reputation. I missed the place the first time, when I left for LA after the first war ended. Ben Hecht used to come here with the boys from the newsroom in the twenties, made this his Algonquin – when I met him in Hollywood, just before the Crash, he told me what became of the city we shared without knowing, made me ache for it; for the feeling of being bright and sharp and deadly, with a thousand miles between you and anyone the same. But by the time he was telling me this, there were a dozen people sharper than me on the same block, and a thousand more between me and the Pacific, a mile away at Marina Del Rey. It'd been hell to think that, and that's what I needed to keep this crew away from. If I left them high and dry now, they'd have to go west, at the height of the boom again, and it'd finish them just as it did me the last time. Max came in the door from the bar to take the order, and Quent grabbed him, waved the menu under his nose.

'What is this, service *compris*? So everyone from the garbageman to the manager gets a tip whether they do a good job or not? It's unAmerican, I tellya. You're headed for a HUAC hearing, buddy boy.'

'And you're headed for Jackson cemetery this hooch you swallow,' said Max, disdainfully eyeing the bottle of Polish vodka by Quent's elbow. 'We cook that shit up in a bathtub round the back.' He tapped the bottle's Cyrillic script with his pencil. 'That label says Fuck you, Imperialist yankee asshole.'

Buddy and Danny were the only ones without an extra bottle in front of them to supplement the wine.

'So what'll it be, Quent?' Max licked his pencil.

'Oysters in brandy, and gimme the real stuff,' said Quent.

I decided that Danny, out on the sidewalk, had been talking out of his pucker. The worth of your life should be judged by what you do, and there's no level of achievement that justifies giving up on trying to do still more: the horizon must be forever retreating. I'd always been the kind to leave things behind, and it was time to change. What was in this room was something good that I did, and I wasn't just going to forget it and die. The forgetting days were over. When shrapnel cut my son to pieces, the army bullied me about the funeral and then I never heard from them again. There was the telegram from the Oval office, and then there were shipping dockets, and then Walt buying me airline tickets and telling me about times and dates at the cemetery. Then nothing, ever again. I didn't get time to feel anything. No one wanted me to. They all thought I should just forget, all over again. I wasn't the kind to, and I wasn't about to start now. I was going to show what it means not to write something off and just ship out. I made movies for almost fifteen years, and you certainly don't forget that. You don't roll credits until everything's been tied up, or until all the strands make one rope. It's only when you find an ending that there can be riding off into the sunset. So here we were, ready to go.

My plan came from an idea I'd had for a long time – the sort of daydream you play with someday because it seems kind of neat; idly and inconsequentially, never dreaming you'd ever be in a position

72

to put it into practice. Or ever want to. But now was the time. I had nothing to lose if it didn't work, but it would.

I tuned back in, and Danny was getting up to leave. He shook hands round the table, slapped some backs, took some crap and bowed out, kissing me on the way. I didn't make a big deal of it. When he was gone, they started kidding about his TV contract.

'I'm not jealous,' Jack said, 'I just want what he's got.'

'TV is dumb,' said Buddy, looking at me.

'It's never going to work,' said Larry. 'He'll be back in six months. You can tell it's peaked 'cos they're giving up on domestic users already. All the ads in the papers now are like, for businessmen. Advertising and shit. If your company doesn't get on board now, you'll be left standing on the shore.'

'And that ain't gonna work either,' said LeRoy LaVerne. 'How about all those scare stories on the same page? How TV's going to destroy the family, give you insomnia, corrupt your children and turn them into morons? Who wants to spend money to be a part of that?'

'And it's such a bunch of crap – Goodyear Playhouse and Royale Revue,' said Jack Ketch disgustedly. 'I mean, compared to radio. When they going to do a show as good as *Johnny Dollar*? Or *Dimension X*?'

'You have to look at the long picture,' I said. 'There'll be all kinds of shows soon. The studios'd have to be crazy not to be thinking ahead. There will be good stuff. It won't be just the theater or the cabaret. Y'know? Ophelia *or* chorus girls. You'll see. People will come back to our kind of stuff. They wanted it once, and they'll want it again.'

They were all looking at me.

'TV is still so new. I mean, it's killing people like us and it's horseshit, but it'll get better. You need to be ready for it, all of you, when it does. It's like electricity. Think about it. There was only one thing electricity did when it came out. People got it hooked up

73

to their house so they could have electric light. That was reason enough. But then, when it was there, there was suddenly all kinds of neat stuff that no one ever imagined – washers and vacuums, and radios and record players, and *blen*ders and re*frig*erators, and – d'you see? Television is the same. Three years ago no TV sets were sold at all – last year they sold eight million. It's *just* neat enough for people to want to get on board, like with electricity. It doesn't do much yet, but boy, you wait. There'll be stuff like we can't imagine.'

'But not now,' said Jack, leaning back to let Max pour him another brandy.

'No.' This was the dumb part. 'People wanted smart stuff from us because they were used to us. Until just now they needed us to give them what they wanted, but not in the way they expected it. But TV is too strange – too new – for them to want anything that's going to stretch them. Not right now. But in a short while they'll be bored of it. They'll want big laughs, big scares and big tears. Big monsters, buddy, because there aren't any in the world anymore. Just little ones. Then they'll tire of that too, and they'll want Isadore again.'

The table was quiet.

'So what're we going to do till then?' Now was the time. 'Max, bring me a martini – bring us all a martini.' He clapped his hands, and I lit a dancer. A busboy appeared with a trayful, went round the table. Everyone took one.

'Mixed with memory and desire,' said Max, bowing and closing the door behind him.

This was going to be tough, but I knew it was the right thing. I'd been to *Cyrano* the night before, with Danny, and though I'd forgotten there was so much about writing in it, it had bolstered those last few hours a lot. I guess it's the ultimate writers' play. It says, writers can get whatever prize they want. It says, we can do your jobs but you can't do ours. It said, to me, that my guys could do what I was going to ask of them. They'd crossed a line anyway, just by having chosen, or having failed to get out of, the lives I knew them by. They'd crossed a line, but they needed to be worked round to it all the same. What I was going to ask of them involved real shit, terrifying shit, and I didn't know how they were going to take that. I stood up.

'*The Dark Hour* is no more, gentlemen, but Mr van Doren has one story left to tell. I want him to go out with a bang, boys. He's been explaining the world, through stories, to ordinary people in ways that they can understand for almost twenty years now. He's improved on reality for two decades, and it's time he got the send-off he deserves. This will be his biggest story ever and I need you all to work together on this one.' I stopped, surveyed the table. 'Which is why you're all here.'

'You are professionals, gentlemen. You have the ability to make a decent job of anything you turn your hand to, whether it's under your own name or Isadore van Doren's – serious literature or monster stories.' All it's got you so far is a fat ass from sitting in front of a typewriter fifteen hours a day, I almost said, but they were looking too serious.

'This is the spirit in which I'm going to ask you to consider what I propose. Our relationship has primarily been one of business, so let's not jerk around. *The Dark Hour* has been a primary source of income to all of you, and I've had to take it away. At any other time you could have turned to writing for the radio or B-pictures, but TV has complicated the issue. We need money – I figure at least a hundred grand, split between you, ought to keep you going until things have calmed down and you can work again. Here is how you're going to get it.

'Every week a bunch of knuckleheads puts together a plan to pull in that kind of money somewhere in this country. You aren't knuckleheads. You're improvers on reality: you're braggers of brags, layers of bets, dreamers of dreams and spinners of webs. You spend all day, every day, thinking up resolutions to complicated situations, calibrating odds, administering payoffs. You are better trained than the finest criminal mind to pull off what I passionately suspect will be the ultimate heist.'

I took a drink of water while they got that down.

'I'm not talking about a life of crime, gentlemen. I'm talking about a minor redistribution of lifestyle arrangements. I'm talking about one quick job that's going to redress the deficit that market conditions over the next few years will make in your lives. I'm talking about security – the one thing you need more than anything if you're going to bring whatever individual quests you're on out of the desert and into the valley.'

I'd thought there might be reaction here, but they were taking it calmly. Still, I couldn't do this alone.

'Did anyone see *Sunset Boulevard* yet? ' I asked, and there were nods around the table. 'How does it start?'

'With the guy dead in the pool,' said Buddy, and added, on automatic, 'With the end.'

'Okay. Well I'm starting with the end. I know how things are going to finish. Everything's got to work toward that now.' I took a long pull on my dancer, crushed it out. 'This will involve killing. Anyone who doesn't want a part of that should leave now.'

No one moved. Instead Jack said, 'Why will it be the ultimate heist?'

'I'll come to that.' That was the only detail that I knew. 'First we need to do what we do. I want you to approach this like a story. What's the best target for a heist?'

'The place with a chink in its armor,' said Buddy.

'No!' Jack was almost angry, and Buddy colored. 'That's how crooks who get caught plan heists. The best jobs oughta be opportunistic, random almost, or they gotta look that way. If they look like they been planned around a chink in the armor, then that chink is the start of a trail leading back to you.'

'He's right,' I said. 'The reality is smalltime. The reality is that

76

crooks get caught. We need things to happen the way they do in stories. We've got to improve on reality. The girl doesn't meet the guy at a dance: she twists her ankle in the fog, and he rides up out of nowhere. That's what we've gotta do. So where?' I needed to do this, because I really didn't know.

'Not banks,' said George. 'It's over, all that b.s. where the outlaw was the little man and the big guys were the bad guys. You can't have anyone rob a bank and get away with it now, however sympathetic you make them. The audience keep their money in banks, get paid from the payroll – this is a boom, and they love the bosses who're rewarding them. They don't think it's smart to see them getting ripped off.'

'Banks, payrolls, whatever – they're too well protected,' said LeRoy. 'They're smart now. One, there's a lot of risk for a lot less reward, and two, you've got a lot of research to do; as soon as you start sniffing around, there's a link that can be traced back to you.'

'So, what?' I said.

'So steal from the criminals,' said Jack, like it was the simplest thing in the world. 'Steal from people who can afford it.'

There was quiet for a moment.

'So, c'mon,' said Jack. 'Why's it going to be the ultimate heist?'

'The one thing thieves never factor into their plans is to allow for death amongst their number,' I said. 'If we're going to pull the ultimate job, as you've pointed out, we should do the most unexpected thing. We can make it the cornerstone of our heist.'

Twelve pairs of eyes looked back at me, and I was ready to take it where I could get it.

'In movie heists you can never pop the hostage,' I said. 'If the bad guys take a good guy hostage, then the bad guys win. The good guys have to back down out of loyalty. That's what the bad guys expect. But what if there are other kinds of loyalty? What if the hostage is dying anyway?'

I swept the table – I wanted to remember this, I wanted (and I

77

was welling up, suddenly) this to be the last thing I thought of – the black sleeves and white cuffs, smeary wineglasses, red stains on the snowy-white tablecloth. I tapped out a final dancer, took a light from Jack's proffered Zippo, and blew a cloud of smoke across the table.

'I have cancer. In my chest, in my neck, in my blood. I have six, maybe eight months. I'm dying, boys, and I refuse to go quietly. I want you to pop me at the height of the heist.'

Susan was working pretty fast, she had to admit it. She hadn't even been on a date yet, and yet she was waking up in his apartment. She had to hand it to herself.

She stayed in bed awhile, though the shafts of noonday sun falling through a gap in the drapes made her feel slatternly. She didn't want him to find her still in bed, in last night's clothes, still streaked with mud and dried blood from the scratches the thorns gave her – that would really have been a little too suave – but she needed to be sure he wasn't home before she got up. When a quarter-hour of silence had satisfied her that the apartment was empty, she pulled off her ruined ensemble and took a shower. She checked out the apartment awhile, in her towel – light-heartedly did all that dumb stuff like checking the medicine cabinet for face-powder or an extra toothbrush – then she dressed, in one of his business shirts, leaving it untucked over a pair of chinos that she had to cuff like a kid. Since she'd lost her purse, with her compact and lipstick, somewhere last night she settled for the natural look, tying her hair back with a silk handkerchief. She was making coffee on the stove when she heard his key in the lock.

He was carrying a brown paper sack of groceries which he dumped on the kitchen table, and pulled out a sixty-four-ounce carton of orange juice.

'You ought to drink this,' he said. 'You're probably starting a cold.' He took a couple of glasses down from a high cabinet.

'What else d'you buy?' she said.

'Toothbrush, some soap,' he said, sitting down, pouring out the juice. 'I figured you'd want to wash up. And peroxide. Your shoulders looked scratched up pretty bad last night.'

'You're quite the nurse, aren't you?' Susan coolly drank her coffee, the small of her back against the stove.

'Someone has to be,' he said, and she snorted, involuntarily. It made her sound like she was being too hardball, and he looked sharply up at her. 'What do you want from me?'

Not nursing, buddy. 'Probably more than you're willing to offer.'

'You know I ought to have you killed?'

'Sure,' Susan said. There was no other way to play it. 'I've compromised you. I've seen too much. Either you rub me out or you let me in.' She held the cup under her chin, blew hard on it, then looked down at him through the puff of steam. 'You said you had guys working *for* you – that means you hire. So why don't you hire me?'

She was making him miserable and she knew it. He was just hoping to maybe knock her off, and now she'd involved him in all kinds of complication. He was just going to have to deal with it. This wasn't going to come along twice, and she wasn't about to let what she felt get in the way of what she needed. But nonetheless she was stopped for a moment by the thought of working with this guy. Movies only show people in their time off, not what they had to do to earn it. She guessed this was because the two things are supposed to be separate (except, she had to admit, in Mafia movies, because Mafia guys earned money with their gloves off); but it might be too weird to be around the same guy all day and then be fresh for him at night too. But, what the hell. It wasn't like they'd be working together in an office or something. She pushed ahead, staring smack in his eye.

'I want to be a cleaner. I'd be good. I could get away with all kinds of stuff that a guy couldn't. I could be *so* useful to you. What?' She frowned up at him, looking like he was trying hard to keep from laughing. 'Fuck you, buster. Open your mind. I'm the last person anyone'd think would be a hitman. Who'd expect a woman?' She was righteously pissed at him. 'Huh? I could get much closer to a target than some knucklehead, and I could get away easier too.'

But when he looked up he seemed pained. 'Sweetheart, no one needs cleaners. All anyone does with hitmen now is pay them not to whack anybody.' He gestured with his juice. 'There's too much at stake now for that kind of crap. Jesus, there hasn't been a hit in this town since . . . Well. Put it this way. Rocky Marcello died last week, and he was one of the last.'

'Well, who whacked him?'

'Jim Beam.' He didn't smile. 'Rocky took up drinking when the old life dried up. Drowned in his own vomit.'

'He worked for you? For Giotto?'

He shook his head. 'Bellini. Some other guy. Look, this is how things are. People aren't at each other's throats anymore. This is 1950, for chrissake. This country is in overdrive, and there are millions going begging for everyone who wants them. No one needs to whack anyone.' He took the jug, poured another cup of coffee. 'Bellini had some guys take Rocky's apartment apart at the weekend, check there was nothing anyone'd want real people to see. They found some old notebook, with maps of his safe places – the places he put the bodies. I mean, can you believe that? Anyone coulda found it. Some guy who worked for Giotto disappeared in '39, everyone thought he'd jumped ship, gone to Canada – he'd taken money all over the place. Turns out Rocky hit him, and he's out in the woods. Bellini let Giotto know, so the guy's mother could give him a decent burial.'

'They're worried about the guy's *mother*?'

'You better believe it. Mothers are the wild card. They're the weak link. Guys like Rocky had to think about people's mothers the whole time. You hit some guy, his mama – who knows

81

everything about him, 'cos that's what moms *do* – she could go straight to the cops and turn in a dozen of his buddies, just like that.'

'*Neat.*'

He drank some of her coffee, grimaced. 'All these guys come from the same neighborhoods, got into the game when they were so high. Their mamas know each other's and everybody else's business. That was always the first question, in the old days. Yeah, maybe we need this guy out of the picture, but how's his mother going to take it?'

'Neat.' It really was. But cut to the chase. 'You said you're the exception. Is that why you're not Italian? I didn't think they let guys like you in.'

'Times have changed. They didn't use to let Polish guys in, and they didn't let guys from Princeton in either.'

'Guys from Princeton don't usually want to be in the Mafia.' Or are they sponsoring a fraternity nowadays, she wondered.

'I wanted to work someplace that had a future,' he said. 'It's all I ever wanted. That oughta count for more than where you're from, but Giotto's one of the only guys who can see it.' He took out his cigarettes and offered her one, lit them both with a match from the stove. 'But let's talk about you. Where are you from?'

'Chicago.'

'No, originally. Where did your family come over from?'

'I don't know,' Susan said. 'I'm an orphan. I grew up at Hull House. I was named for one of the sisters.'

'Really?'

'No kidding. I meant it about it being hard to get to college.' She took a slug of his juice.

'Well,' he said. She gave him back the glass, and he went on, after a moment. 'When my grandparents came here from Poland, they wound up in some tenement on the lower East Side with no work, no money and no food. They nearly starved the first winter. It's the poor who emigrate, not the rich. But the Italians . . . well sure, the ones who were stepping off the boat'd left their inherited land behind, spent all their money on the passage, and had nothing to live on in the new country. But some of the Italians here were already in City Hall, so they sorted out work and lodging for the new arrivals; handed out free coal in the winter, and turkeys at Christmas, fixed things up if anyone ran foul of the law, and all they wanted in return was your vote. What did anyone care? Giovanni and Maria had never seen a ballot box in the old country, and the idea that graft is a bad thing sounds pretty stupid to people who'll watch their kids starve otherwise. So that's how the Outfit started. People who'd come to the cities because they didn't have the capital to start farming, being looked after, and repaying it with votes. I mean, compare that with the rest – the white trash, who don't have anyone to look after them. You know? The rednecks, the hicks, the Klan. They're America's real invention – a mass of undignified poor, who're never going to learn to tolerate anyone else because they despise themselves. The padrone system doesn't look so bad, compared to that. I found out about it when I was taking a course in political history at Yale, and that was when I started to dig beyond that dumb *Scarface* thing.'

This guy was driving Susan crazy. She sat down at the table opposite him, propped her chin in her elbows so she was leaning forward with her cleavage framed. He lit another cigarette.

'The big guys soon realized there were better ways of making money than at City Hall,' he said. 'So they bribed Prohibition through Congress. In 1919 there were nine thousand legal saloons in Manhattan; ten years later there were thirty-two thousand illegal speakeasies, all controlled by the guys who paid for the legislation: the guys who got liquor outlawed so that they could control the supply. That was the first step toward what we really do.'

'We?' Susan didn't get it. 'I thought the Outfit was like, families and factions and stuff.'

'Naw. That's just for public consumption. It's much more

organized than that. That's one of the things that attracted me to it. That and the chance to have someone take my ideas seriously.'

'What ideas?' This sounded like it was going to be useful.

'All kinds of stuff. One thing I'm working on is new markets. Europe was in ruins five years ago, and this boom we're riding now is from exporting to help them rebuild – that's what really got us out of the Depression. But it's drying up now, so we have to find new markets. We can't do what England did a hundred years ago – India and shit – because we've just fought a war to stop that kind of thing. So we're going to have to invent new markets, at home. I got the idea when I was down in Tennessee one time.'

'What were you doing in Tennessee?'

'Doesn't matter. But I got talking to this motel owner, told me he'd just got married. Scrawny old guy, maybe thirty-eight, thirty-nine, with bad teeth and a wen. Then the blushing bride came out from in back, and she was thirteen. And I was like, whoa! This is too weird. It wasn't to them, but it was to me – would be to anybody. Down there, they don't have any kind of transition between being a child and being an adult; but in the cities it seems we do. So there's a new market, right there. Kids who aren't kids anymore, but aren't adults either. Their parents grew up in the Depression, but now they're richer than ever before, so they want their kids to have what they couldn't; so these kids have got money to spend, and they'll all go off to college – they'll have more independence than anyone their age ever did, and we can provide whatever they want.'

'What, hookers?'

'C'mon. Something much bigger. You ever hear that Tony Bennett guy? Frank Sinatra? These kids love those guys. But I figure, what if we get a load more like them, but make the songs a bit more about what the kids're interested in? Booze, cars, dating – whatever. But we hold on to the contracts. We give the singers special clothes to wear, then sell them to the kids too. If we can keep shifting what glamor *is* – like, what you've gotta *wear* to be a popular kid – and we get a stake in the clothes stores, we can clean up. And the coolest thing is, we can export it too. Because Europe's had nothing for ten years now, our stuff is everywhere already. American goods have become the desirable standard. We can carry that through. It's beautiful.'

Susan didn't want to interrupt. He was like an ugly girl buying jewelry for herself with her first paycheck.

'But there's all kinds of other stuff. Another thing I'm doing is a remake of that Prohibition gag. I'm going to get a link established between cigarettes and cancer.'

'I thought that was all horseshit.' She'd seen some dumb story about it in the newspaper.

'It is,' he said. 'But we've dug up some nasty shit about a few of the guys in the Health Department – how they've been using Nazi research from the death camps – that they're anxious not to see in the papers. So they're being a little more receptive to our laboratory's findings than they might be otherwise. Pretty soon they'll recommend that cigarettes get banned, and then we can control supply of the one habituating luxury that even the poorest – *especially* the poorest – will pay for. We'll make billions.'

'What if the tobacco companies can pay Congress more than you can?' Susan pointed out.

'We're not about to let that happen,' he said. 'But that's just one of the simpler things we do. We've got way more than that going down.'

'So that's what you meant about McCarthy, when we had breakfast.' Susan was beginning to understand.

'Sure. If McCarthy hadn't existed, I would've had to invent him. That's what I do. I look for things that are going to be big and try to get in early. McCarthy's finished things for the studios. Good deal. The guys on the West Coast are just smalltimers, who can't see beyond servicing the movie business, with narcotics, with women: they don't invest. Now the studios are done for, the industry will be small guys who need money. And they'll come to us. It's a fantastic industry for us. I always hated being so far from that.'

'You're not so far.' She meant that there was nothing between Chicago and LA except dustbowl and desert.

'I used to be. I'm a transplant,' he said, in a tone he might've used to announce himself an archangel. 'I'm a New Yorker.'

This was a surprise. She'd checked the place out already, but he didn't have any evidence of his background anywhere. But then she guessed it might've been a bit unlikely to find a yearbook or anything. Freshman year, *Cosa* College, 1947. 'So how did you get into this in Chicago?'

'I was only at Yale the first year you were at Smith. I was in County the rest.'

'You were in *prison*?'

'You used to live in Brooklyn, huh? Then you know the Armor Security depository.'

'Sure.' Anyone who lived near the bridge couldn't've missed it – the place was like Fort Knox.

'I had a plan to knock it over. I worked on that heist all the time I was in high school, while all the other kids were constructing science projects or making out behind the bleachers. I planned it for five years, till I was halfway through college. None of the New York guys were interested so I took it to Giotto: he gave me money, but he said I was crazy. I was the only one who ever believed it could be done.'

'It can't be done.'

'I know,' he said. 'I got ten years.'

Susan laughed; and, thank god, he did too. 'Out after six for good behavior. But because I did time and kept my mouth shut I got respect when I came out. No one remembered that I screwed up; all they remembered was I kept it tight, and did what they said while I was inside. Giotto's got a lot of business that way, and I acted on his behest while I was there.'

But she still didn't get it. 'So what does Giotto want with Earl?'

'He just needs to use that place as a front for the benefit of the cops – use it as a clearing house for contraband cigarettes, bootleg liquor, whatever. We make it kind of obvious so the cops think that's all we do. They *want* to think that's all we do. This way, we let them think that, and give them a few little kickbacks to turn a blind eye, and we get on with our real business unhindered. It suits us for them to think we're a bunch of *paisans*, y'know? Fucking guineas, whacking each other, skimming it off – if they ever got wind of what we were really up to, it'd kill them.'

'So why're you telling this to me?'

He looked up. 'I have a feeling about what you do.' And Susan was like, sure you do. No kidding. You and every other guy. She gave him the old eyebrow.

'No, really. People have all this free time now. Play is the new growth industry. Ordinary people never had too much time for it before – too busy scratching out a living. But now there's the whole weekend.'

'So, what, people're going to be makin' whoopee all weekend? They'll get tired of it. Jesus. It must've been hard enough staying with the same person forty years when you only had to put out for them once a fortnight. What're you saying? Everyone's going to start playing around?'

'You crazy? No. People are going to want to play around, but with each other, do you see? I did a memory improvement correspondence course when I was in the joint that said we only use a tenth of our brains, day-to-day. Well, I think we only use a tenth of the sex part of us, too. But people are going to need prompting – they're going to need someone to sell it to them. Which is where this stuff comes in. Toys, for grownups to learn to play again with.'

'You really think there's money in this?'

'I think it's a goldmine. To be American is to live in a permanent escalation of desire. There are millions to be grabbed, and all you need do if you want some is inflate that desire. We're all real good at wanting things badly.'

Susan'd been around the stage long enough to know a prompt when she heard one. She looked hard at him, and he looked hard back.

# The Rewrite

The primary aim of modern warfare . . . is to use up the products of the machine without raising the general standard of living . . . if leisure and security were enjoyed by all alike, the great mass of human beings who are normally stupefied by poverty would become literate and would learn to think for themselves.

– George Orwell, *1984*

*Somewhere near the 38th Parallel, Korea.*

Six months passed and, except for the first couple of weeks, Lucky hardly knew it. Two years ago he'd had an original story kicking around Paramount for a few months, about a newspaper guy who pretends to be crazy so he can get inside an asylum and uncover an old crime there: instead of winning the Pulitzer Prize, he goes mad. Lucky really ought to have known.

'Incoming!' screamed Coolidge, down the line, and Lucky dropped his yellow legal pad into the slime at the bottom of his foxhole, hunched down over it, whimpering as the mortar shells burst shrieking and whining around him. He jammed his pencil between his teeth to prevent their breaking off against each other – he was used to this sort of thing. Once the shelling started, that was pretty much it for the day, until you passed out from nervous exhaustion. And then it started again. He put his head between his knees, clamped the meat of his thighs over his ears, and screamed to drown it out.

89

The noise was the worst. Then the shit. The Koreans used human manure to fertilize their rice-paddies, and Lucky had begun to suspect that they'd been making contingency plans for a nation-wide constipation. Every foxhole Lucky dug, it felt like he was tunneling into shit. Every time he pulled his shelter half over the top of the hole, he sat back and admired his house of shit. This whole country was made out of shit. And he'd thought Burbank stank.

When the worst of the first was over, Lucky salvaged the legal pad, wiped it off as best he could, and shoved it inside his battle-dress. He wondered what time it was: he'd been working since maybe mid-morning, and it was easy to lose track when the sky was perpetually dim with smoke. He'd left his watch at the barracks in Japan: it was his father's watch, and he hadn't wanted to end up losing it. Everyone did – left wallets, snapshots, address books, the works. No one thought they wouldn't be back there by the weekend.

There was no reason not to. America was the big bluff cop of the world, ready with a clip round the ear for any of the neighborhood kids who stepped out of line. It was going to be enough just to show up, let the hoods know who was here, and watch them go scurrying back to their moms. It was going to work a treat. Officer America was going to show the world who was boss, then maybe go for donuts – and Lucky would get first-hand material for his war picture, be back in Japan for Sunday lunch; then desert, jump ship back to the States, and hide out in Hollywood. Have it sold inside six weeks, no sweat.

That had been six months ago. It seemed the Irish cop had been taking a few too many pulls from that flat black bottle inside his tunic. Lucky didn't know what he'd been doing. He glanced upward a moment then snapped his head back down as an .88 burst almost directly overhead. It could've been anywhere between lunchtime and dusk – the air above the foxhole was thick with smoke. Lucy had said, when she was through screaming at him after he joined up, that the sky would be their only common ground all the time he was out there. They'd been at Santa Monica, looking at the ice-blue stars above the trees, above the sea. They'd both been pretty crocked. The stars are ours, she'd said. Me and the stars – we'll stay up for you: you take a moment out whenever you can and look up, and you'll know I'm looking up too. They'd forgotten about the time difference but it didn't matter. He could never see the goddam sky anyway.

The shelling had settled to a regular pattern of screams and thumps. He sat back out of the hunker, felt around on his ration belt and found a half-squeezed tube of steak paste. There were some damp crackers in a crumpled K ration box under his knees, and he fished them out, spread paste on with a shitty finger and wolfed it. He always snacked when he worked, but here there was never enough food to do it right. It wasn't like you could run down to the deli for a pack of Ring-Dings when all you needed to push a scene just that little bit further was a sugar hit. But you got used to it. You may once've thought the rations sucked, but after six months they started to taste mighty fine. You got used to every- thing – the food, the lousy weapons, the lack of almost everything you needed. You learned to cut the tops off your combat boots, so you could slosh the water out without having to take them off everytime. You learned to ditch most of your equipment as soon as you got it, because it was all pretty much useless. You learned to crouch, screaming, in stinking mud twelve hours a day. You found out what it was like to be constantly driven into holes in the ground by a few peasants. This was not, it had to be said, what singing the Star-Spangled Banner through twelve grades of school had led Lucky to expect.

What it was, however, was the armies of the North bursting through the parallel and pushing south to Seoul. This was the UN observers in Seoul waking up on a Saturday morning six months ago to find themselves in a war zone; this was those gravy-train bastards basing their reports on a few garbled speculations and then hightailing the hell out, leaving their records behind and making verification of the facts a little tricky. This was the US suddenly committed to the least expected of wars in the least predicted of places, under the worst field conditions possible. This was, Lucky (who knew none of this) had thought, an excellent opportunity to pick up the kind of field detail that would make *The Beardless Dogs* a surefire seller. It was going to be cool.

Because no one had expected a war. It ought to've been no more than a police action, a containment. America was the only country in the world with neat automobiles, air conditioning, atomic bombs. Anyone with half a brain would take one look at a US task force and bug out, but not these crazy bastards. These sonsabitches knew there wasn't anywhere we could just drop a bomb and say, there. Stop *that*. These little shits knew there wasn't anything except the big one to throw at them. These stumpy retards dug trenches below trenches six months ago. These yellow motherfuckers knew there was nothing to use against their tanks and artillery. These little bastards just didn't get it. *But we're American!* screamed some Idaho fatneck the first month Lucky was here, standing up in his foxhole to protest the third order to dig in like cowards in as many hours. Then a chunk of shrapnel the size of a baseball took off half his face. The North Koreans seemed to be having some kind of problem with comprehending the new world order. They just didn't get it, the fucking hicks, thought Lucky, as shrapnel buzzed over his head like lines of angry bees.

Things had started to jar on Lucky two weeks after this thing started, when they were stepping off the boat from Japan at Pusan. His unit found itself filing down one gangplank as American stretcher-cases were loaded up another. Pusan itself was a hellhole shambles of corrugated iron, stinking street markets, twelve-year-old hookers and organized crime. They'd been told they'd be training in Pusan for a couple of months, but they were out of there in two days, going north by truck and train, sleeping in sidings and schoolhouses, and trying to ignore the backspill of refugees streaming past them in the opposite direction.

There'd been nine casualties in his unit by the end of the first week: eight grunts, from drinking the water, which no one had bothered to check; and the Lieutenant, from a cinder blown into his eye by a train engine. The remainder of his unit – still talking excitedly about the PanAm plane that had ferried them out here, the first flight most of them had taken – was switched to another division, to buddy up with a new bunch of bored smalltown kids about to find themselves at the frontline ten days after signing up in the Midwest. The 38th Parallel'd had about as much reality for any of them as the rings of Saturn.

When they'd finally got to the battlefield, they'd been told that they'd find a South Korean unit to anchor their positions to, but there was no one for miles this side of the enemy lines. Their field radios refused to work in the constant rain, and they'd been reduced to raiding an abandoned schoolhouse for a child's atlas, tearing out the Korea page and using that to navigate with until it got dark. They'd scraped foxholes among the rocks, in drizzle and darkness under poncho capes, and settled in to wait for morning. This was when they'd gotten to experience their first artillery bombardment; and, when it finished, their first Bugging Out – wild-eyed Americans streaming back past them, with Lucky's unit scrambling after, out of fear they'd be the only ones left; while, over their shoulders, files of mustard-colored North Korean tunics padded doggedly, carbines raised, a few hundred yards behind. This set the pattern for the next few weeks.

As they'd retreated back from the first town they'd come across, they'd seen local peasant women and children come running from the battle lines as if they were refugees; then pull rifles and grenades from their bundles and bring down withering fire on their asses.

93

The grunts that survived ran into roadblocks and ambushes placed by local residents. The ones that survived *that* gave up on trying to distinguish between civilians and guerrillas, and just learned to lock and load on anyone wearing the native dress of white pajamas. The fact that the women wore pants there too somehow made it easier to kill them. They'd started burning villages suspected of harboring guerrillas, or simply to deny hiding places to them. It was around this point that Lucky had found himself saying 'gooks' for Koreans – he found that he'd had to, or he wouldn't have been able to shoot children and old people so disinterestedly.

He soon gave up on *The Beardless Dogs*. He couldn't do an action picture now he'd seen what it was like. And besides, after they'd retreated all the way back to Inchon, he got a letter from Lucy saying that Vincente Mantegna, who ran a production company that Lucky owed four thousand dollars to, was keen to break her legs if he didn't get another B-picture script from Lucky inside a month. It wouldn't have been such a hot career move for Lucy to get busted up because she was a stuntwoman. The letter had been postmarked two weeks before. So Lucky had swallowed a quart of water from the river, and used his subsequent hospitalization to rework *Beardless Dogs* into a monster movie in three days flat. Mantegna was only temporarily appeased, and the yellow legal pad inside his battledress was Lucky's fourth script for the bastard in as many months.

It had been crazy to get mixed up with Mantegna, but it had seemed like a good idea at the time. Lucy had hurt her back in a fall, because some asshole prop guy forgot to cut open the corners of the cardboard boxes she landed on – the air hadn't been able to whoosh out of them fast enough and she was going to be laid up for at least ten weeks. Meantime, Lucky hadn't sold a story since the summer before last, and the money was just about gone.

Mantegna's lousy production company had got hold of one of his boxer stories, after everyone else in town had swabbed their asses with it. Lucky had, in the last five years, made boxers do just about everything except fend off aliens (he'd had baseball players do that). Mantegna had offered to put up two-thirds of the money to make it, and give Lucy a contract for all his movies, if Lucky could come up with the other third. Lucky should have smelled something – the story reeked, one of his worst ever – but he'd reached that point of despondency where it made sense that the only thing that anyone wanted was the worst thing he'd ever done. He'd told Mantegna there was no way he could raise that kind of money, so Mantegna put him under contract too, working out his stake with new scripts at two hundred bucks a pop. Lucky and Lucy had been already into their landlord for three months' back rent, and with her not working it'd looked like they'd be spending their first anniversary on the sidewalk. He'd signed up the same day it was offered him.

Which was a seriously bad call. Mantegna was an asshole who had no business being in the business. He didn't understand the first thing about B-pictures. Lucky may not have made many movies, but he'd watched plenty and he'd written a pile – *She Lives*, whose fourth draft was now on the floor of the foxhole, was his seventh piece of crap for Mantegna in a year. It was only ever going to be some dumb bride-of-Frankenstein type thing, but it could have been okay had Mantegna not gotten his dumb ass on it. He just didn't get it – didn't even know the basics. If you want to make something scary and you don't have any money, Lucky figured, then you never show the monster. If there was a monster in the shadows or behind the door, then the shadows or the door were what's frightening. If you opened the door and showed the monster, then, however horrible it was, the audience would know that that was the worst thing you had to throw at them, and they'd sit back in their seats. If you never showed them, they didn't get a chance to, and they'd stay scared right up to the pay-off. It was kids' stuff, a no-brainer.

But Mantegna, the dumb guinea fuck, wanted monsters he could put on posters. *She Lives* first draft had been cool – the mad professor's daughter and the hick boy running from shadows. This hadn't been good enough for the asshole, despite the fact that it would've cut his production budget in half. But Mantegna had presold eighteen states, he was in production next week and Lucky had no choice now but to give him what he wanted. While the mortar shells burst around him he wrote in some dumb piece of hokum – for a scene Mantegna planned to put on the posters – with an old Indian spear that the monstress was going to use to skewer the daughter. Lucky put her on top of the battlemented clock tower – the clock stopped by lightning, naturally – playing her fingers over the ancient blade, blue fire telegraphing from her talons to the metal and back. Lucy wouldn't have a problem with that, he figured: run a wire up one leg, under her dress, down her arm and under her palm to her fingers; earth the blade and there you go. He wrote in the instructions on the script; Lucy didn't know electrics, but he'd done it in high school physics. She'd be able to rig it up, no sweat whatsoever. So he pulled the forage cap over his eyes, and waited for quiet, waited for sleep.

It was only four days later, and two days after the mail drop, that he thought about her unearthed leg, and by then it was too late.

A pair of craps dice the size of Maytag washers were showing double-six. Susan stood like Betty Grable between them, smolder-ing at Earl over her shoulder. On a plinth behind her, Alice was twining one nyloned leg around the stem of an eight-foot martini glass.

'Hold it,' said Earl, and the flash popped and fizzled. 'Sweet,' he said, looking up, and grinned. This would've been unthinkable when Susan started working for him, but he was doing it all the time now.

Susan had to hand it to him. The man-size Perspex martini had been on its way to the Fez Room, a nightclub downtown that Giotto was refitting, where it was going to wind up spuming a spotlit blue fountain behind the orchestra; Earl had shanghai'd it, and got a couple of set-painters from the Rialto to knock up the rest out of plywood, chicken wire and paper-mâché. This was going to look neat. It was her first magazine shoot – for *Eyeful*, Earl's first magazine – and she'd wanted it to look just right. She strutted across the set, gave a swift tug to her rolled nylons, and entwined herself around a diamond ring so big you could step through the gold band without ducking your head. Dice, rings, booze and cards: the spread was going to be straplined 'Man's Ruin'. Susan shook her hair round her shoulders and looked ruinous at the camera, as Earl snapped and snapped away.

Giotto's money had worked on this place like spring. This was a proper studio now, not just a rough-walled basement, and upstairs, amongst other personnel, were an art director and an editor, pasting down pages and writing captions to the pictures ('Isabella has recently returned from Rome, where she posed for leading European sculptors'), along with men's-interest features about cocktails and free love, and syphilis and cirrhosis. The House of Whacks was now aka Eyeful Towers, and Earl was going mainstream.

*Eyeful* was for news-stands, and either Susan or Alice was going to be on the cover. Susan had spent most of the last couple of weeks poring over back issues of *Vogue* and *Harper's*, coffee-table editions of Horsts and Cecil Beatons, thinking about what made a cover shot and then trying to do it in front of the mirror. She realized one morning that she couldn't leave it up to Earl – that there was more to being a model than being a mannequin – so she'd got a bunch of books from the library – *Photoplay* annuals, cinematography textbooks, anything with movie stills – and looked at how the actresses *used* the camera. It was no good just looking good, she decided – you had to be a vortex, pulling light toward you for the camera alone. She was getting pretty good at it, and she knew she'd be more than a walk-on if she went back to actressing now. And besides, Alice was starting a run in her stocking that Earl hadn't noticed yet – if he tried to blow her up it'd show, and Susan was certainly not going to tell her. She put her hands in her hair, and leaned back into an eight-foot plywood royal flush.

By now a couple of wiseguys had come in from stacking crates of cigarettes upstairs to watch. There were almost always a couple of Bellini's or Giotto's guys around now, in case the feds came calling. There'd been three busts since they set this up. The cops came over, cuffed whoever was around, impounded whatever was in the storeroom – pre-tax cigarettes, whiskey, furcoats – (Susan got a swell silverfox from one of the guys a few weeks ago) and everyone went down to the station for a couple of hours while the pay-off was negotiated. Susan had gone herself, the first time. It was swell. They put them all in a room of their own, sent in some pizza, gave them a pack of cards to play poker with. The guys who were watching now considered this to be a perk of the job, a cool afternoon off – it was like they'd almost've felt cheated if they didn't get busted regularly.

Joey Volante stuck his head round the door to call the goons back to work, and Susan caught him looking at her, gave him a little shimmy and a wink. He leant back against the doorframe, folded his arms coolly and watched a little while, and when Earl wrapped it up to roll back his film Susan and Alice tottered over in their heels, Alice leaning over to kiss his cheek – but while she did it he was looking at Susan.

'You ladies got your dancing shoes shined for tonight?'

Ladies – he always said that. Susan was like, he's kind of an asshole, but he grows on you; the same way ugly jewelry does when a girl finds out how much it's worth. Alice had her arm round him now, and Susan didn't need X-ray eyeglasses to know she'd got her hand on his butt. Alice'd vaunted Joey all over her, these last couple of months.

'Did your cousin show up?' she asked him, looking theatrically solicitous over at Susan.

'Sure,' said Joey. 'He called me just now.'

'You'll like him the most,' put in Alice. 'He's a fun guy.'

'A fun guy,' said Joey, looking insolently at Susan.

Alice was rubbing it in because she knew Ben was an organ-grinder and Joey just a monkey; but now Ben was gone, and she was the one with a boyfriend. Joey, meanwhile, however much he shot Susan glares that would melt steel, was pissed at her for getting him stuck with Alice when he thought he could've had Susan from the start.

However, Susan was prepared to put up with it. She wasn't about to clear out of here just yet – the money was too good – and besides, if something was going to happen then maybe she was prepared to let it. Joey Volante was easy, and you had to take it where you could get it, Susan had decided just lately. She'd taken to keeping a bottle of

Wild Turkey around her apartment, and this was what suggested it to her. Life, she'd come to suspect, was like liquor stores. You can buy your booze at the market where it's cheap; but you can only do that during the day, when you swear that the way you felt at midnight isn't going to happen to you again. But of course it does, so you go to the liquor store and pay the mark-up like every other asshole. If you don't want to be an asshole, then you take it like a man and buy it at the market, however much your morning head tells you that you aren't going to need it.

It irritated her, thinking that way, because it was the kind of thing Ben would say, and what the hell did he know about anything? Susan hadn't seen the gimp in four months. She'd had six weeks of heaven, thinking this was it, this was what all the fuss was about – sleeping over at his apartment, leaving clothes there, bringing up cold cuts and salad from the deli, talking, drinking, making love. It had felt like she was finally stepping into the spotlight in her own life.

Then he had to go to Cuba – Giotto had some interests in a bunch of casinos there, but lost his shirt in the revolution. He was only supposed to be gone two weeks, but Susan hadn't heard from him since. His phone had been shut off and his apartment had a padlock across it. She was quite flattered at how crazy he must've thought she was, that he actually felt he had to move to avoid her when he came back, but it hurt like holy hell. No one had ever pulled the rug out from under her quite so completely – not even her husband, when he'd walked out on their three loving weeks of marriage. She wasn't exactly unaware that the whole thing had been a mistake that time, but she really hadn't had the slightest intimation it was going to happen this time. She figured Ben must've forgot himself while he was with her – forgotten that if you're a guy you have to sit on your humanity – but then the moment he was away he must've come to whatever passes for his senses, and decided to get out like every other sonofabitch Susan'd ever met.

She must have a sign over her head, she figured, like one of those whistles that only dogs can hear: a Coney Island arrow of strobing neon that only jerks can see. Here's my heart, assholes – drop it on the sidewalk and stomp all over it. It's okay, I'm used to it. I don't expect anything else. She'd gone back to his apartment the day after he left – she couldn't sleep, so she went over to sleep in his bed. Next morning she was just kind of putzing around, and found a florist's receipt in a stack of junk by his phone, with some girl's name on it, dated last Wednesday. She told herself it must be his mother or something, tried to forget it, and didn't go back to his apartment until a couple of days after he'd failed to return; and then there was a big old Titus padlock on the door, like the ones they used to hand out for high-school lockers on the first day of every new year. She stared at it for about a day, then went home and lost it bad.

The worst thing was that this shouldn't still be happening. She was twenty-five, for chrissakes. She'd thought by the time she was this old everyone would be driving jetcars and she'd have four kids, but both remained equally remote. The Smith old-girl newsletter that she really ought to stop having them send her – she was sure they must get a big old bang out of it, bunch of waspy Betsey-Anns in the alumni office all falling over themselves every time she sent in the latest change-of-address slip – was full of girls from Susan's freshman class having babies. It seemed like there were little kids everywhere she looked just lately, doing little-kid things, and breaking everybody's heart. They were calling it the baby boom or something dorky – there was a spot about it on the newsreel once. It wasn't like Susan was desperate to turn into some cow-eyed production line, but – she didn't know. She could see how it might be kind of nice to have something to define herself against. This is a baby – I therefore am a mother. She'd never talked about it with anyone, and she suspected it wasn't going to happen, but whatever. It was no big deal. But she felt that it might just be nice to have some guy stick around longer than a couple of months anyway. Just for the sake of variety.

But until then she was going to get on with her life, and since the upturn in business here had put her back in the black, she figured why the hell not. So she moved out of that crappy hotel, got an apartment, got her first ever listing in the phone book. Two rooms, kitchenette, her own bathroom. It was cool apart from the furniture – a bunch of nasty old Frank Lloyd Wright stuff from the thirties, some old Shaker chairs and shit. She could never believe what landlords expected a person to live with – every place, the same old horrible junk. She was going to throw it all out, get some modern stuff – nice, bright blues and lemons and pinks, plastics and teak veneer, maybe a swirly deep-shag carpet – there was just bare, varnished boards right now with William Morris rugs to match the dreary old drapes – but it turned out that all the barfy stuff was on inventory, and she wasn't planning to be there long enough to make losing her deposit worthwhile. Besides, having stuff that you like makes it hard for a person to drop everything and clear out and she needed to stay mobile. It was excellent not to have to see anyone if she didn't want to, and she was still in the Loop, in the middle of downtown. Sure, she had to high-step over the bums and the boozehounds some mornings, and if she tossed a cigarette carton into a trashcan about a dozen heads would turn, but she would've hated to be out in the sticks. The Loop was the only part of the city high enough: Susan hated to be down near the ground. She liked to look out the window at the towers of a city, and know that it was her that'd got her here and no one else. It was cool to go out and not have to worry about finding a cab to get her home. That night she was going to the legendary Continental Ballroom, and it was only just around the corner. You're never late for anything when you live downtown.

And she wasn't that night – though it wouldn't have mattered if she had been, because it took Alice half an hour to read a menu anyways. She smoked a last cigarette out of her window, enjoying the traffic, feeling the heat rising off the terracotta facing of her building, from where it had baked all afternoon in the July sun; watching her smoke drift away on the thermals into the sweetest soft evening, watching the clouds to the west turn a gleaming red. Then she skipped down to the street, rode the sidewalk two blocks to the Continental, swinging her purse through the heat and the downtown hum.

It didn't start until Alice got up to dance with Joey's asshole cousin from Los Angeles. He was totally knocked out by the Continental – maybe they didn't have jazz in LA – and he pestered Susan for a dance all through dinner. She blew him out because one, she couldn't really dance and two, he was a real jerk, kept telling her he was going to get her on television. When she seemed less than impressed by this and it turned out he had no other conversation, he took to playing with toothpicks, making little stickmen and stickgirls, with cocktail onions for heads.

It was turning into a real boss party. Joey was snickering to himself all the while because Susan and Alice told the cousin they were actresses – this was before Susan decided that she'd rather die than have the dork touch her, which didn't, incidentally, take too long. And Joey wasn't much better when the subject was what she and Alice did for a living. Susan'd thought – he was such a jock and everything – that he'd be down on Alice hard to give it up, the moment she started being his girl. But he never did. If either of the girls ever mentioned it, he was less a thirty-year-old wiseguy than a fourth-grader, peeking into the cheerleaders' shower-room without really knowing why he was doing it.

So Susan was rapidly getting to the point where she suspected that the reason people go to nightclubs all the time is so that, after they're married, being able to stay in the whole time will come as a relief; and then, while Alice was dancing with the cousin, Joey commenced to come on to her. Susan's only surprise was that it'd taken him so long since Ben; she guessed it was mostly precipitated now by his having competition – his cousin – coupled with the fact that he'd been going out with Alice for long enough to treat her pretty rough without having to worry about her taking a hike, meant he could do what he liked. He used to be real sweet to her, sending her flowers with poems, no name, on the card – she got a bouquet once with a couple of lines from *Leaves of Grass* on it, and she was like, wondering out loud about it to Susan to get her jealous, so Susan said, maybe it's from Walt Whitman, and Alice was like, so why didn't he sign it? No kidding. But that was then and this was now.

So Susan complimented him on his tacky new pinky ring, just to see if she could do it and keep a straight face; but he lifted his hand to show off the diamond like a newly engaged girl, turning it this way and that to catch the light better.

'This is America,' he said, finally curling his fist around the stem of his glass. 'There's millions out there, if you wanna get up and grab them. And your only competition is jerks. You make money, you gotta show it. Gets you respect. Gold is good. You oughta get some guy who can provide you with things like that. Whaddya say? Some necklace, show off that pretty neck?'

'I hate cold things touching my skin.'

'Guess Mr Kahane didn't get too far with you then.' He smirked, insolently.

'What's it to you?' Susan'd had enough of Alice rubbing it in that Ben was not around anymore – she really didn't need it from anyone else.

'He's an asshole.' Volante leaned back against the plush, gesturing with his cigar like a bigshot. 'College asshole. He ought to go work with the rest of those Ivy League jerks. Somewhere safe. General Motors or whadyacallit, IDM . . .'

'IBM,' she said.

'Yeah, well, whoever. Not us. Giotto's lost it. I dunno what they did to him in jail but word is they took out half his brain. Why he wants guys like that around . . .'

'He did six years in County.' Susan didn't know whether she was defending Ben or just trying to explain to this guy why she was ever with him. 'Can't anything make up for being Ivy League with you?'

'He got caught.' Volante spread his hands in the air. 'This is what I don't unnerstand. I mean, can someone explain this to me? He got caught, but Giotto makes him. And guys who didn't get caught gotta keep on doin' all the dirty work, same as before.' He took a slug on his Scotch and lounged back, glass in hand, talking way too loud. 'He earned himself a lot of disrespect, you know what I'm sayin'? Even before he did anything for Giotto. The guy just walks in from nowhere. I worked for Bellini six, seven years, the whole time he was sat on his ass with Giotto in some deluxe suite in County. Tough work, not a dumb kid's idea of some half-assed caper. Sheez,' he exhaled heavily, 'you know why they call it the Mob? 'Cos that's what it is. Four, five hundred guys, all pushing to get their head above the rest, get their face noticed by the big guy. I had to do it all – do the kind of shit that doesn't just get you six years, you better believe it. And yet the wallet that ought to be riding on my hip is bumping round on his. That can bust a guy's hump, y'unnerstand what I'm saying?'

'So the money's what really gets you?' She was teasing him, but he probably didn't know it.

'It's a matter of honor,' Volante said. 'He's not a Sicilian. He's not even Italian. Fucking Polack. He should go work in the concrete, the iron. They got all that sewn up pretty neat, and hey, who's got a beef with that? Each to his own, and that's how the Polacks wanna play it. But this is how we look after Italians. Giotto had no business bringing in a gimp.'

'Well, he's out of your hair now, isn't he?' She figured Volante might know where he was.

'Yeah,' he shrugged. 'He cleaned out. Guess he can't take the heat. Word is he's in Mexico.'

Fucking Mexico. She bet he'd got himself some little mamasita already. What the hey. He was history, and tomorrow was anothah day. And besides, Volante might be kind of an ape, but some women go for that. His unintellectualizing vitality could make him attractive, if you were in the mood. Susan was tired of guys who don't know what they want.

Right on cue he slid around the banquette and started snowing her.

'You forget about him, sweetheart. I think you did already.'

'Yeah, whatever.' Susan picked up her drink – but her glass was empty and she was like, déjà vu. Getting pretty crocked now.

'Hey, you see this?' He hitched up the sleeve of his jacket and unbuttoned his cuff, pushed his shirt back. There on his forearm was a tattoo of some hourglass dolly, in a corset and rolled nylons, her arm behind her head and her legs folded under her. It took a moment for Susan to register that this was, in fact, her – a cartoon Susie, copied from one of Earl's photographs.

'It's somethin', huh? Pretty neat?'

'Jesus.' She gaped. 'Is that real?'

'Are those real?' he said, looking hard at her chest, but she played hardball.

'What does Alice think?'

'Alice hasn't seen it. Only got it last week, and she's . . .'

'She's what?'

'She hasn't . . . been there for me for a week. She's not . . . see, I'm a man who needs a girl . . . to be there for me. I got a lot of pressure. And she won't . . . when she can't do the right thing for me, she won't do anything else. You know what I'm talking about?' Susan had a pretty good idea. 'Even one week a month is too long for a guy like me.'

But Susan was like, a week? What a lightweight. Try four months, buster. So,

'Excuse me?' she said. 'Did I have a blackout while you broke up with Alice, huh? And was I in a coma when you spent a couple weeks lavishing flowers and attention on me?' He gave a kind of sheepish grin, and dropped a heavy paw on her leg.

'Whoa,' Susan said, pulling away but not too far. 'We got a speed limit in this city, mister.'

'So you're, what, going to give me a ticket?'

'I need to see some identification first,' she deadpanned, seeing if he could go the distance – hardly any guys could.

'Will this do, officer?' he said. And that was when he opened his fly, and Alice saw Susan's face from across the room.

So there was kind of a scene. Alice threw a drink in Volante's face and he stood up, his fly still open, and slapped her with a straight arm. Her clothes collapsed like there'd been nothing in them all evening; and then she was out for the count, with the-cousin-from-LA kneeling over her, gawping like a goldfish. Volante buttoned himself up, and stood there for a moment, breathing hard. The whole room had gone quiet, and Susan took time out to consider the situation here. Joey hauling his equipment out in a club was kind of a shock – guys usually did it in cabs, empty El trains, in her experience – but, let's face it, four months was four months, and she never bought anything sight unseen. And besides, she could really care if Alice never talked to her again. So she scooped up the box of toothpicks on the table, walked over to her date, and tossed them down to him.

'There,' she said. 'Go crazy. Knock yourself out.'

And then Volante was hustling her out, into the night and into a cab. The cool air brought her up kind of sharp, but this was something she'd learned on the high-school bleachers: if a guy was pushy enough then there really isn't much you can do about it, and you just have to go with it, lie back and think of the relief of your own bed when you finally make it home. She'd been a few places since high school, however, and when he started getting kind of fresh in the cab Susan good-time-gal'd him all she could, implying that the town should be painted several shades of sunset before the lady lay down, and that the wait would make it all the sweeter. By the time they got to the next nightclub he was along for the ride, showing off, scanning the room for a source of some entertainment.

It was some dive on the Near North Side, a lowdown joint with an uptown address, and exactly the kind of place an out-of-town bigshot looking for some action might get recommended to him by a bellhop. The hayseed was alone at a table, scanning the room for someone to send champagne to like his life depended upon it. Volante locked in on him like a crêpe-necked hooker on a college boy. He left Susan alone at a table long enough for the hayseed to commence making eyes at her, then pointed him out to her and suggested it.

She thought, what the hey – I'm stuck with one asshole already, may as well make a party of it; so Joey went to the bar to give the patsy a chance to send a bottle of champagne over, and when they were halfway down it Joey went over and sweet-talked the guy. Pretty soon the hick was practically falling into Susan's cleavage. This was his last night in the city – he was some middle-aged chickenfeed magnate from Iowa – and he was obviously pining away for something to brag to the Elks about back home. Joey did a spiel about needing someone to show him some action – about how you had to be careful, an important guy like him alone in a city full of sharks. Strictly cornball stuff, but the moron swallowed it all. After he'd ordered a second bottle of French champagne, Joey mentioned a little party across town – very small, very select. The hayseed took this to be some kind of coded invitation to get Susan alone and slope off with her back to his hotel room; like Volante was a pimp and Susan was one of his girls, and that this was a way of introducing the transaction in a slightly more intimate setting.

Susan really ought to've been climbing out the powder-room window by this point, but she was pretty drunk and ready to drift anywhere the night was going to take her; besides, this was one over on Alice, and she wanted to see what kind of shit Joey could pull, given half a chance. It was weirdly fascinating to watch, and she wanted to know how the story ended. So once Joey'd seemed to give him the green light, the hick practically choked trying to get his champagne down his neck fast enough, and hurried them both out into a cab, almost rubbing his hands at his luck.

But this wasn't his night for double-sixes. The 'party' turned out to be a card game, a hustle to get the hayseed drunk and winning, then take him for every cent he had, and maybe his watch and wallet too. It was a polite way of shaking him down, without using any muscle, and was calculated to be nothing anyone could file charges about. As soon as Susan realized she got sick of it. It wasn't any moral objection – the hayseed was an asshole, and maybe this would teach him to keep it to himself and not go bothering girls in nightclubs. It was more that it depressed the hell out of her because it was so smalltime. It made her homesick for Ben – she never had to do this kind of usual-guy shit with him. So she got up to leave, but the hayseed assumed this was his cue to leave too, flush with the two hundred bucks he'd just won. Joey went over to him, and whispered that he needed to brief his girl a moment before he gave her up for the night; the hayseed made a show of protest but agreed to take one more drink while the cardgame took five. Joey followed Susan out to the corridor.

She didn't like the look of him. Volante could've swaggered for America when he had his nose in his first champagne cocktail, but that was four bottles ago. Now he was scared for his life, his skin gone white and sweaty, his eyes avoiding Susan's as he came out of the room. His good-time, cock-of-the-walk demeanor had retreated deep inside him, behind whatever was really him; and it was this that animated his face into a snarl as he suddenly grabbed Susan's shoulders and slammed her up against the corridor wall.

They both looked anxiously at the open door to the suite, in case anyone heard, but they could hear the wiseguys inside still oiling up the patsy under the guise of shooting the breeze. One walked past the aperture, his arm around the hayseed's shoulders, pushing a drink into his hand.

'You go back in there and make him stay,' Joey hissed. Susan pushed his hands away.

'You do it. I'm out of here.'

'Taking him with you? Forget it.'

'What's it to you? It's not your fault if he wants to leave.'

'Get wise, kid. They only let him win two hands to get him loosened up. Now they mean to take him, and shake him down *good*.'

'So that's why you brought me here? You said it was a party.'

'There was noplace else to go. Places close at night here, y'unnerstand? This is Chicago, not Manhattan. I thought we could drop him off at the game, maybe have a little party of our own.'

'Well you thought wrong, buster. I'm going home.'

But he grabbed the fleshy part of her arm, squeezed hard enough to make it turn white under his fingers.

'You get back in there, and you make him stay.'

'You do it.' She twisted away.

'I'm not the reason he came,' he hissed.

'Then why can't you go?'

He laughed, but there was no humor in it.

'Because *I brought him*.'

And then she understood. Susan pushed his arms away, and he glowered at her, half in anger, half desperation. But she was like, bite me.

'So,' she said. 'Not such a bigshot, huh?'

'What the hell you think this is?' he hissed. 'These are serious guys, okay? This is serious shit. This ain't no fucking game.'

'So why'd you bring me here? I thought we were playing, not working.'

He exhaled, heavily. 'I thought you'd wanna, I dunno, take it to the edge a little. Get yourself some big money. Then maybe we could cut loose, you know. Big time.'

'And what about Alice?'

'The hell with Alice now! You gotta play along here. I thought you were different. I thought you were up for the play. I thought you had guts. Guess I was wrong.'

This was strictly playground stuff but it worked. Ain't nobody called her yellow, especially when she was loaded.

'Watch me,' she said.

She went back into the room, and slipped her arm around the patsy's hip as he stood talking with one of the wiseguys. Or rather, the wiseguy was talking and the hick was staring at the drink in his hand as though he wished he could fall into it and swim away.

'Say, honey,' Susan breathed. 'I've been bringing you luck, haven't I? What say you let me sit in your lap a couple hands, huh? Hold your cards for you? Huh?'

Either she wasn't very good at this or the patsy had clicked that she was as much a part of the scam as the rest of the guys. But hope sprang eternal, if not in his breast then his pants.

'I could use a bite,' he said, turning away from the wiseguy. 'What say you and me go get a little dinner somewhere?'

'Hey,' interrupted the wiseguy, 'you don't need to go anywhere. We can order up from the restaurant down the street. We usually do, around this time, don't we, fellas?' Chorus of assent from the guys at the green baize, now rather desultorily dealing out cards and chips. 'Why don'tcha join us?'

'I have an early start in the a.m.,' said the patsy, and went toward his coat.

'Say, you're not going to walk out on us now, are ya?' said the wiseguy, still trying to sound light about it. 'I took you for a sportsman.'

But the patsy drew himself up. 'Took me for a fool is what you did, sir.' He took out his wallet, tossed the two hundred bucks he'd won back on the table. 'Here. There's your money, and not a cent more. Thank you, gentlemen, and goodnight.' He put on his hat, nodded to Susan. 'Miss.' Susan was genuinely shocked; she hadn't thought he had it in him. Suddenly she needed to pee pretty bad.

But the other wiseguy put himself between the patsy and the door. The guys at the table were all on their feet. The first wiseguy grinned, all teeth, and put his hand inside his vest. Susan wanted the floor to trapdoor beneath her. And then the door opened, and Ben walked in.

Some knucklehead who was by the elevator when they'd first arrived followed Ben at a slight distance, showing his palms to the other guys. Ben stopped short, and gaped at Susan like she'd come out in her underwear; but then he snapped out of it and opened the door wide for the hayseed, who got the fuck out and didn't look back.

Ben jerked his head at Joey. 'You too. Scoot.'

Volante looked uncertainly at the wiseguy by the door, who was staring at Ben in disbelief, but took a step toward the exit anyway.

'Hold it,' said the wiseguy, and turned to Ben with a big smile, showing the kind of teeth you usually see on a Wanted poster. 'Am I missing something here? Tell me, 'cos I don't know. I'm kind of dumb that way.' He burlesqued puzzlement, spreading his hands in the air. 'At the movie show I have to take Cheech here along, or I don't get the plot. Ain't that right, Cheech?'

One of the guys at the table grunted assent.

'So you gonna tell me what kinda shit this is?' appealed the wiseguy, but Cheech just shrugged.

'Y'see?' He beamed back at Ben. 'Even Cheech don't get what

you're doing here, fella. So that makes me think, dumbass that I am, that you walked into the wrong picture. Now that ain't any good, see? If you're in the wrong picture the audience, sittin' there in the theater, they're not gonna know what you're doing. They're gonna get confused. You upset the plot, see? Now I ain't no Hollywood bigshot, but my guess is, we gotta take you out. Whaddaya say, Cheech?'

Cheech shrugged. 'Whatever you say, boss,' and he took a step toward Ben.

'I'd stay where you are, if I were you,' Ben said, languidly.

Cheech snarled, and his hand went to his waistband, onto the butt of his gun.

'I couldn't recommend it,' Ben went on. Susan gaped at him. He was in a room full of guys whose names ended in vowels, and he was talking like some preppy kid out on a lark. But Cheech grinned, pulled out a .38 that he flipped round in his hand, catching it by the barrel, holding it pistol-whipping style. Susan was like, she wouldn't've minded watching Ben get creamed, the bastard, but she suspected that whatever he was going to get would be coming her way soon after.

'You,' Ben tossed at Volante, 'tell coach here the score.'

But the wiseguy interrupted.

'Just put the brakes on there, copper. Fellas.' He snapped his fingers, and the knuckleheads at the cardtable all drew pieces. 'Cheech,' the wiseguy ordered. 'Shake him down.'

Ben raised his eyebrows, and made no move to assume the position; Cheech patted him down anyway.

'He's clean, boss.'

The wiseguy curled his lip, and started pacing around. 'So what kind of fuckin' rookie they sendin' me now, huh?' he demanded of Ben. Susan glanced at Joey Volante, who looked like he was about to drop a load in his pants. 'You skate on up here without hardware? This what they teachin' you at cop school these days, huh kid?' A knucklehead sniggered behind him, and the wiseguy began to circle Ben now, playing to his gallery. 'How long you been out, boy? You still a little wet behind those ears?' He put one boot up on a chair, and drew out a razor that he opened with a *snick*. 'I think I'm gonna take me a look,' he grinned, burlesquing tugging hard on Ben's ear, and slicing it off. This went down a storm with the knuckleheads, and even Ben's mouth twitched at one corner.

'Oh, I amuse you?' said the wiseguy, baring his teeth. 'I like that. I like it that I'm uh, here to please you.' He mountebanked a stage-ham bow, but when he straightened up his face was sour. 'I think that's pretty fuckin' chuckalicious, cop, 'cos you amuse me. What did you think, boy? You could dance on up here, tell me you're City Hall's new nigger . . . and I'd start payin' you off tonight? Huh?' He pushed his face at Ben, who gazed back evenly. 'Where you from, boy?'

'The North Side,' said Ben.

'No, where you from originally. Where they post your ass from?'

'Manhattan,' said Ben lazily, stretching out the a's like taffy.

'Oh, New York motherfucker, huh? Well lemme, uh, give y'a little advice here, kid. Lemme give y'a little welcoming party. This is Chicago, unnerstand? We do things a little different here, and we been doin' things a little different since you New York assholes were still shootin' each other in the streets. We got arrangements, see? This is the city that works. We do business.'

'I don't need your business,' Ben said quietly.

'*Then what you come here for then, boy?*' the wiseguy roared, sick of this shit.

Ben put one hand in his coat pocket, and Susan was expecting him to pull out some horse-stopping .45 that he'd somehow managed to secret. But then she realized, with horror, that he was actually *lounging*, one ankle crossed over the other. 'I came for the girl,' he said, as though it were the most obvious thing in the world. He caught her eye, and winked at her, suave as hell.

And then Susan got it. He wasn't worrying because he didn't have anything to worry about. Joey, who was flattened up against the wall now and looking desperately around, was scared of these guys because no one was going to care much if he got slapped around; Ben, however, was the kind of guy to do, not to be done to. This didn't let him off disappearing for four months, but it was kind of a relief to know, right now.

Ben turned to Joey. 'Go ahead,' he said. 'Introduce me to your little sewing circle here.'

This was killing Joey, Susan could see. He hated Ben's guts, but he'd got to take it. He was out of his depth here in a way Ben wasn't – in a way, it occurred to her, that Ben wouldn't be anywhere. The expression on his face showed him torn between the suspicion Ben had been fooling around here just to land him in it deeper (and he was probably right, Susan guessed), and relief that this little scene was drawing to a close.

'This is Ben Kahane,' Joey Volante said. He almost spat it.

'Drives me crazy,' said Ben in the cab. 'These little creeps. Wouldn't have known Al Capone if he'd worn a sandwich board.'

'How'd you know I was there?' Susan had meant to be pretty pissed at him, but she was too surprised to do it right now.

'I called Alice when they said you moved out of your old place. Say, where're you living now?' Totally breezy and all.

'Oak Park,' Susan said. 'I'm married to the mayor and I've got three kids.'

He chuckled, but this pissed her off even more.

'I don't see anything so funny, buster.' She scooted right over to the window. 'What the hell do you mean, disappearing like that? Not calling me for four months?' She said it good, like she'd planned she would – not whiny, but righteously affronted.

He shrugged and said, 'They didn't have any telephones where I was.'

'Which was?'

'Jail,' he said. 'Or more precisely, the secret police interrogation suite in Havana. Just here,' and he motioned to the cab-driver to stop.

Four hours later Susan had traced her fingers wonderingly over the burn scars on his chest, his thighs, and a whole lot else besides. They were at the House of Whacks, though he hadn't wanted to go there. He said that he'd got worked over good his first week in County, eight years ago, and spent a few days on the floor above the regular wards at the hospital, in the cons' sick bay. These were the medical school's old animal experiment rooms, where doctors who'd apparently failed the auditions for Auschwitz put questions to living flesh that no one really needed to ask. There were still gutters down the middle of the floor, and Ben'd had a horrible suspicion that the dust was rich with motes of dried ape blood. He couldn't believe anyone could get well there – it was a bad place, he said. Not like a haunted house in a comic book, with hidden doors under the basement furnace that were portals to hell: rather, there were echoes, through time, of the kinds of things that put your hackles up; a place of contained ill-will. He said he felt the same thing at the House of Whacks, but Susan was like, you ought to try working here, pal. She'd felt it herself, which wasn't cool at all – this was the place she worked, and she shouldn't have needed to have all her armor on, not the whole time.

But locked in the studio, lying on a chaise-longue that she'd been tied to a dozen times, but with no ropes now, no weird shoes or clothes – sex like momma used to make, at least she assumed – she'd been able to forget it for an hour. This was the last thing she'd thought they'd wind up doing, even after Ben showed up. After they got out of the card school, he took her to a restaurant – he'd come looking for her almost straight from the airport, and hadn't eaten a proper dinner in three months – and she'd been prepared to go along with it. Let him spill out his tale of woe, then hit him with the evidence – the florist's receipt she found four months ago, with some little strumpet's name on it. So she did, over dessert. And,

'They were for the dead girl,' he said. 'The one we found that night in the woods.' And Susan crowned herself Miss Dogpiss of the Year, 1950.

She was the only person he'd seen since he got back. He didn't know jack about what'd happened since he was away, so Susan took him to the House of Whacks to show him – the paste-ups of *Eyeful*, the stockrooms of contraband, that guy Mantegna's new office and screening room, hung with lurid posters of his drive-in successes. Then she'd been planning to show him a few of her new costumes, to complete his tour of the business; but when she took off her cocktail dress to change, neither of them had been able to wait any longer.

But now tonight was pretty much over, and far from feeling sweet and lazy and generally like the cat with the milk-mustache, this bad place was getting to her. Ben was smoking a cigarette, laying back; she decided to call him on what happened earlier. She raised up on her elbows, rested her breasts on his chest and looked him in the eye.

'I didn't mean to be along with Joey,' she said. 'We doubledated, and Alice started a row.'

'Yeah, so she said.'

'Aren't you pissed at me? For being with him?'

'I think you can do better,' he said, but seriously, pushing an errant bang back behind her ear. Susan didn't really know how to take that.

'Aren't you worried you've pissed him off?' she said. 'He's kind of been running the place since you've been gone.'

117

'Volante is as big as I let him be, and no bigger,' Ben said, not playful. 'Tonight's been good for him. He has to be kept down. I can't have guys like him getting ideas.'

Susan was like, one pro to another. She took a light from his cigarette, talked tough around the filter-tip. 'He's kind of a hair-trigger, though, isn't he? I mean, he does stuff first and thinks after. Aren't you worried he's going to resent being shown up in front of those other guys?'

'Those other guys were just about to bust his fingers and he knows it. I've done him a favor. And besides, it's good that other people see him getting slapped down. He's always been kind of partial to shooting his mouth off around town, and we can't stand for that. He works for Bellini, and Bellini owes Giotto – the only reason Giotto tolerates him is on the condition that he remembers his place. If Bellini forgets it then everything will go to hell. Giotto runs this town because people think he runs it – the moment they stop thinking it, he'll stop running it.'

'Why'dja have anything to do with guys like him anyway, if he could get out of line?'

'Guys like him will do what they're going to do regardless. So we let them, but we use them.'

Lighten-up time. Susan got up, wrapping herself round in one of the prop sheets that'd made their extemporized bed, and walked over to the back of the set.

'So what do you think of my career?' she asked over her shoulder. 'You see all this stuff?' She pulled out a clothes-trolley of rubber, hanging limp as dead fish, buckles and zippers jangling as she ran her hand along the garments. He sat up, cross-legged, the sheets pooling in his lap as he peered through the candlelight.

'They look better with me in them,' she said. 'Wanna see?' She didn't wait for an answer, but dragged the rail away behind a backdrop. She wasn't quite ready to go to sleep yet, but his voice

118

was getting drawlier and drawlier: she figured she'd put some snap upside his turtle a little.

'Go over to the make-up table and pass me some powder, will you,' she called out from behind the screen, selecting a short-sleeved catsuit with a zippered front. His hand appeared with the Johnson & Johnson's, and she shook it down inside the latex then inched it on. She couldn't be bothered with the knee boots – too much lacing, and she didn't want him getting bored – so she grabbed a pair of six-inch pumps from the rack, pulled the rubber up at her shoulders and tugged the zipper down mid-cleavage. Then she strutted out from behind the white paper, her heels clocking on the concrete floor. She put her hands on her hips and stood facing him, feet apart.

'So whaddaya think?'

He gaped at her.

'Close your mouth, babe. And switch on those arc-lights, why don't you. It's in back.' She turned away and doubled up at the waist, ratting out her hair then tossing her head back. He got up, sheet wrapped round him, and then the *chunk* and hum of the lights filled the silence. Susan stepped into the brightness.

'Well?' She arched an eyebrow, pirouetted on a heel.

'Why this . . . rubber?' he said, eyes round and shiny as quarters.

'The same reason as the ropes and stuff. You can't photograph flesh, so this is flesh, plus. Which makes it more so, don'tcha think?'

'You look like a dolphin,' he said, running a hand over her taut second skin.

'Fresh,' she said, and winked at him. 'Neat, though?'

'Neat,' he said.

'You want to try some?' She was daring him. 'It's okay, it stretches.'

'Sure.' He couldn't back down, and she led him round, helped him into a pair of long rubber pants. He winced as the latex pulled the hairs from his legs, and Susan giggled.

'How do I look,' he said, finally.

'Swell,' she said. He did too. He had a pretty good body from the waist up, his skin the color of sugar-cones in the glare of the lights. Susan walked away to get her cigarettes. 'But you know Bellini's cutting up rough about this stuff?' Of course he didn't, and he didn't say anything. 'He wants to drop it all. Alice told me. He doesn't like it – and neither does Joey, but he's torn in two. He doesn't want Alice to stop earning this kind of money, but he's kind of an asshole about other guys looking at her, you know? And I guess he doesn't want to be disloyal to Bellini.' She sat down on the chaise, lit a cigarette. 'But I figure it's like you said.' She blew out smoke. 'Bellini's more interested in the booze and cigarettes. He wants to keep things like they are. Booze and cigarettes are needs he can understand.'

But Ben was putzing around with the stuff on the clothes rail.

'Say, what's this for?' He held out a latex hood.

Susan laughed. 'That is the weirdest thing. Bring it here,' and he did. 'Kneel down.' He bowed his head, and Susan molded it onto his face, strapped it up at the back. Then she went over to the rail, got the airbag and hose, while he watched through the eyeholes. 'This clamps down over your mouth here, and the airbag is to control your breathing. The idea's the same as letting someone tie you up; you let them have the power. But you have to trust them.'

He was still kneeling, looking up at her.

'Trust me?' she said.

His eyes were wide as he nodded.

'Then lay yourself back up here.' Susan patted the chaise behind her.

*Jack Willard hunkered down on the smooth metal floor and, dismissing the claustrophobia, gave his full attention to the situation. Anyone else his age might've panicked, but it was not in his nature to. He was a serious kind of guy, which had always singled him out at college. When they were cutting up cadavers the first time, for example, he had been the only kid in his class not to crack a smile when two of his fellow freshmen commenced to play catch with some dead guy's liver. He was probably the only med student at Harvard not to have a human skull – tricked out with party hat and sunglasses, with a cigarette between its teeth – grinning down from the bookshelf of his study-bedroom. It wasn't a question of respect; simply that frivolity, or indeed any deviation from his singular purpose, was anathema to his nature. It detracted from the job in hand.*

*Regret, had it ever warranted consideration, Jack would also have found an impractical distraction. Other guys squatting on that floor might have expended useless energy in railing at their own stupidity in taking such a small economy, hopping freight cars between school and summer job rather than taking the bus; but again, this wasn't Jack Willard's style. All he had to rely on in this world was himself, and he had learned long ago the uselessness of after-the-fact reproach.*

*All he needed to do was assess the situation. He was in a pitch-dark freight car with no apparent cargo. There had been no markings on the outside of the car to suggest it, but, now he was inside, he was pretty certain this was a meat-wagon. He'd climbed in through a hatch in the roof, pulling it shut after him against discovery; then had hung in space a moment before he dropped, expecting to hit wooden crates a foot or so below him in the darkness. As it was he fell the full fifteen feet onto cold metal, and considered himself lucky not to have fractured an ankle. The absence of payload told him immediately that something was wrong; it also told him that there was no way back to the roof-hatch until the car was uncoupled in Chicago. A thorough, groping exploration had discovered smooth metal walls with no handholds, and nothing that might be pressed into service as a platform from which he might launch himself hatchwards. The only furbishment he discovered, feeling his way in the unnaturally total darkness, was what he sincerely hoped weren't a row of butcher hooks suspended from a rack on the wall.*

*But after a while he forced himself to admit it. This was a refrigerated freight car, and before he was going to be let out there were around fifty hours to kill, if the cold didn't kill him first. Even though the car was empty, he suspected it was still kept close to freezing, to deny bacteria the conditions to flourish. He was stuck in there, it was below zero, and there were fifty hours to Chicago.*

*He had begun to shiver shortly after he found the meat-hooks. It was June, and all he was wearing was a light cotton sweater over a button-collar shirt, cotton pants, and summer underwear; the rest of his clothes, or those that he'd need for packing meat in the stockyards, he'd mailed ahead to his lodgings in Chicago. He'd had the foresight to come prepared with food and water – he had, in his pack, a foot of Italian sausage, a loaf of Wonder Bread, and a bottle of water – on reflection, he stowed these inside his sweater to prevent them freezing. But that was it. He wasn't far enough through med school to have studied the effects of prolonged exposure on the human physiology, but he had a notion that fifty hours at a degree or so above freezing at best were not felicitous conditions to the support of even a young and vital metabolism.*

*Panic was something that was new on Willard, but after a moment's honest puzzlement when he woke, he was forced to concede that this was, in fact, what he was feeling. According to the radium dial of his watch, he had slept for around ten hours, and this in itself was worrying – he never slept more than six. Furthermore there was a hard, relentless ache in his muscles that, however much he tried to explain away as a consequence of sleeping on hard metal, he suspected nonetheless was the result of sustained and vigorous shivering as he slept. He extricated the leather bottle from against his skin and allowed himself a mouthful of water, then took a bite of sausage and a couple of slices of bread.*

*He had dreamed while he slept – this too was unusual – dreamt of a jumble of ice floes, of fishmonger's red hands, of canvas frozen solid and I-may-be-gone-some-time's. He was cold now, deep cold, the chill wedged into his bones as unyieldingly as it lodged in the bricks of his Boston rooming-house for six months of the year. The food sat in his belly like a block of ice. There were thirty-six hours to go, and he was tired. He had no feeling in his hands and he slapped them together, rubbed them hard, forcing blood back into the wooden slabs they'd become, then dug around in his pack for his address book and a stub of pencil. He opened it to what he thought were the Z's, pages he knew to be blank, and began to write in the dark.* Hour 15. Fatigue and mental disorientation. Circulation poor. *As far as he was aware, there was no first-hand account of death from exposure in the medical canon. He had never assumed that medicine would grant him posterity – he had simply wanted to be a good physician. But if his life had taught him one thing it was that you took what fate handed you, and made the best of it. He would chronicle his sensations as his body shut down its functions, as he froze to death. It would undoubtedly be of use to the profession in some small way. He sat back, quite satisfied, licked the pencil, and concentrated on the job in hand.*

*When the Chicago crew opened up the wagon and found him, they thought he'd died of dehydration; but couldn't figure out why there was a half-full bottle of water in the pack that lay by the body. Even when the coroner read the shorthand pad he couldn't understand it.*

*The temperature he recorded in the freight car was steady at 8°C, and had been since the dial was set to defrost in Massachusetts.*

I was at Schlagl's with Buddy, having lunch; but in the big room this time, where the silver dollars were set in the floor, and stripes of sunlight fell buttery-yellow through the row of vermouth bottles in the window. We were meeting there because I didn't have an office to meet in anymore, and besides, I figured every day could be lunch from now on. I didn't even need to do any of that lunch crap, stuff I'd been doing twenty years, like that thing I learned in script supervision, when writers used to take me out to schmooze me as cheaply as possible; you order the special and house white, as if you're too captivated by the other person to look at the menu – makes being cheap look like panache. Work was over now, and the dumb economies that used to govern my life made no difference at all anymore.

I leaned back in my chair, tossed the sheaf of double-space onto the tablecloth, lit a dancer. I proffered the pack at him, but he switched his head demurely.

'You really oughta smoke,' I said. 'I don't see why you won't. Don't you get tired? Of breathing air, and nothing else?'

'Air is free,' he said.

'My point exactly,' I said. 'Not wanting extra is unAmerican. Really, we should lock you bastards up. Fifty years ago the anti-tobacco lobby got smoking outlawed in thirty states: by the twenties the same people were being indicted for treason. It was the war, of course.' I gestured to the typescript. 'So you want out?'

'Out of what?' He put his hands in his lap.

'The robbery. I take it this is supposed to make me think about beating the cancer?'

'It's a true story.'

'So if your mind can shut down your body, your mind ought to be able to shut out a tumor?'

124

'You just oughta think about it.' He looked up disconsolately. 'You said they told you you'd be dead by now.'

'They tell you anything,' I said. 'They don't really know shit, except it's going to kill you. C'mon,' I crushed my cigarette, waved to Max for my coat, and tossed five bucks in the dish. 'Want to show you something.'

I'd got a letter from Danny that morning, out in LA. Breezy, didn't say much. The kind of letter you write as a prompt, in the hope that, by not mentioning the real business, you'll get one back telling you what you want to hear. I mailed him back a copy of the last issue of the magazine, with a comp slip.

I had to sit on Buddy hard. I couldn't permit any doubt because I had too much of my own. I'd had to do this with all of them, to various extents; Buddy was always going to be the hardest, so I saved him to last. But it was tough. I was too close to him. It made me think that I really oughtn't know too much about other people; maybe if I hadn't, I wouldn't have had to do what I was about to.

It's a terrible thing, to be old and to discover that you've been wrong. All my life I'd thought, just connect. Know *people*. Every different life, no matter where it's from, will make you the gift of a larger one. And the sharper the relief, the greater the effect. Whatever, I was wrong. Quite apart from the obvious scam of filling your gaps with a fast parade of whoevers (to stop you from thinking about why there are gaps and where they might have come from), interrogating other people's lives to avoid looking too hard at your own isn't even much of a dodge – shrinks, so it goes, top themselves more than anyone. The trouble begins when you've picked up a few handy facts about someone: before you know what you're doing, you're constructing histories for them, and making them fit so neatly with the way you want to feel that they just massage whatever was wrong with you to begin with.

So, as I'd seen each of the gang alone since that lunch, I'd been thinking that maybe this wasn't such a hot idea. Maybe I only felt I had to do the heist because I knew too much about my gang of putzes. Because I'd made it personal. If I coulda kept it just business, then I could've just let it all go, and just disappeared – gone off into the wilderness to die, like an elephant. Too late now. I had to go looking for something more, like I did when I got married. But it was done now and I had to make the best of it. Maybe I was too involved. I figured the hell with it. They knew nothing about me, and that was the way I wanted it. I needed them to think that something had exploded inside me, and that to go along with whatever I wanted them to do was going to be easier than trying to deal with whatever fallout they'd get from me otherwise. So I paid the check, got Buddy in a cab, and did something I wasn't proud of.

Shit ends and shit begins all the time, without anyone even noticing. Maybe three times in my life I'd had a letter delivered by a mailman on his last route after fifty years on the job. It was probably nothing, probably a bill, probably a subscription reminder that I didn't want – but the significance, the tremble in his hand, as the last letter slips from his fingers. Happens all the time. For something else to start, something has to end. When I was a kid, my nurse used to make me stop crying by telling me that someone really sad, someone who needed to cry if they were ever going to get better, was waiting for me to stop before they could start. She said there was only so much unhappiness to go round.

So I was damned if I was going to let Buddy or anyone else make me feel lousy. If you find yourself feeling emotions that don't fit, I always thought, then you just need a spiritual overhaul, or to work harder at organizing your life. I knew I ought to be setting my affairs in order, but I figured there were ways and ways of doing this. Like, I knew I ought to be getting rid of stuff – one of the few things I'd dredged up to feel good about when I found out was that I only had to buy one more bottle of window cleaner, two more boxes of floor soap, one more package of Drano – but rather than giving shit away I'd started buying it. I guess I must've figured, what the hey, enjoy it while it's still there. I could totally understand that thing about Vikings and Egyptians and whoever, keeping all their effects about them in their tombs. I wanted all my goddam effects. I'd just got a really neat Clarice Cliff ashtray that was definitely coming with me. I didn't know what else to do while I was waiting for it to start happening – waiting to have something to show I was dying by. Dr Casey, forever revising his projections, said I had about three months of that to get through and then everything would change.

So while there was still time, I took Buddy to see someone who it happened to a while back. At the Columbus hospital, in a room looking toward the lake, a character actor named Robert Cummings had been dying for most of a year now. I knew him a while in Hollywood, and though I'd heard he was here I'm afraid I only visited him after I was diagnosed. What can I say? You lose touch. If I'd kept tabs on everyone I used to know I wouldn't have had time to do anything else.

Besides, it was lousy to visit him. He used to play cowboys, trappers, whatever, spent most of his working life in flannel shirts and denim; now, he hadn't been able to take a leak by himself for four months. I didn't plan on getting this bad. I was still at the initial phase, where the cancer is diagnosed, and I didn't plan to go any further. I'd watched him go through the intermediate phase, where treatment was undertaken, and was hugely traumatic, with the outcome totally uncertain: that had really sucked, and that was when I made my mind up. But now he was in the advanced phase: his treatment was solely palliative, if ineffectual; if he was anywhere in there, then he was waiting to die, like everyone else.

He was sleeping, or unconscious, so we talked in whispers.

'He has the same as I do. This was where I can expect to be by spring.'

I'd thought Buddy might be totally freaked out, but he had a writer's – or a kid's – curiosity.

'Does he sleep all the time?'

'No. If you charted the efficacy of his medication as a bell curve, he's at the top of the arch right now. It's rare to have caught him asleep, believe me.'

'He's allowed *whiskey*?' Buddy pointed at the bottle and glass on the nightstand.

'The tumors have altered his metabolism,' I said. 'If he doesn't drink he won't feel like eating. He's quite severely emaciated, as you can see.' This was the worst thing for me – the floral hospital-issue wrapper draped over this mummified chicken-wing of a man.

'Do you want to wake him up?' Buddy said. 'Let him know you're here and all?'

'No. This is his best part of the day. He'll spend most of the next twenty hours wishing for this again.'

'How much pain is he in?'

'It's useless to speculate. We don't know. We can't have any idea. I mean, I can kid myself I know more about pain than you do. Guys think they know pain, but they're only good with impact pain – getting clipped on the elbow by a baseball, hitting a finger with a hammer. Women know a little about tissue pain: about tearing and swelling of the soft parts of you; but you can't remember it too well. We'd stop having kids if we could.' I pulled out my cigarettes. 'We can't imagine what he's feeling. Chronic pain has no foreseeable end, tends to get worse not better, serves no purpose, and takes up all of your attention, making life not worth living. Trying to live with it is like swabbing the decks of a sinking ship.'

Buddy had gone quite pale. 'Can't they do *anything*?'

'He's getting morphine, but not enough to give him more than a couple of hours off a day. Doctors figure that if they give you any more you'll get hooked on it. You're going to die anyway, but

128

you'd be amazed how stupid they are about it. Bob told me that if he asked for it too often they seemed to figure he was hooked on it already, and held it back even more. So as the pain got worse, they gave him less and less to help with it. It's probably some kind of religious hangover – Christ died in pain so therefore we should too, and painkillers are gonna cloud your repentant faculties – but mostly it's this whole dumb drug thing.'

This was what really decided me, and it was partly my fault. Neat, huh? I had a part in engineering one of the first drug panics this century, and this was part of the fallout. One of the first scripts I edited was a picture called *Cocaine,* a hack job that we put together in six weeks after an English actress named Flora Kempton took an overdose. I've still got one of the notices from the *Film Renter & Moving Picture News* in a scrapbook somewhere. *If you're down in the mouth, dull, depressed and feel like nothing on earth, take a dose of COCAINE. It will buck up your box-office receipts. It will drive away Depression.* It really did. It did crazy business. Twenty states banned it, to outrage from the gutter press, who, paradoxically, argued that morality tales ought to be shown. They won, naturally, so as soon as they got the movie shown, the papers started on the scare stories: Southern cops having to use elephant-caliber guns to stop crazed coked-out negroes with superhuman strength; white girls getting hooked on it, lacing cigarettes with cocaine to knock out doughboys on weekend passes. It was like, that thing about white girls getting slipped Mickeys and sold into slavery, but turned on its head: no one seemed to care much what the effects of the drug actually were; as far as the press were concerned, it was more or less the same as a bellyful of hooch. Still, the hayseeds and the mayors wanted to read it, so it ran and ran. I felt bad about it at the time, but I wanted to get on the other side of the camera fast, and I knew *Cocaine* was the biggest break I was going to get – it was supposed to be a flapper's drug and they wanted a flapper to write it. But this was where it had left me – too scared to die naturally because if I ask for medicine for the pain, a doctor's going to think I'm some kind of dope fiend because of a panic I helped start thirty years ago. Story of my life, I swear. But it was time to lay it on thick with Buddy.

'Even if you do get morphine, and don't have the indignity of begging for it twenty hours out of the day, you still don't have much quality to your existence. Morphine binds you all up, Robert said. The laxatives they give you work erratically and make you lose control in the night. You have to lie on a rubber sheet, and get cleaned three times a day.

'They could surgically knock out the pain-bearing nerves – either by local anaesthetic or by permanently damaging them – but they never do. It's almost like they think pain has a cathartic function, when it really doesn't. What it does have is a link to morale. The more pain you have, the less will to live. And then you're off their hands forever.'

I crushed out my cigarette in the arm of the chair – they all had little ashtrays set into them, like on the Greyhound, I guess to stop people stealing ashtrays from the hospital – and glanced over at Buddy, who had his hands folded in his lap and his eyes on the floor. It looked like I was winning.

'You never went to Europe, did you?' I may as well have asked him if he'd been to Jupiter. 'Over there they have a real old church almost everyplace. Really. Three houses and a farm, but there'll be a big stone church too: it's like nowhere was too small to franchise. And I mean *old* old – five, six hundred years is nothing. They used to bury the dead around the church, right up until this century, and you can see where each successive congregation is under the ground now from the gravestones. It's the strangest thing, but most of them offed in their forties. It makes you realize that most of us really ought to be dead by now. People aren't designed to last this long. You'll notice your first gray hair in a couple of years, because the time for you to have plumage is over. *You're* pretty

130

much through, Buddy, let alone me. It's just because we've got heating, and clean water, and, jesus, refrigerators, and antiseptics and laughing gas. And what's the point? When this is what you come to?'

'Okay, okay,' he said, finally. 'You made your point.'

'So you'll do it?'

He exhaled and stared at the green lino. I said,

'Any other way of dying has got to be better than this. People die other ways all the time. A million Americans a year can't be wrong.'

'It's not that. It's the . . .'

'The heist? You have a problem with that? Forget it. You won't be any danger at all. We're going to plan this down to your breathing. We're the best-qualified people in the world to do it. Don't you see? Between us we've written almost two hundred heist stories; and those were just the ones I could track down. Even me. I did four at RKO. Funnily enough, you're the only one who hasn't. But you will. And in the meantime you have nothing to worry about. No one's going to be in any danger that we aren't in complete control of.'

'It isn't that.' He gazed miserably down at his folded hands.

'Then what? You have a problem with *stealing*? Oh, Buddy.' I reached for my dancers again, offered him one but he refused. I fired up and took a long, long whoosh. 'Okay. You're clear on why we're doing this? Even though you're good at what you do, you aren't going to be able to earn a proper living, through no fault of your own. You'll have to, jesus, flip burgers until this rides out and the industry stabilizes again. Work on a road crew. That Chatterton kind of crap is all very romantic, but if it doesn't finish you off it'll kill you as a writer, Buddy. You'll turn bad inside. Everywhere you look you'll see people who are lazier than you, people who are stupider, meaner, less honest and more conniving, all earning a fortune and whooping it up, right in your face. This is America, and this is the start of the 1950s. Now all that stuff in

131

Europe's sorted out, the rest of the century is going to be ours and you better believe it. And you're one of the most valuable people this country's going to have, because you can tell it about its nightmares and its dreams: no one's going to wake up to this for a few years, but you need to be ready for them when they do.' I squashed my cigarette, lit another. 'You've crossed a line already, Buddy. Yes you have. Just by doing what you do, you've chosen to stand outside. Are you going to refuse to do something you'd make a character do without giving it a second thought? Huh?'

This was a new one on him. I'd been saving it.

'And besides,' I went for the kicker, 'we're not going to steal anything that hasn't been stolen already.'

'What are we going to steal?'

'I'm working on it. But it's not going to be real money, trust me. It'll be share-dealing profits, gambling dividends, that kind of thing. Money that's been dishonestly generated, out of nothing, by people who can afford not to miss it. We're not going to be stealing from real people, trust me.'

This didn't seem to be working.

'Is there something you never told me?' I went on. 'Did someone die on you?' I wondered if he knew about what happens when you're a griever: what happened to me, anyway, when my son, though an .88 had blended him as efficiently as a Moulinex into gray German mud, came back whole in the small hours to punish me; as though the fact of my grief had made me complicit, responsible somehow.

'You're killing yourself,' he said flatly. 'You're getting us to do it, but however you dress it up you're killing yourself. You might not get a whimper from that bunch of wash-outs but someone's gotta slap the cards on the table.'

He sat back but wouldn't meet my eye; and then I got it. It explained a lot. He was a Hades-fancier, a coffin-craver, a Lethelush. This was why he was cutting up rough. Suicide junkies, like any aficionados, don't like weekend dancers waltzing onto their floor. But I needed him on the team – I wasn't having the one I believed in most excluded from the reward. The only thing I could do was call him on it.

'I don't see the problem,' I said. 'You read that Dorothy Parker?'

'Sure.'

'Don't you think it weird that all she ever did was write about it and never do it? She'll live to be eighty if the booze doesn't get her.'

'That's the balancing act to do,' he said. 'Acceptance of death is an initiation rite that qualifies you for life.'

'But you oughta read Seneca,' I said. I'd gone through it all: when I first discovered that I was going to need to compress my last twenty years into twenty seconds sometime soon, I did my research. '"You see that stunted, parched and sorry tree? From each branch liberty hangs,"' I quoted, unfairly. '"Do you enquire the road to freedom? You shall find it in every vein of your body." You know the Senate used to keep a supply of poison especially for the citizens? All you had to do was go plead your case, and they'd give you a vial. Don't you think I've got a case to plead? Do you think I want to take my last breath after months of stupefying agony? C'mon. All that sanctity of life stuff is some dumb Christian thing. Really. Contrition through pain. Gimme a break.'

He wouldn't meet my eye, again. I glanced at the clock, and figured it was time to get out – visiting time was almost over and besides, I was dying for a drink. I went over to the bed a moment to hold Robert's hand, just in case he could feel it – and to my surprise he seemed to. There was a pressure back, from his hand to mine, and his head moved a little on the pillow. For a terrifying few seconds I thought he was going to wake up, and I really didn't know what to say to him these days. But he didn't move again, and then I was leery to let go in case my relinquishing the contact did the same thing again. I heard Buddy's chair scrape softly, and figured he was standing behind me. This was just irritating now. I really ought to've been sweeping him out of there and getting him in a cab before he had time to think or argue anymore. But when I looked round, the room was empty, and he was already gone.

In a room just the same but two thousand miles west, Lucky couldn't take his eyes off the photograph Lucy'd had framed, and placed on the bedside cabinet beside her. It was of her, a week after it happened, and Lucky couldn't help thinking that if he put what it showed in anything but a melodrama, he'd have to start with the visitor addressing the mound of bandages and plaster at the wrong end. There'd been more wrapping than there was Lucy. Both her legs were in casts, as was her right arm; her back was in a complicated brace, and the whole shebang was suspended on a network of wires and pulleys. Her left arm was sleeved in a kind of plastic over the burns, and thick swathes of bandages were wrapped around the compound fractures in her skull. But she'd been in Cedars-Sinai four weeks now, and was sitting up in bed with just the casts and the brace still intact.

'It was a concealed lightning conductor,' she said. 'It was under the asphalt. Could've happened to anyone.'

'They shoulda checked,' said Lucky. 'Damn his fucking eyes, Lucy. Did he send you *any*thing?'

'Check for a hundred. Get me some icewater?'

He poured it out. 'A hundred? Is he kidding?'

'I get fifty bucks a day, you know that. Nothing, if he doesn't get the shot. He didn't have to give me anything.'

'But jesus, christ. Doesn't the actors' guild . . .'

'Actors' guild doesn't cover stunters and you know it. Jack Kehuma fell twenty feet more than I did last year and he didn't get a penny.'

135

'Well, he's not going to get away with this. He should've checked that building out. He shoulda gotten the damn blueprints.'

'Mantegna? Yeah, right.' She snorted, then smiled with pain. He saw it and picked up the buzzer.

'You want I should get you some more painkillers?'

'I just took some before you came. That's the wrong way to call them anyways. If you need a nurse real bad you just find a good show on the TV and turn the volume up. They don't have a set at the nurses' station.'

'I can't believe they have them in here.'

'It's a sales pitch,' she said, 'one of the night nurses told me. A dealer round the corner figured that he'd got a captive audience here who'd come round to e-zee credit terms by the time they got out. You get a coupon when you leave, she said.'

'Maybe if I got sick too we could get a free one,' Lucky said, but he was thinking that something they had to try and sell to people when they're sick couldn't be as hot as it was claimed to be.

'But you're glad of the TV,' Lucy said. 'This is like having an endless two-day waitover at a bus station – but, bonus, they torture you too.'

'Lucy, I don't know what to do.'

'How long've you got?'

'Pardon me?'

'On leave.'

'Eight days. But I'm not going back.'

'You're what?'

'I'm going to desert.'

'You crazy?'

'C'mon, what're they going to do? Bust me down from a private to a civilian?'

'Fuck you,' she said. 'They can put you in prison.'

'They'd have to find me first. I work for cash, and I haven't made a tax return in my life, you know that. I cashed in my back pay on

136

the passage back, and I gave them a false address when I signed up. C'mon, I was always going to do this. I just meant to do it six months ago, is all.'

'But that was before it went crazy out there. They care now. They'll find you.'

'They've got enough problems, trust me. Unless I walk right up to them and flip them the bird, they're not going to waste people or time on looking for me.'

But this wasn't what was on his mind at all. All he could think about was that there was no way they were going to be able to pay for this. Stunters don't carry accident insurance because the premiums would cancel their earnings. He'd sold the car and borrowed two hundred dollars from his sister already – that'd cover another three weeks, but they said she was going to be in here another three months. He suspected he was going to have to take money on the street, and he'd written that into enough low-rent gangster pictures to know what it entailed.

The bell rang, and a sister bustled him out. He was almost glad. He hated to see her and not touch her; and, though he'd gone over it in his mind till he could almost dismiss it, he still felt bad about writing that scene. And besides, he thought, as he lit a cigarette on La Cienega, hospitals are creepy. The nurses were unnerving, because it seemed like they expected the patients to die. If you lived, that was a bonus play, and if you got better, they'd hit three bars in a row. But that place was the House of Death. They wouldn't bat an eye when you were gone. They wouldn't have any problem at all adjusting to a world without you. He got a cab downtown before he could think anymore about Lucy in there.

Lucky was not the kind of writer to sit around in his bathrobe all day. Quite aside from anything else, he needed to write such quantities of stuff to keep eating that he couldn't rely on things just occurring to him. Everyone with a real job needs someone to get a six o'clock drink with sometime, and Lucky'd made it his business to be that someone for as wide a diversity of LA nine-to-fivers as possible. The cuttings librarian at the *LA Times*, the Orange County Coroner's secretary, the admissions clerk at Cedars-Sinai emergency room . . . Lucky knew pretty much everything by now about how tough it was to find a good man in this town, how hard it was to date someone when you worked with them, and about how it was when the most you had to look forward to at the end of the week was mowing the lawn and taking the kids to her parents'. But this was also how he got the skinny on what was up at City Hall, what was going down at 5th precinct, how the movie mogul's mistress wound up on a slab at the morgue, and a whole bunch of other stuff that he couldn't put a price on, germs from which screenplays could be coaxed.

This five-thirty martini was another of the same. Tom Collins was the press agent for the Defense Department in LA; Lucky'd known him four years, and ought to've spoken to him before he signed up for Korea, but Collins was out there already. They were both back now, but Lucky shortly ought not to have been; so top of the bill was how he might manage to avoid ever wearing green serge again.

'You don't have anything to worry about,' said Tom when he finally showed, dumping his brown leather case by the side of a stool and hoisting himself up next to Lucky. 'Dry as you like, two olives. Word is, they're pretty much resigned to losing anyone who can get themselves out of there, and they don't have the energy to go looking. You wouldn't believe what this fucking fiasco's done. I have to keep checking the flags on the wall to remind myself I'm working for the American army. We're all over the place.'

They were at the Oak Room, where they could say what they liked, pretty much. No one who went there was unimportant enough to want to listen in.

'Get this,' Tom said, and took a big old slug on his martini. 'The best idea so far is to put the draft on a rota. You serve your term and you're out of there, and the next batch comes over. That's how bad it's got: they're actually ready to admit that no one's going to stand for being in that shambles more than a few months.'

Lucky could sing hallelujah to that. The grunts he'd enlisted with – assholes in need of a uniform, jerks who'd failed even to make prison guards – even they had come to look like the novelty of being shelled, sniped at by children, and running away three times a day was beginning to wear a little thin by the time Lucky bugged out.

'But there's the kicker,' Tom said. 'No one wants this over. You know how many steel factories, how many chemical works have gone over to munitions? How much napalm, how many helicopters, how many for-chrissake *uni*forms are rolling off the assembly lines? The banks and the corporations and the Pentagon ain't just happy, buddy, they're fucking delirious. This war is going to fuel a boom without inflation, wreck the British Labor administration, and generate a massive growth of power of the military–industrial complex. The CIA is going to be able to do pretty much what it likes if it can keep Congress voting it the kind of money it's getting now for another couple years. Which they will. Everyone's a winner. Look at McCarthy – would have been out on his crazy ass a year ago without this. This is turning into the last crusade against Communism, and no one gives a fuck what it costs.'

'I have to say it, I never saw any Chinese,' said Lucky.

'That's because there are none. The best that Intelligence has managed to dredge up so far is a bunch of North Korean trucks with suspiciously low mileage on their odometers. But if you believe what we're feeding to the press, there're more Chinese troops south of the border than wrinkles on Mamie Eisenhower's butt. We've got rumors but no proof that the Soviets have funded the North Korean army, but get this: they're loans not gifts, and at the same bank rate as US mortgages.'

'They musta been talking to my landlord.'

'But really. This is getting out of hand. Truman said, three months in, that it looked like World War Three was here, but that was for the birds. It's going to be far nastier than that. Curtis LeMay wanted to raze the five biggest towns in the north to stop it, and he got shouted down as a maniac: but what the shouters want to do now is raze *every* town, north *and* south. Because that's going to take lots more bombs, lots more napalm, lots more tinned pork-and-egg-yolk, lots more bootlaces. They don't want to stop this war until there isn't a single bush left for a gook to hide behind. Hey, can we get another martini here?'

Lucky lifted his glass into the bartender's line of vision. 'Won't the UN try and broker something?'

'*Yew*-nited nations my ass. You know that when we release press pictures of guerrillas surrendering we have to drop in the odd Limey and South Korean to make it look like this is a team thing? When they capture NKs they have to take 'em back to the battlefield a week later to get the pictures. I tellya man, this is us and no one else. This is the first time since Alexander the Great that a first-rank power has been making the running on the world stage like this. Scary, huh? If these guys can engineer and sustain a war until they're satisfied there isn't a nickel more profit to be made out of it, then where's it gonna end?'

Lucky only cared as far as he could use this. Maybe Jimmy Stewart as the pacifist president? And who's that guy, William Holden, as the chief of staff, and maybe some broad caught between them – Lana Turner? – cool. But he'd never get a shot at that kind of budget. Maybe in the next life. He shrugged.

'I'm tellinya man,' Collins went on, still in fifth gear. 'What if this goes on until the next presidential election, and some Democrat rides in on a stop-the-fighting ticket?'

Lucky looked blank.

'They'd blow his fucking head off, is what. I can't tell you the half of it, but this is setting a helluva precedent. Power is shifting from Congress to an elite group of generals and industrialists. Think I'm crazy? Talk to my wife. She thinks I'm screwy too. But I swear . . .' He shook his head and picked up his drink. 'Ah, shit, hey. I didn't ask about Lucy once.'

Lucky took out his cigarettes and proffered the pack. 'Sends her love. Said there's nothing she'd like more than a weak martini with a couple of losers but she has to stand us up this time.'

'Ah, shoot,' said Collins. 'Couldn'tch've wheeled her down here on a gurney or something, huh? I'll go visit her with Marcie at the weekend. She in County?'

'Cedars.'

'Sinai, huh?' said Collins. 'Finally rubbing shoulders with the stars.'

'Rubbing body casts,' said Lucky, without humor. He pulled out his wallet and cocked another dollar at the barkeep. 'County doesn't have the equipment she needs.'

'But mucho pesetas, huh amigo?' The bartender set up two and poured them out.

'Si,' said Lucky. 'El gringo sawbones, he say: I take your *casa*, your car and your *cojones*.' He took a rueful gulp at his shot-glass. 'If that fucker Mantegna didn't break my balls already.'

'You gonna face him down?'

'He skipped town.'

'I got some buddies in Washington. You want I get them to run a track on him?'

'No need,' said Lucky. 'It'll be in *Variety* soon enough. He's moved into the skin-flick racket. He's gone to Chicago.'

141

'*Satin Rough and Tumble*, reel two, take two,' said Earl, and the boy snapped the clapper, stepped back out of the frame. Alice and Coco Brown went to it, and Susan rolled around in the background looking horrified. This was the second take because she hadn't looked horrified enough in the first: Earl was concerned that this might cause the viewers of this little epic to lose faith in the plot, and abandon the essential suspension of their disbelief. The story was, after all, what a person would be watching it for. So concentrate.

In reel one, Alice, in black satin lingerie the same as Susan's, was tying the latter's hands and ankles, and giving an ornate ottoman the gladeye all the while. Enter stage left Coco Brown, in white satin, who hammed claiming to be Susan's rightful owner. End reel and reload. Then Alice slapped Coco, Coco slapped Alice, and hostilities escalated to hair pulling and rolling around on the floor, while Susan writhed against her bonds in the background. Reel three was going to feature Coco and Alice making up, then taking it out on Susan over the ottoman together: Susan wasn't looking forward to this because, since this was live action, they really were going to be spanking her instead of just posing it. She'd tried to schmeichel her way out of it but Earl hadn't been having any of it. 'It's the best-lookin' girl gets tied up' had become his one direc-torial tenet. Next life, Susan swore, she was coming back ugly. 'It's the looker who oughta pull focus; that's the girl audiences re-member.' If she didn't get born ugly she'd do the job herself – take a baseball on the beak, let her eyebrows run wild, go crazy with the Cokes and devil's food. Enough of this shit.

But she'd been trying not to argue anymore. When Giotto and Bellini hooked up with this Mantegna guy and Earl got to borrow his 16mm rig, Susan had thought for a moment that he was going to be shooting real movies; but these were stag reels, strictly mail-order, same as the photosets. Even if it weren't for the money, Earl would be practically delirious at being back in pictures. And, it had to be said, the money was crazy. This was the third one they'd done, and the first two had sold truckloads, at thirty dollars a pop. They were just girlfights – physical contact that got past the censors – and they were only advertised in *Eyeful*, but it seemed to Susan like every stag party, every roadhouse basement and every revue-bar backroom in the country must've been playing her every weekend. It was almost beginning to make her nervous – some-times when she was out on the street she felt like one guy in every ten she passed must know who she was, like her face was a timebomb planted in their heads, that'd go off when they saw her for real. So far she hadn't had a reaction beyond the double-takes that she always got, but she figured it couldn't be too long before some crazed square-eyes stuck her up in the Stop&Shop to tell her he was her number-one fan. The terrible price of celebrity was something she always thought she could've got used to enduring, but she'd never figured on it being like this. She guessed that maybe you do get what you want, but just not in the way you want it. Whatever. She was going to buy a car with the pay-off from this one.

Peachy, peachy, peachy. And then there was Ben. He'd told her that he loved her but she didn't believe he meant it. Like the asshole with the tux and the microphone used to sing – if love did not exist/Would anyone bother to invent it? Susan knew it didn't mean shit. She figured that if either addresser or addressee was in a state of advanced undress at the time of declaration then it didn't count. She felt that you ought to be able to put a tattoo on a guy every time he said, I love you, so that all the other dumb broads he was going to say it to could see how much it meant. It had still felt pretty good though.

'And, print,' said Earl, and turned to find a light for his cigar; Coco and Alice got up and started dusting themselves down; and Susan had to *humph* around the ball-gag, until the lighting boy came over to carry her to a chair. And then a fat Studebaker in midnight black rolled through the loading bay doors and Susan was like, I don't be*lieve* this shit.

Three hours later, and Susan'd seen this scene so many times in the movies that it wasn't even boring – it was just making her late for the party. She'd wanted to go get a purse to match her new shoes; and she knew she was going to anyway, regardless of how long this took her, but now it was going to make her feel flustered and late and guilty, which kind of shanghai'd the fun of going to Carson, Pirie, Scott and giving those snotty bitches in the millinery department holy hell. She glared at the two clichés – the eager young rookie and the hell-with-it old-timer – and gave them eyebrow number nine, useful for wisecracking dorks on street corners, and traffic cops who pull you over to try and get your phone number – the don't-you-assholes-have-better-things-to-do curl and corner-flip.

But the rookie was clearly eyebrow-illiterate, and continued methodically to verify that Susan had total recall on everything she'd put on her rap sheet.

'So you're an actress?'

'You always make me feel like I've got the next line, what is it with you?' she said.

He tossed the sheet down on the table.

'Okay. Enough of this b.s.' He couldn't even cuss like a grownup. 'You're seeing a lot of Mr Kahane.'

'He's writing a musical comedy about some dumbass cop who doesn't know shit from Shinola. I'm doing the typing.'

'Is he paying you?'

'It's a labor of love.'

'Are you in love with Mr. Kahane?'

'Tell me,' Susan said, leaning forward and lifting her chin, 'how are you recording this? Tape or wire?'

'Tape,' he said, nodding to a box on the wall. 'There's the mike.'

She turned toward it and enunciated, boomingly – her old voice coach would've been proud – 'For the record – I am in love with Mr. Kahane.' And she sat back, while the rookie looked poison at her. The 'timer was gazing beatifically out the window.

'Do you hope to marry him?'

'What's it to you?'

'Let's just say that if you did we'd be seeing a lot more of each other.' He pulled out some gum. 'Usually around five a.m., with a bunch of uniforms breaking the door down.'

'I'm an early riser.'

'Don't go for that beauty-sleep routine, huh?' he said, folding the gum into his mouth.

'I'll take a stick of that,' said Susan, and he handed her the package after a moment's thought.

'So here's the deal,' he said, after the BlackJack was back in his pocket. 'You're some doll-faced hick from the sticks. Some guy takes you to swell nightclubs, sets you up in an apartment, shows you a good time. You don't look too closely at what he does to fill his wallet. Am I right?'

'I've lived in Chicago longer'n you have, hillbilly boy.' Susan looked at him evenly. The 'timer turned round from the window for the first time.

'All my partner is trying to tell you, miss, is that Ben Kahane isn't the kind of horse a girl oughta be thinking of hitching her wagon to,' he said. 'You may not be familiar with what he does, but a lot of people in Chicago are. And a lot of them don't approve, exactly.'

'Well, I'm over twenty-one,' Susan said, and added, with a

glance at the rookie, 'fourteen too, for that matter. I guess that means I can hitch up to whatever I like, even where you come from, Bobby-Ray.'

'So you'd marry him?' the rookie said, making no effort to keep the Ozark out of his voice now.

'If I do I'll make you maid of honor.'

Which just about did it. So he stuck her in a holding cell, with Alice, for the three more hours he was allowed without charging her. Alice chirped on kind of how you'd expect for a while, then fell quiet, smoking cigarette after cigarette. She was as pissed as Susan: both suspected that their boyfriends ought to've been getting them out of this, but since neither appeared to be, they were damned if they were going to bring it to the other's attention by talking about it. There was no sign of Earl either; Susan didn't know where the hell he was, though she had an idea he was getting a harder time with Detectives Clearasil and Pepto-Bismol than she did.

When the cops finally sprung them, it was well after seven.

Susan was going crazy by then, and not just from being banged up in the zoo with Alice; if they'd been held for even a few minutes more, Susan was going to be late for the party that night. This was almost too cruel, because it was going to be money, and she'd been looking forward to it for weeks.

It went like this. Since some outfit in Michigan had commenced making with the competition, Earl had hit on the idea of mailing subscribers in the Lakes area with invitations to hire out Susan and the others for private photography sessions. It had gone down a treat. Twenty or so guys bristling with Rolleiflexes and flashguns all paid twenty bucks for Susan and another girl to go out to the beach and do swimsuit stuff, to the woods for hiking shorts-and-sweaters, or back to some guy's mansion for open-air underwear. They were all rich guys, and Earl was almost going crazy trying to figure out how he could wring more out of them; but meantime, it was a hundred bucks each for an afternoon drinking champagne with a bunch of harmless old sweeties, and Susan didn't mind a bit. She'd seen Giotto around the House of Whacks once or twice, and had been not a little surprised to see him at one of these camera-club things a couple of weeks back. Turned out he was paying for the whole session, as kind of corporate hospitality for some associates from out of town. So she'd introduced herself; and he'd looked like a tuxedo'd father walking up the aisle when she'd told him that she was the one putting that snap in Ben's turtle these days. So this was what the party she was late for was. Giotto had been sixty yesterday, and since all his friends and neighbors were the guys who came out on the parties, Susan and Alice had been invited too.

This, Susan figured, was her chance to chummy up to Giotto. She wasn't still on her the-mafia's-the-only-place-my-talents-can-be-recognized kick, but she guessed that being close to Giotto was never going to hurt. And besides, he was a one to take favorites. to recognize and reward the special when he met it – she only had to look at Ben to confirm this. So since she figured she was going to have to step formally into his circle someday, as Ben's other half, she was glad it was sooner, and from something done on her own terms, rather than later, as just an appendage to a man.

Susan hit home, showered, and lightning-changed, then went straight over to Alice's – but she was still in the stuff she had on at work today, and still semi-hysterical. Susan groaned, deep, then brusqued it up, set about sprucing the dozy mare. She would've called Ben up and got him over, but he'd been in a meeting at Giotto's all day, and the idea was that he was going to stick around and meet her there. So she had to manhandle Alice into the shower alone, then drag her out, towel her down and shovel her into a cream, raw silk, off-the-shoulder number. She still wasn't co-operating.

'C'mon Alice. You want to see Joey in a tux, don't you?'

147

'Seen him in a tux,' she sniffed, and of course she had – he would've worn one when he proposed to her. This had been as much a surprise to Susan as it was to Alice. Volante had oiled round to Susan's apartment a couple of Saturdays ago and asked her to come shopping with him uptown. This had kind of weirded her out a little because he must've known she was with Ben again, and from what she'd heard from Alice (and more obliquely from Ben, because he wasn't too interested) there was a greater gulf between him and Ben each day than there is, yea, between the rich man's coffers and the vaults of the kingdom of heaven. So she'd hemmed and hawed a bit.

'You gotta come,' he'd said, looking all little-boy-lost on her stoop. 'I need you to help me pick out something. I never did anything like this before.'

And Susan was like, no kidding. Although he'd evidently had no little commerce with jewelers before, carrying as he did several pounds of nine-carat around the thickness of his fingers and wrists, these had clearly been representatives from the Joe DiMaggio House of Crap rather than the sleek merchants of North Michigan Avenue.

So she'd gone. Apparently Alice had had no idea – this was Joey's scheme alone, a brilliant career move that had been gestating in the depths of his consciousness ever since he started running numbers all over the South Side in his youth. He needed, he said, to marry in order to consolidate his position.

'I can be one of the guys or I can be one of the Men,' he'd said in the cab uptown, twisting the doubloon on his left pinky. 'Guys have girls, Men have wives.' And he shrugged.

'But she's not Italian,' Susan had pointed out.

'So she can dye her hair black.' He'd put his hand on her knee. 'C'mon, this is 1951. No one comes from anywhere anymore.'

She'd wanted to ask him whether it wouldn't be some kind of loss of face for him to be married to a girl who ties people up in her underwear for a living, but this was something she'd been preferring not to think about, with relation to Ben, for her own part. She liked to see it as the equivalent of the rich benefactor falling in love with the penniless-but-talented chorus girl, with a plan to make her a star that can only be derailed by the materialization of the Happy Home, honeys till the end of time. Just kind of updated, was all.

And so she went along, mostly to make sure he didn't buy Alice anything with a decent resale value, but had had her night with Ben spoiled by the thought of Alice's phone call next morning; of the coerced lunch date, and having to coo for hours over the proffered hand.

But it wasn't all wasted. Susan didn't want to show up at the party on her own, and this was how to get to her.

'C'mon, Alice,' she urged. 'Don't you want to show off your sparkler?'

Which bucked her up no end. Inside ten minutes Susan'd gotten her in a cab, and they sailed out to Oak Park and beyond, to Giotto's palazzo by River Forest.

It was a kind of a garden party thing, a big white mansion set back from the road and veiled from the friends 'n' neighbors by a thirty-foot band of conifers, now throwing long shadows across the front lawn; which itself was the size of four football pitches, rolling around in groves to the sides of the house, and milling with women in pre-Labor Day frocks, guys looking a little early in white tuxes. Everyone looked beautiful, everyone looked like they knew each other, and everyone looked like they lived in the kind of place that had white telephones. Susan could've pulled this off a lot easier if she wasn't stuck with Alice, so she steered her over to a rank of liveried waiters, got a glass of non-domestic champagne for herself, and put up with Alice demanding something called a Horse's Neck, which, she explained to the incredulous sommelier, was ginger wine, ginger ale, and a piece of lemon peel.

'I don't like cham-pagne,' she said, 'tickles my nose.' Susan was sure that the monks who spent eight years lovingly tending the stuff that was sending sparkles through her front lobes already would concur with Alice's gourmet assessment. 'Hey, I don't see Joey *any*place.'

'I don't see Ben either,' Susan said, lightly. 'They're probably talking inside or something. C'mon, let's take a prom.'

An hour or so went by. There were plenty of guys Susan knew there, and none of them the slightest bit abashed to say howdy in front of their wives, treating her more like an indulged and favourite niece than a girl they paid to take her clothes off. They all seemed to want, not to give her stuff, but to do stuff for her. One guy had an airplane and went flying over the city on weekends, offered to take her up when it was cooler: he said it was no good just then, because there was a fug over the city that you couldn't see from the ground – you looked up, the sky was blue, but when you were up there all you saw below was brown. Susan told him he could call her anytime. Another old guy said he could fix it so she got to throw in the first ball at Wrigley Field on her birthday – she told him that was for movie stars, and no one'd know who she was: he countered that the crowd mightn't know who she was, but they could sure as hell see what she was. It was really fine – reminded her of the kind of thing you had to do and say at the few last-night parties she'd been to – and she got off on knowing the moves so well: all the girl-stuff you had to remember at parties, like when someone walks away from you, even if they've just told you to go to hell, you have to look as though they've just promised you the best of sex and money. As the sun was winding up to call it a day, Bob Kravitz, an accountant in his late forties, hadn't just promised Susan a tax-free annuity, or offered to fuck the red out of her hair, but he'd told her where the bathroom was, and that was almost as good right now. Susan offered to get Alice another Horse's Ass or whatever it was she liked, but she didn't want one – she was pissed because Joey hadn't shown, which added to Susan's irritation at Ben. Where the christ was he?

The leading edge of the party had begun to mill up the steps through the grand double-doors by then, and Susan ditched Alice, wandered in with them, and drifted up the stairs like she owned the place. She found the bathroom as directed and took a leisurely rest stop, making free with the perfumes and unguents provided for the use of the patrons. When she was done she didn't go straight back: she felt as though she'd had the preliminaries; now she wanted to find Ben and Giotto, and crank up the main feature. So she strayed down the corridor, away from the main stairs, looking for a library, or billiards room or whatever little treehouse they had their circle jerks in. All the same, she felt kind of like that other Alice, a little leery of opening any of the white doors that punctuated the corridor walls as regularly as colons in a contract; so she walked toward the light at the end, which it turned out was a picture window above a second staircase. She could see the back yard from here, which was as different from the front as a midnight kiss from one two hours later.

The house, she could see now, was at the top of a small ravine that cut down to the Des Plaines river, with log cabins and horse paddocks half-concealed beneath tall pines and oaks. There was a tennis court, gardens of various degrees of wilderness, and, just below her, an abandoned glasshouse stuffed full of dying palms. Here and there, in the overgrown borders, peacocks were putzing about between the sumac and the poison oak. It was almost like they were in the wild, foraging around, and Susan stopped to watch them awhile, following their progress and forgetting where she was. The voice behind her made her jump.

'I only put out one sack of garbage a month – the birds eat the rest. Isn't that something?' She turned, and there was Giotto.

'They're beautiful,' she said, resisting the urge to stare at him, looking back out the window.

'They were my wife's,' he said, still standing behind her, gazing out at the garden beneath the falling sky. 'In her last few weeks she had me move her bed to the back of the house so she could see them. She never understood why they wouldn't stay out front.'

'They look happier in all this green stuff,' she said.

'That's what I thought,' he said, with a smile in his voice. 'The front yard was hers, the back was mine. She hated all my mess – drove her crazy. But I think, what good is a beautiful garden, when you can never look at it without seeing some *paisan* with a wheelbarrow?'

'But you keep the front so nice.'

'For my guests,' he said.

'And perhaps for her, still?' said Susan, looking for a way in.

His mouth widened a little. 'Perhaps,' he said. 'You know a little about loyalty, I suspect.'

'I know that once you've found someone worthy of it you shouldn't let it go,' she said.

'And have you found?' he asked, twinkling benevolently at her.

'I think so,' Susan said. 'I'm . . .'

'You,' he interrupted, 'are the girl who's been taking so much of Mr Kahane's attention this summer.' And he took her hand, kissed it. 'We are always going to be in competition, I suspect.'

'We already are,' Susan said, but nice. 'He's been letting me be a wallflower since I arrived at your party.'

'Only an honest man would be so foolish,' said Giotto, and offered her his arm. 'Shall we?'

So he led Susan down the second staircase, through a galleried corridor hung with tapestries of green and gold and ocher and umber, to a library so large she could see the curvature of the earth in the parquet floor. Ben, about three lines of longitude away, was up to his shirtsleeved elbows in the green glow of a desk lamp, his collar studs unbuttoned and his tie undone, an untouched balloon of brandy and a cigar gone out in a heavy ashtray by his elbow. Giotto remonstrated with him, and he acceded good-naturedly, once he'd emerged, blinking, from whatever subterra of paper he'd lowered himself into. Susan kissed him, leaning down and holding back a veil of hair with her hand; then stood behind him to tie the black silk round his neck, recalling, for a moment, the actor who first showed her how to knot a bow-tie, in a green-room four states away, in a life five summers away. It had reminded her of a Chesterfields ad from *Harper's Bazaar* then, and this did even more. Giotto was charming in a way rich guys generally weren't. Since they had no need for charm, she figured that it just kind of evolved out of them. There might be a coccyx-type residue, she guessed, occasionally activated to make them feel that whoever they were using it on liked them for their wit or intelligence rather than their power or their money, but she'd never come across anything like this. If he'd been thirty years younger, he'd have made her feel like she was the first woman he ever met, after a youth marooned on a desert island reading Dante and Shakespeare and Donne. It was like being rich and married, out at Bar Harbor and being indulged as favorites by some charming old guy, who just also happened to be Ben's grandfather and the proprietor of his legacy. She would have loved to have gone along with it, but a mean little voice kept reminding her that, far from being a couple of Rockefellers, a war hero and his society girl, they were a mobster, his jailbird right-hand man and a porno star.

Giotto even had a daughter, to complete the fireside group, though maybe not how a Norman Rockwell would have drawn her. She only looked in the library by mistake, as part of her project of avoiding the party altogether, but Giotto's face lit up and he hauled her over, presenting her as proudly as if she was wearing taffeta and satin, when in fact she stood before them with a ponytail, cuffed blue jeans and a fading phone number inked on the back of her hand. She was back from college for the summer, and if she was meant to be a mobster's daughter, Susan felt, then the casting director ought to be sacked. She made Susan realize that Giotto had, in fact, pulled it off. She was as far removed from the world of Joey Volante as she was from the world of debutantes and Mayflower surnames.

She went to a liberal arts college in Vermont: precisely the kind of school Susan should have gone to, but scholarships had only been available to the really snooty ones. Giotto and Ben pointedly left Susan alone with her for a while, so the gals could do gal-talk; Susan thought she was going to have to try hard at it, but the kid seemed quite happy to make with the chit-chat for a moment, as though, hearing the high color drifting in on the air through the open windows, she were maybe regretting sequestering herself off from the party quite so violently. So Susan talked about Strindberg and stuff, and Frost and Hopper and Pollock. She asked her if she couldn't wait to get back to school, but she said she liked Chicago.

'But don't you have yourself some boy back east? Some math wiz? Some football star?'

'I don't really meet anyone,' she said.

'C'mon, at Bennington? Sure you do.'

'Well, I guess.' She picked at the thread on the seam of her jeans. 'But then I think of all that dumb talking you have to do and I get discouraged. It's not going to kill me if I leave it a couple years.'

She was a riot, alright, but Susan was fascinated by her in the way you are if you find yourself looking at what might have been you, had the variables been different. Susan kept her talking, with an almost indignant curiosity, but finally Giotto came over and commenced importuning his daughter to go take the midnight waltz with him, which was enough to send her back up to her room. So it was just Susan and the two men who walked back out into the party.

In the huge rooms at the front of the house the wood of the long tables beneath the windows remembered long-melted snowfalls as it flexed beneath the weight of spiced baked hams, and pastry pigs, and turkeys burnished mahogany brown: and gins and liquors, and champagne served in glasses big as finger bowls, with silver bowls of sugar cubes on the side to sweeten the wine for Italian–American palates. On the steps, emotional reunions were enacted almost continuously between women who didn't remember anything more than each other's names, and beyond, the green baize of the front lawn was now blue as a pool table in the moonlight. Susan was introduced to guys – Manny, Doody, Wesley, Ferdie, Filey, Sam-Ray and Sonny – and though she tried to stand on one side and make a conversation with Mandy, Trudy, Wendy, Fergie, Heidi, Sarah-May and Sandy, Ben would have had to've been missing almost all of his faculties not to have seen she was dying. Eventually it got through to him and he excused them both; she had him wander around to the back, took him into an old summerhouse and tried to neck awhile, but he didn't seem too interested. It occurred to her that she'd done something wrong, shown him up somehow; she knew she hadn't, and tried to dismiss it for the foolishness it was, but it wouldn't go, and she picked at it like a scab.

'You didn't even come out for half the party,' she said eventually.

'We were busy. I'm sorry.'

'What was so important that you had to leave me with Alice three hours?'

'We got a break on something we're doing. It was worth looking into,' he said, throwaway.

'During his sixtieth birthday party?'

'Sure,' he said. 'C'mon, I'll show you.'

'Show me what?'

'You'll see. The sun ought to be up by the time we get there.' he said.

'Get where?' she said, but he was already pulling at her hand.

★　　★　　★

155

They drove out to the lake, or at least Susan thought they did. She assumed that's where they were going because, if you're in love, you go to the water almost as though you can't help it. To the edge of the city: Battery Park, or the Golden Gate; or to its heart, by the Seine or the Thames. You go to the edge, and hold each other, and look over the water because you're on the edge of the rest of your lives, the leading edge of the future. And this was where Ben drove, back across the city and then out, along a rural road, its asphalt crumbling at the sides in the far edge of his headlights' sweep. But he stopped where the road ran out, in front of eight feet of chainlink fence, and still a quarter-mile from the lake.

'So, what?' said Susan, hiding her mystification. 'This where you take broads parking?'

'Maybe later, doll-face,' he said, giving her leg a pat. 'C'mon.'

He popped his door, came around the car and handed her out, then held back the sagging gates, to let her inside whatever kind of compound this was. But Susan wasn't dressed for hiking, and made more of a big deal of getting through than was totally necessary. He didn't seem to care, though.

'This is my big thing. This is the biggest thing we've ever done. Isn't it great? I found it by mistake. It was the fence that gave me the idea.'

'What? A bunch of trees?'

'Oh, right. No, c'mon, just the other side.' And he grabbed her by the hand, dragged her along the scabby road and around the trees. Then, sudden as summer, there in front of them was a ghost town, falling away down to the lake.

'It's a housing development, from the twenties,' he said. 'Hardly anyone remembers it's here. It got abandoned when the bank collapsed in '29 – they foreclosed on a whole town. C'mon.'

He took her hand again and they walked, along pavement ruptured by the roots of trees, exposed through the skin of the asphalt like the broken veins above an old man's ankles. Set back

156

from the road were rotting frame-houses, with green moss growing on their tar roofs, and lawns colonized by crabgrass; occasionally the line was broken by dark holes in vacant lots, like sockets from which molars had been pulled – 'They took a couple dozen houses out on flatbed trucks,' Ben explained.

Clouds of bugs, skeeters and katydids were already rising above the sumac and poison oak grown wild between the lots, and in the pre-dawn light Susan read a faded, barely legible notice for a lost cat, tacked to a tree with pushpins grown orange with age. A block further on, she peered through a rusty screendoor, and saw a copy of *Little Women* on a kitchen table, swollen with damp to the size of a Sears catalog. They came to a half-collapsed Dairy Dreme at an intersection, stopped a moment to admire the huge carved-wood clown's head on the verge outside, then noticed the hornet nest inside its grinning maw; so walked on, past a slumped hardware store, a dead post office; finally they came to a narrow street that dead-ended at a blistered clapboard church, and Susan walked up to it, sat down thankfully on the steps.

'So what do you think?' asked Ben, lighting two cigarettes and handing one to her. 'Don't you think it's neat?'

'Sure.' She was tired. She couldn't even bring herself to inhale the cigarette – she must have smoked a hundred since the cops busted her, since the movie shoot, since she'd woken up that morning about three lifetimes ago – so she just let it burn between her fingers. She thought it was a bad place, and she didn't want to stay there. Her bed was a good place.

'This is the big thing,' said Ben. 'This is what everything is for.'

'I'm cold,' Susan said. He held out his arm to go over her shoulders, so she assumed the position, her arms round his waist, her cheek over his heart. He talked on, but she didn't really hear. She was falling asleep, and she drifted awhile before the idiocy of what he was saying brought her back up. It was so dumb she wasn't sure if she dreamt it.

'. . . And we'd rebuild that fence, run barbed wire along the top, just in case the Klan got any ideas. Maybe have a roadblock at the gate. You see, a colored family is never going to be allowed to move into white areas, however successful they might be. It's not even prejudice: I'm guessing that most people don't care. But what they do care about is the price of their property, and if they're the first neighborhood to let in the coloreds, then of course they have reason to worry, purely because of the ruckus there'll be. The Klan'll come bowling along whether they're wanted or not.'

He stopped talking a moment and all she could hear were the katydids, and his hot blood flexing in his chest. She didn't need to ask him to repeat himself. One really low period she'd lived in a rooming-house in Bangor, Maine, with her sash window over-hanging Track 3 of the railroad station: inside of two months she knew the name of every stop of the NorthEast railroad – Portland, Kennebunk, Ogunquit, Morningtown – from hearing the an-nouncements in her sleep. It was the same now, listening to him talk; but then she heard the rising intonation of a question, and she had to sit up.

'Huh?'

'You know anything about the native Americans?' he repeated.

'You mean, like, the Indians? Apaches and Comanches and shit?'

'Yeah.'

'Sure. I know plenty.'

Actually, she didn't. There was some guy once, some Princeton psych major who was snowing her onetime, telling her about his dreams. Like, that was really attractive – hey, I'm not self-absorbed at all. Just let me finish telling you about my potty training, and then I'll feel you up. Suave. Anyway, he was like yada, yada, how he went camping in the Catskills onetime and discovered that his Indian name was Son of Spirit-Dog; it came to him in a dream one night. And this guy's father was like, some whitecoat little beetle in

158

a DuPont lab, cooking up new recipes for nylons. Spirit-Dog, her ass.

'You know what really did for them?'

'Sure,' Susan said, not seeing what this had to do with anything. 'They got slaughtered.'

'Their buffalo all got slaughtered. There were thirteen million a hundred years ago, until someone cottoned on you could cure their hides; twenty years later there were only a couple hundred left on the plains. Buffalo Bill got a cute nickname, and the Indians got the way they lived kicked out from under them.'

Susan had seen some Iroquois once, boozehounds, all dent-faced and saggy-looking, panhandling for change on the street in South Dakota. The guy she was with made a big show of bustling her away while shaking his head over how sad it was, but she'd suspected that this was mostly so he could avoid contact with them without looking like a cheapskate. She guessed that maybe it was kind of unfair, but that was a hundred years ago. She was like, this is the twentieth century – get a helmet.

'It's the same for the Africans,' he said. 'They got their land taken away too. Everyone who's come here in the last couple hundred years has had the same problem – what kept them alive, they left behind. If you had land in the old country, all you had here was your body. You know Chicago was like, the promised land for the slaves? Down on the plantations they'd look to the north, and Chicago was what they saw. But then they come here, get work, have kids and educate them, but can't get out of the ghetto. They try to move out of the city, the white neighborhoods go crazy. So the plan is, we turn this place into a town for the affluent colored.'

Susan gaped at him.

'It's going to take most of Giotto's assets to do it, so the whole future's riding on it,' he went on, almost as though that was a minor irritation. 'But, christ, no one's had a chance to do this in a hundred years. We're going to build a town, and instead of having it grow

159

like a bunch of weeds, we can plan it. We'll give them their own hospital, their own shops, a school . . . and I'll give evens if it isn't pulling the best grade point averages of the county inside ten years. This is something to dream about. Out of nothing, we're going to make the future, for a thousand kids who'd go to hell on the South Side. This is what I always wanted: this is taking a leap through a mirror that most businesses barely glimpse themselves in. Giotto knows it too. We're way out front. We're going to do it first, do it ourselves, and keep on doing it.'

Susan could see that ugly-girl-buying-jewelry look again.

'We'll have to tear most of it down, sure,' he went on. 'Even if the wood was good, which it isn't. But we'll keep the foundations, put on exterior shutters and period roof lines. Styling and details is what's gonna sell it. I got the idea from cars, all the crap they're sticking on the grille and fins now, the way you can choose from twenty colors when you order one – they're customizing the mass-produced to disguise the fact that they're all the same. You see all those horror newsreels about how in Russia they all live in the same boxy apartment, all have the same lousy car: the joke is, America isn't so far from Russia as far as lack of choice goes, but we've got the money to tack crap all over the basic design, so you get the illusion of choice. Any color so long as it's black is still pretty much it, but we can customize the details. The future is in styling, not design.

'Can you imagine? Everything modern with none of the crap of the city. Kids who can't go out of their apartments now because of all the white trash slumped on the sidewalk are going to be playing hopscotch on the streets. Having bake-outs in the woods and catching fireflies in jars. Playtime isn't going to end here until mom calls you home. And this could just be the beginning. If this works we can look at white towns too. You remember all those bunga-lows that got built for the war-brides? That was the last big phase of construction. Well now the war-bride's got kids, and she'll want to get out of the city too.'

He was crazy. Giotto had to be crazy if he was swallowing this crap. *How crazy was she for being with him?* That was the worst thing.

Susan had thought, when she was first getting mixed up with a mobster, that it was going to be easy. It'd been simple to see where the motivation was: she just had to be the sweetheart, and soften up his hard-boil a little, like Jane Eyre and Rochester, or Claudette Colbert and Clark Gable. But, christ, this guy. One moment he was ordering knuckleheads around like James Cagney, the next he was Cary Grant in *Monkey Business*. She knew she didn't want an angel with a dirty face, but she wasn't so sure she wanted a nutty professor either.

Besides, morons were much easier. Dorks she could deal with. You knew where you were with a bonehead, even if the only way he could get into your pants was to bore them off you. She guessed there was an outside chance Ben might be the boy wonder, but prodigies, like Oscar-winning actresses, tend to be people you don't know. She was like, you hear some girl you were in high school with is in the movies now, but you think automatically she can only be appearing in a bunch of real dogs simply because you know her. She can't be anything special because that would be too weird; and by the same token, Susan was pretty sure Ben couldn't be the one man in a hundred million who could pull something like this off. She couldn't just sit there and let him throw away his life on this crap. It was their life together, too. If this went belly up, and it was so crazy she couldn't see it any other way, then he'd be bankrupting the one person in the world who believed in him. It wasn't like some rival firm was going to come along and pick him up out of the ruins, because all the rival firms were interested in was cathouses, and bootleg booze, and fixing the numbers on races three states away. What the hell was he doing in the mob? What the hell was Giotto thinking of, listening to this crap? Who the hell was Giotto anyways?

He sure wasn't the guy in the movies: he was just some sweet old guy now, regardless of what he'd been once. Susan had thought she just wanted someone who could use her, so she'd never feel frustrated again. She couldn't help wishing she'd met him when he was still a Medici, a Borgia – a duke of jealous vigilance and furious angers, someone who might've taken the two of them to a high place, and shown them the world . . .

But this was typical her. Ben kept talking all the way back to the car, pointing out things, gesturing excitedly. She tried, but she couldn't make it out. Maybe this was the big time, the kind of break she always wanted. Maybe you do get what you want after all, but just not in the way you expected. Maybe building a whole new town out of nothing and solving, in one stroke, the worst problem this city was ever going to have ought to've been enough for her. She read the news: there'd been riots everytime a colored family had tried to move out of the slums into a white neighborhood, and she didn't necessarily think it was unrealistic of Ben not to think black and white were ever going to be able to live on the same street. She guessed this was a reasonable idea. But kitchens? And window shutters? And color-coordinated dishwashers? Was this the most the Outfit could give her? She wanted doubloons, and stakeouts, clinically planned heists and . . . invasions and containments and control. She'd cried when the boats sailed for Korea. Traffic flow analyses and schoolbus pickup plans weren't her idea of heroic. They weren't what she'd had in mind when she got mixed up in this. But you didn't get mixed up in this, she hissed at herself. You just wandered into it, and only because someone fancied your ass.

Realizing that made her feel like seven shades of shit already, and as they stepped back through the gates, she was back to the question she'd started with.

'Why's this so urgent?' she asked him. 'Why were you doing numbers instead of being at the party?'

'They were some big numbers.'

'And you usually do them in the middle of the night.'

'Urgency is a factor now.' He broke eye-contact.

'Something happened, didn't it.'

Suddenly, she knew. The balance had shifted. If the wind blows, the top of the tree sways further than the trunk; and at ground level – she could see it now – at the House of Whacks, Earl was getting to be monkey to this new guy Mantegna.

'Bellini's getting heavy, right?'

He flicked his butt over the sidewalk, a firefly arc through the air.

'You're trying to get away from Bellini.'

'Yeah,' he said quietly.

'What happened?'

'As of this morning, we had five unions in our pocket. Tonight we have two.'

'Damn.' Susan said it in wonder, rather than anger or exasperation. It occurred to her that that was why she hadn't seen Alice again at the party. Joey Volante couldn't have shown, out of loyalty to Bellini, and Alice must've got sick of waiting for him.

She knew Volante hated Ben, with a passion, but she was pretty sure he wouldn't be so obvious about it unless Bellini had it in for Giotto. This wasn't business at all: it was entirely personal. She thought of the groaning shelves in Giotto's library, the paintings on his walls, the way he'd been able to name the green things in his garden; Giotto's daughter had told her how he liked to play the piano to himself, on Sunday mornings, in a room with the door shut. Bellini and Joey would hate Giotto and Ben because of stuff like that. This was the American way. It was the Nazis in Hollywood war movies who knew all about the histories of the châteaux they'd commandeered, and could talk for hours about the art on the walls and the vintages in their cellars: the good guys loved their mamas, baseball and a shot of bourbon. Frank Capra movies – how

163

more American can you get? The dork, the hayseed, the patsy who stayed behind in the hick town, he was the good guy. Bellini's mob, so insistent on their being more Italian than anyone else, were clearly more American than they thought.

'You know we got busted this morning?' Susan said.

'Yeah. They give you a hard time?'

'Naw. They were civilians. It was okay.'

'Attagirl.' He reached for her and kissed the top of her head. She wrapped her arms round his ribs, lay her cheek on his chest.

'Did Bellini set it up?'

'I guess. You were right. He wants that side shut down. He had a bust-up with Giotto over it a couple weeks back. But nothing like what's coming.'

'What's coming?' She didn't realize until it was out how coldly she'd said it.

'We don't know. We've got to be prepared for anything. We're hoping it's not going to be anything we can't contain before we can move out of that small-time forever. You've got to see it. This is just the start. This is just something that's ready. For every one thing I want to do there's a hundred I can't because it's not time yet. But it's going to be soon, and I'm in the right place to do it. This country may as well be the only one on the face of the planet. Look at the intake scoop on this thing' – he gestured toward the bonnet of his car – 'It's one in the eye to the rest of the world. We have air-conditioning in our *cars* – there are maybe a dozen buildings in France and England that have it at all. See what I mean? Here and now, honey.'

But Susan, even as she turned her face up to be kissed, was thinking that now is never good enough because you can't send it back. You can't send what you have now back to when you didn't have it. The rich guy can't send a winter coat back to the shivering newspaper boy he once was. She couldn't send some of Ben back to when she didn't have anyone. It had been four years, and she was changed now. But now was tomorrow's then. It could work both ways, she realized. She guessed. She kissed him back, harder than she knew she was doing, and he pulled her tight against him.

Lucy hadn't even the pleasure of being paralysed, and it really would have been a soft option. She was aware that her feeling that way may have seemed 'wicked' to the nurses, several of whom were pious and flinty-hearted enough to have made things more difficult for her had they suspected it, so she kept the sentiment unaired in front of them.

But this was the worst of all. At least total paralysis would have meant no pain, and no hope for the future. As it was, she was fucked up pretty bad, and there was nothing to look forward to except prodigious, scarcely credible exertion, if she was going to get out of this damned place. And to achieve what? It wasn't like she was ever going to work again. There was no way she was ever going to come out of this at a hundred per cent, and if she tried to work when she was firing on less than all four cylinders, it would make her so dangerous as to be unhireable. It had happened too often before, to scores of guys – shit, she'd seen it herself. She was doubling some ditz in a chase-picture Shorty McFallon was stunting only last June, and it turned out he'd smashed his wrists and popped his shoulders one too many times before. The gag was that Shorty was to transfer from a plane to a speeding train, climbing down a rope ladder from one to the other. But the pilot was a novice, and kept missing the tag; by the time he was making his third run at the speeding locomotive, Shorty's shoulders – which, by this point in his career, were held together with Scotch tape and hope – popped out for the last time. The worst of it was that Shorty didn't tumble but fell straight down; hit the ground feet first, and Lucy had seen with her own eyes his shinbones pushed out through the heels of his shoes. He crumpled up like a concertina, hence the posthumous nickname.

She didn't want to end up getting a nickname too, but what else was there? Mornings when she was slated for the gym (which was every day but Sundays and Tuesdays) she didn't want to wake up. She'd always kept herself in shape, but this was something else. Hoisting weights and climbing ropes used to feel good; even the sour miasma of spent masculinity that seemed coated over everything in her old gym hadn't been able to dent it; or even getting up at five a.m. just to avoid the assholes who hogged the place after seven – several of whom, her first week of going there, had assumed that if she was a broad in here then she must be a cleaner, and counseled her to leave the equipment be. Alone in the dusty white room, with the sunrise flooding through the windows, she'd felt like she was giving her body what it was built for, and her muscles responded gaily, obedient and eager to reach the goals she set.

But what happened in the hospital gym wasn't in the same ballpark – wasn't even the same fucking sport. Lucky hated it even more than she did. Was it better for him to witness her frustration and shame, or for her to endure the therapist's tortures without his support? He was fucked if he knew. *Get to the end of the bar! You can do it honey!* And she was like, *Urrrghhhh!* – her hair tumbled sexily around her shoulders, the tendons under her jaw and above her clavicles taut and defined, the sawdust-hot-off-the-blade smell of her sweat, her knuckles blanched around the parallel bars – but then her useless legs, trailing behind, her feet bent back perversely at the ankle. And after, when she'd say, *So this is the way it's going to be? If I want to walk from the stove to the kitchen counter I've gotta take the whole morning off?* There was nothing he could say, except that this way she was never gonna be able to walk out on him.

But neither of them felt like laughing. This was going to throw them out of joint forever. They'd never sat down and planned anything, but the idea had been that it was easier for a woman to specialize and get noticed than it was for a man. So Lucy was going to stunt her way up to being a second unit director – the kind who was in charge of shooting discrete segments, like a car chase, a gunfight, or a river run. Once she was in there she could start getting him production assignments, and he could slowly let that take over the strain from this maddening, furious writing. Eventually they'd power-couple it up to the point where they had director/producer status, work a few big projects and then retire, laughing all the way to Cancun. In the meantime, Lucy's money had been what underwrote the present. They'd thought about what would happen if she got hurt, but decided they were too young and swell for it to have much of a chance of featuring.

It was tough for Lucky not to be angry with her. However much he railed at Mantegna, to see Lucy reduced from the woman who held the reins to this was too ass-backwards. Between visits to the hospital he lay around the apartment, until the loneliness drove him out onto the streets of West Hollywood, to walk and walk till he was tired enough to sleep. The one thing that was clear – the only thing that didn't fade in and out of his consciousness like the dashboard reception on a cross-state drive – was that this was the end. Some kind of an end, anyway. He and Lucy had been together long enough for it to seem improbable that there'd been much to them before, or that there would ever be an after. The idea that they might not always be on an upward trajectory had always been too perverse to be contemplated. It had been obvious to Lucky the moment he met her, at a traveling carnival that he'd joined to pick up detail for a love story he was writing. She was a sharpshooter and he swept up elephant shit, and the moment he saw her he knew. It wasn't anything like he imagined: he'd always written these scenes as, you're-beautiful-I-want-you; but what he'd felt at that moment was, *so that's what you look like*. He couldn't get enough of her. He'd stay awake all night so he could look at her face. He'd picked up from one of the women's magazines he occasionally read that you were supposed to be attracted to someone who is more or less as attractive as you, but that was never going to work for Lucky. He needed his kids to have someone better than him to look at, and here she was. They never married, but were as good as within a week.

Looking back now, it seemed crazy that they'd ever thought it was going to work. Lucky's hit-rate hadn't been much better than any other hack's, but Lucy, they figured, could always work to cover the lean periods. It had seemed wide open: there just weren't enough female stunters to go round, and since the studios were churning out, on account of the war, pictures where the women did pretty much the same as the hero and gave as good as they got (even if, for the sake of form, they suddenly turned into simpering sack-sirens at the end), it had seemed pretty damned astute for them to take on the business together.

But then the business started to change. It seemed, as the half-century tightened into focus, that the parts getting written for women called for little more than a cooze on legs, and a sedentary one at that. In consequence what Lucy really needed was for a boozehound actress who looked like her to become famous, so that she could get exclusive work filling in for her. This wasn't so likely. There were a couple on contract here and there who fit the bill, but they were too damn tall to play opposite any of the guy leads at the time, who were themselves so short that they probably shopped for clothes, as they certainly did for mistresses, in the junior section. There'd been a girl over at MGM a while ago whom Lucky had his eye on, and he almost went so far as to write a stunt-heavy story for her. But then he got talking to her at an opening, and decided she was never going to be smart enough to buck the business – Norma Jean something or other – nice tits, but jeez what a ditz.

Worse still, Lucy's union folded. Lucky only got her to agree to do stunt work to begin with after he took her to meet the organizer of a new union of stunters, who were negotiating with the Academy to fix compensation rates and insurance. This was unprecedented: stuntmen had always been the assholes of the industry through tradition. The first stunt guys were Indians who couldn't get work anywhere else, knew how to handle a horse and weren't concerned with things like liability insurance and sick pay. A culture of bravado and superstition evolved around the trade, and because stunting was full of such a lot of guy-type crap – technical calculation, mechanics, brute physical strength and (however anyone tried to jargon it up) a certain degree of recklessness – it was allowed to seem kind of pussy to expect anything approaching the same terms and conditions as a bunch of faggy actors. So – lousy pay, no security, no recompense for industrial injury – the new union was set to change all that. It had all been going fine until TV came along; then suddenly the studios, scared witless, dropped negotiations on the grounds that all overheads had to be cut. Soon the only stunters getting contracts were those who signed compensation waivers, and things were back where they began.

By then it was too late for Lucy to back out of what she was doing, so they'd started working for Mantegna; the idea was that since Lucky would be writing the scripts, they'd have absolute control over the stunts. And then everything had gone to hell.

Soon there was no point to her being in the hospital anymore, and they used the last of the money to move out of the city to a stairless bungalow in Torrance. While Lucky sat with his Remington on a card table in the bare kitchen, smoking cigarette after cigarette while he tried to trashy up his best story enough to sell, Lucy would wheel herself out onto the blistering sidewalk, turn into the street, and then just spin and spin, until the hot metal rims cooked dark stripes into her blistered palms. However hard she pushed herself, she never got beyond tract houses, never got to the edge of anything, and every foot of the return journey was salty with pain.

After a few weeks of this, Lucky commenced to goof off, for the first time in his life. He moved his card table to the bedroom; this was the one room in the house at a lower level, with a shallow step by the door, so she couldn't get into it without calling for him. He claimed to be working on paper now, so that she wouldn't notice the absence of typewriter clatter about the place – even bought some yellow legal pads and arranged a bunch of sharpened cedar-sweet 2B pencils in a jar. But all he did was lay in his underwear on the bed when she was in, and rummage through her personal effects when she was out. He didn't seem to be up to much else. He lived in fear of personal callers – Mormons, salesmen, repo men – and didn't think about anything. This was actually pretty cool with him. For the first time in as long as he could remember, his head wasn't full of aging boxers, alcoholic surgeons, malcontent gangsters, and ghetto-tainted baseball stars. Without them he felt okay; relieved, even. He still read the trade press, but mostly to gloat over stories of how the studios were all going to hell now – these made him feel less alone. They'd started a while ago, and he hadn't understood most of them; it had actually seemed like kind of a good thing, at first, for fewer and fewer pictures to be made centrally and more on tender. This meant, it appeared to him, that there would be more spec work floating around that he could reel in, and not just for B-picture merchants like Mantegna. But now the imminent end of motion pictures was all the trades talked about, though mostly, Lucky suspected, because people want to be told everyone else is fucked when they themselves don't seem to be. It was in a special *Variety* feature about why no one needed to be in Hollywood anymore that Lucky saw Mantegna's name, as vice-president of Bellini Productions in Chicago, with an office address printed underneath it; and it was then that he thought of something to do.

In the newspaper that day was a story about how tuberculosis had ended. The thing I'd grown up in daily terror of, and now it was over, just like that. I used to have nightmares, when I was a girl, of the day when I'd cough over my homework late one night, and see the red spray settle on the page in a misted airbrush of dots. And then the fallow years, the foul inversion of everything natural, in sanatoriums, Michigan and Minnesota, long enough to have changed completely, but without changing: the cards left face down, the smiles uncoaxed, the flesh unpressed; the careful, wasted life, from the kid who couldn't play to the woman who couldn't live.

Had it ever happened I always figured I'd strap myself to the front of the Hudson Bay Express, right over the cow-catcher, and see if a thousand miles of icy air couldn't run those tubercules out of town. But now it was finished: it was done. On the next page, the story was about the latest acronym in the rollcall of horror – InterContinental Ballistic Missiles, and what a warhead can do to a city. In a badly mimeographed pamphlet Walt sent me two years before, I saw the spreading ripples, the concentric circles, with Chicago the red eye of the last storm. They were going crazy out in LA. This was the scariest shit ever, but no one dared make a picture about it because that might be unAmerican.

'Say, Jack. You see this?' I held the *Defender* out to him.

We were at the beach, with hampers and rugs, in light cotton trousers and shirtsleeves against the humidity. I was wearing penny loafers, and a white silk kerchief knotted around my old-lady's turkey-neck. The others were playing softball on a diamond marked out in wet sand; with Buddy, the catcher, berating every flyball so much that LeRoy had just fouled four consecutive pitches upside his head.

'Sure,' said Jack Ketch, too old, as I was, for that shit. He'd spent half his life on Venice Beach, letting agents do the work while he kicked back, and only cranking a fresh sheet of bond paper into the Remington when there was really nothing else for it. McCarthy had taken away his deckchair; he'd been working for me back here on a strictly extra-curricular basis.

He'd got a little fire going, of brushwood or driftwood or whichever, and was making coffee cowboy-style, in an indigo enamel pot suspended from makeshift A-frames. He was trying to be cool about it, but I knew this was the kind of thing he thought he'd never get a chance to do again. They were all trying to act like they did this all the time, but I knew this was part of a life that they'd denied themselves, way back (along with having someplace to go on holidays, establishing a connection between sex and love, and ever having a date New Year's).

I looked at Jack speculatively as he examined the newspaper. He wasn't so bad; and once you found out he wasn't a mailman or a salesman, a certain kind of woman might think, wow, neat, I could be with a writer. Especially at my age. But they aren't like regular guys. Most of the time they don't do doodly-squat. If you're hocked two months for the rent this can be difficult to understand. Even if things are on a roll then they don't come home at six and turn it off, as I knew from Walt; and if it's not going good then they're clingy, when you need them to be forthright and full-of-the-world, like the first man in your life used to be. It's no way to live. Ask a writer how his day was and he'll either mutter obscenities, or, just once in a while, say, oh, okay — y'know. The only thing they're really good for is planning heists. Maybe I ought to've tried it with old Walt.

Jack returned the paper, having studied the columns, the diagrams, a moment. He knew what I wanted.

'Sure could squeeze a monster movie out of that story,' he said, pushing his fisherman's cap back on his head. 'College kids on spring break – because no one's going to get tired of sweater girls in bathing suits, and a beach lets you show all the flesh the censors are going to allow. All-American, cornfed boys and girls . . .'

'But with one krazy kid who wears his cap backward like a catcher. Called Skeeter.'

Jack screwed up his eyes at the horizon. 'You want to scare them about something else, you gotta scare them with the things they know about. Puberty.'

'The curse,' I said, having just come full circle with mine.

'Vampires. Body fluids. There's a bunch of little punks like to stand on my street outside the corner drug and *spit*. Don't need to be Dr Freud to work that one out.'

'Werewolves,' I said. 'The sleek child on the change. Waiting for the moon, with those scary new hungers you can't quite satisfy . . .'

'Ought to be able to get a pretty gross monster out of that,' said Jack, turning back to his fire, 'even if you didn't have it caught downstream of an atomic meltdown a few years in the backstory.'

He didn't care too much – it was too easy. This was why none of them wanted to work in movies. They didn't see what I did. I'd have loved to do a movie again, just one more: even if it was just some creature-feature. I didn't care. Horror movies aren't sophisticated, and because they aren't they let you remember how it is to be a kid, and what it means not to know. The best monster movies are the cheapest ones – Walt taught me this – where they can't afford a monster, so they have to keep it behind the door or at the bottom of the stairs. Then the door or the stairs is what's scary, because you don't know, just as you didn't know when you were a kid. Walt used to say it was the same principle as bluffing in poker – when you open the door you're showing your hand, and the game

174

is over. The human imagination can deal with almost anything once it knows what it is – it's not knowing that's scary. All I had to do was open the door. I wondered, briefly, if Buddy grew up dreaming of the fucked-up atoms, like I dreamt of the twisted microbes, of the enemy within; then I tossed the paper aside.

Over the lake, thunderheads had been gathering all morning, sloping up to each other like wiseguys outside a pool hall. It was a perfect day; and besides no one else wanting to bet against the storms, it was midweek too, the city was at work, and happy to be there. However the citizens jammed this place at weekends, however they beamed at the long sweep beyond the milling flesh, while their kids whooped and yelled behind them, however they kidded themselves this was what the gray drag of the week was for, I was sure the whole thing was still kind of unnerving for them. We grew up without weekends; we still weren't sure what they were for, or what to do with the pesky things. No one was: after two hundred years of going crazy trying to coax a living from the raw country, it was tough to slow down. You live through a Depression, when you'd sign away your firstborn for the chance to drudge yourself into an early grave, then it's tough to give it up. It's kind of hard to deal with everything in the world suddenly telling you it's somehow unpatriotic if you don't take two whole days a week and fritter them away on painting by numbers and visiting monuments of national interest. You can't change this late in the game.

We don't like to stop. This had been the toughest thing for me too. All the time you can bury yourself in work, you don't have to think about what you are, and why you do the things you do. I always bought that crap about, unless you work hard you can't play – that without the filter of toil you won't see the time off for what it is. Now I was beginning to think it was the other way around: without the downtime you can't appreciate the up. It was like, the difference between skyscrapers in Chicago and skyscrapers in New York. In Manhattan they're crowded in on one another like bottles

175

on a pewter drinks tray; here, there's just one a block. It's the gaps between them that make you see how beautiful they are, and how wonderful the imagination and industry that put them there.

The softball game was breaking up, despite Buddy's outraged imprecations; the contagion of recumbence spreading inward from outfield like a ripple in a pond, transmitting its symptoms of lit cigarettes and horizontality. These guys didn't have that fear of interruption, that horror of stopping, because they were never really off the job; even with nothing especial to do, they were collecting, like cops or like hermits, going about their business with bucket and sieve on the shoreline. But having had, in this life of mine, a husband and a son, I knew what was needed; if I'd given them another couple minutes, then half the slackers would've been asleep already, wriggling their shoulders back into the sand.

So I did what I do, and three minutes later they were wading into the beer and fried chicken. I wasn't eating – not so hungry those days. Those tumors of mine were flowering in my system like time-lapse clouds in a June sky. Even if I weren't nauseous the whole time, I wouldn't've felt much like eating anyhow. It'd given me a sore mouth from vitamin deficiency, but I figured what the hey – I was finally getting the cheekbones I'd wanted.

So I picked at some chicken salad, mostly to stop anyone noticing I wasn't eating. About the twelfth or thirteenth worst thing about being ill the whole time and knowing you're never going to get better is everyone else knowing it too. Maybe a year before, when no one knew what the hell was wrong with me yet, I sat down at the clinic one day and some fourth-grader next to me turned round and said, Hi, I'm Marty, and I have leukemia. And I was like, oh, okay. That's nice. Should I call you Marty? Because it might be easier to remember you as Cancer Kid. Or maybe Tumor Girl, or how about Scary Brat Who Tells Everyone She Meets For The First Time That She Has Cancer. Or just, That Child With

Whom I'm Having The Most Awkward Conversation Ever. I did not want to do this to people.

It was bad enough sometimes just to think that I was roping those guys in at all. I swear, I coulda made a great bishop ordering his tomb, a real doozy of a dying king. The honorable thing, I was finding myself thinking too often, would've been to die quietly, not to lay this guilt crap on anyone else; but it was too late to go back. So there, at the beach, I was trying to pull myself together enough to marshal my dotard generals and washed-out grunts for one last mad tilt.

I had to be crazy. These were no Horatios, or Sanchos either. My getaway man, sitting down opposite me, lived with his mother, a suet-faced woman with stringy hair, partial to torn floral housecoats and listening at the door while her forty-year-old son took a leak. On the sand next to him was my post-job swag-laundering operative, a guy who parked his car on a public lot, a block and a half from his apartment, to avoid the repo men. My elite team of strategists, standing around Jack's driftwood fire, consisted of one guy who'd spent the last thirty years writing about a Philadelphia girl he probably only met once, who died of the Spanish 'flu in '18; a thirty-nine-year-old drunk who lost one arm, four toes and both heels in a flooded uranium mine six years back; and a blue-skinned, sleepy-eyed Keats-boy whom I didn't know whether I wanted to mother or carve my name in his back with my nails.

I was feeling like, gimme a break here. I wasn't grown up enough to do this. I felt as much an impostor doing it as I ever did in LA, screaming deadlines at fifty lazy, shiftless, good-for-nothing writers when all that was really concerning me was Long Island iced tea and the roof of my apartment; or when I came out of the hospital with Nicky, a week after he was born, thinking I had to watch every little thing I did now in case it turned into the thing he came to blame for messing him up; or twenty years later, when I gave away his little wire-hair terrier, because he'd written that every

177

day, as he sat under a dripping shelter half in German mud, he'd thought of me walking her the four long blocks from Lexington to the Park. I ran away, I ran away, and then I ran away again. I wasn't going to do it anymore. It was time to set my lands in order, and I was damn sure I wasn't going to die having no idea why. Though I was trying to think of it less as dying than as redistribution of matter. Like some guy told me once, everything came from stars and when I look into your eyes, baby . . . it was either Walt – or some actor whose face I can't remember, tried to kill himself jumping off the Hollywood sign, broke his back but lived another twenty-four years till cirrhosis copped him in the war. Whatever. I was going to know what it was to see something through, and not have to be somewhere else wondering about what it was that I'd left behind.

So brusque, and to business. I outlined the target. Jack used to do a lot of heist stories in Hollywood and he'd buy some guy from Siemen-Marcus a few Michelobs every now and then to get the skinny on how to blow the latest safes. The guy was a big wheel in the security business now, covered both sides of the Rockies, knew where new vaults had been sunk in any city west of Indianapolis. Like any tech-head, what he wanted most in the world was to talk to someone who seemed interested, so with Jack making with the 'say, how does that work again?' we got plans, blueprints, electrical circuit originations, storm-drain flowcharts, alloy composition graphs, and the brand of liquid soap in the men's room at Earl's place.

Then I'd gotten the cream cheese from my slice-the-pie-guy, who was looking after the dividend division afterward. He was the same accountant who came up with the tax-scam I'd been running at *The Dark Hour* the last couple years. I'd decided that since Isadore's was the only name on the books, he may as well be the only name on the books, if you see what I mean; so I got him a social security number, an employment history, and a permanent address from a street-numbering quirk, where the numbers jumped from 1263 to 1267 with nothing in between – there was a whole bunch of them downtown, where there used to be a stables or whichever. I loved that kind of thing. Anyway.

'The target is a shitload of Nazi gold,' I said. 'It's gonna be stored in the safe at this guy Earl's place while it gets laundered. I said we wouldn't steal anything that belonged to anybody, and I meant it.' I waited for reaction but there was none. 'It's bullion. Ingots. It got snuck out through Switzerland into Italy, where the Outfit took over – they sent it to New York and then here, in the hope it's going to cool off a little.'

All through legitimate banks, if you can believe it. One cool thing about this business of ours is that everyone you meet wants to feed you stuff for stories, so that, should anything ever make it into a book, they can buy it, put it on their shelf, and take it down to show off when they have people over. We'd all picked up a bunch of them, and that was how this came to us. One of Jack's other sources was a banker downtown – a guy who never quite got used to the idea that he was in Chicago now, and still watched Wall Street like it was after his sister. The summer before, he noticed the gold prices failing to go crazy at a time when they really ought to have, which suggested that some of the banks must've had un-disclosed reserves in their vaults; so he put Jack onto a couple of people in New York, had them sniff around a little, and soon there was enough to put two and two together. The Israeli secret police had, it seemed, followed the heat out of Europe and as far as Manhattan, but then lost the scent; this was because it had been brought here and stuck under the ground, where it was closer to hell and less obvious.

'The fact that we're stealing from the Mob doesn't mean shit,' I said. 'It's nothing to be afraid of. They're not going to know what's hit them. The only threat they worry about is from rival factions, and they're all in on this together.'

'But the place is still going to be crawling with Mafiosi,' said Jack, 'so we go in when their pants are down. The stated business of this joint is the production of one-handed literature – art pamphlets, *kapeesh?* – and they use the basement to take pictures of broads, then paste them up into magazines upstairs.'

'How d'you know?' said LeRoy, teasing.

''Cos I jack off over them, okay? I did some work with one of the paste-up artists years ago. Donnie Hood?'

'No shit,' said Quent, 'I thought he was dead.'

'He says the same thing about you,' said Jack. 'But before we go arranging a high school reunion let's remember that he's our man on the inside. No contact and I mean that, however long any of you go back with him. He's our ticket in. The joint is always full of footsoldiers, but these guys are knuckleheads. However much contraband is passing through the place, they all make sure they've got nothing better to do when Earl's using the place to photograph broads. Donnie's going to tell us when that's gonna happen.'

Jack was my man. This was kids' stuff to him – truth is more facile than fiction, he always said. He continued, talking around a fat inch of cigar.

'You wouldn't believe the scene in that place. I mean, this is the major fucking Mob outpost on the South Side, and it's staffed by shitheads. Donnie says most of them don't even bother carrying pieces – just sit around drinking up the contraband and ogling the girls. They're not gonna bother to smarten up their act because this is just a stopgap, till they can get the gold shipped out through the Pacific.

'But the noise we make when we blow the vault door open is going to be loud enough to make even an Italian guy tear his eyes away from two girls in their underwear. Shit will hit, and they'll come looking for us.'

'Can't we get out underground?' asked LeRoy.

'In any other city, but not here,' said Jack. 'After the '71 fire, city ordinances specified six feet of firewall in all new foundations – so if

180

it happens again, it won't spread through the sewers. Methane.'
Heads nodded all around the circle, and I could see this snippet
getting filed away for future use. The hero and the girl in the
burning building, blasting their way out through the water main –
the bad guys vaporized with a matchbook tossed down a storm
drain. 'The South Side may look like it's falling down, but the
foundations are gonna stay solid till the river runs over the
mountain. There's no way we can sneak out once we're in. We're
going to have to face them. So what we do is send in a ringer.'

Which was me. I'd show up just after the explosion, when the
*paisans* were running round like Chicken Licken, claiming the sky
had fallen on their heads. Looking like I meant business – black
jumpsuit covered in webbing and D-rings, gas mask, rubber soled
boots, black leather gloves.

'They're panicking,' I said. 'I'm an easy focus for their anxiety.
They assume that we detonated from outside – that we expected
the explosive to take them out – and are moving in to mop up.
They take me hostage.'

'What if they just shoot you?' Buddy suggested, missing the
point.

'I come in through a window on the fire stairs and jump down.
I'll be clearly unarmed, and looking like I expect the cavalry behind
me any moment. These guys are dumb, but not that dumb. They'll
see that I'm the general – no hardware – but for all they know there
could be five or fifty behind me. If they can get a gun to my head so
that it's the first thing my back-up sees, they'll have won a stand-off
rather than a shoot-out straightaway.'

This struck no chords of amazement or outrage amongst the
faithful. We all had a utility with structure, a facility with reversals,
without which we wouldn't have been there. It'd occurred to me
early on that whatever gameplan we conjured between us, we ran
the risk of appreciating it a little too much for its own sake, for its
neat!-factor – for the kind of thing that makes you sit back and give

yourself a little sock in the arm a moment when you're at your typewriter. What works in a ten-cent storybook mightn't cut it so much when you're staring down ten wiseguys with ten nine-millimetres on their home turf. So the plan was, for once, to leave the story out of the plot, and put the beginning, middle and end into our own lives. We were going to get closure, in this B-picture life, then maybe we could think about the main feature.

'Which is when we let them wait,' said Jack. 'We let them sweat while we load up with bullion – six ingots a man. We're not taking it all because we don't need it all. This is still going to be twenty bags of sugar, gentlemen, and you'll still need to move fast. Training will be stepped up a session a week until we're doing it once a day for the last two weeks.'

George – who did boxing stories for *Sir* and *Gent* as a sideline – had had them all punching bags and hoisting weights at a gym three nights a week since the start of the month. I hadn't gone along because they felt they'd be too embarrassed to have me see their chair-spread asses crammed into track shorts. I swear, this is the one generalization you can safely make about writers. Ten years of fifteen hours a day in the same chair, and when you bend over, your neighborhood goes out to take its laundry off the line.

'So then you guys come blinking out of the rubble into the daylight, and we make the stand-off.' I lit a dancer, more for the feel of it in my fingers than anything else. 'The situation becomes clear to the knuckleheads. I underline it further by ordering you to shoot me and blast your path out. You feign horror. They meanwhile will have got a bolt across the doors, and will have grouped in front. One thing they don't expect you to do will be to pop the hostage. Still another will be that you've pre-wired the doors with explosive. Buddy.'

Who was our ballistics guy, but if I could've changed this I would. There was too much responsibility, but he was the only one who had any kind of facility with math. The others were the kind of guys who, in order to work out the tip in diners, simply doubled the bill, however strapped they were. Really. Maybe money wasn't even the best thing for them. My projections suggested that they were going to make enough from this job to keep them going as though *The Dark Hour* still existed, but perhaps that wasn't what they needed most. I was probably flattering myself, but maybe having me to work for – feeling somehow responsible for me, because if they didn't write anything for me then I wouldn't have had anything to do – maybe that'd been worth more to them than the money. Because they'd changed, most of them, into something that money might not've been any good for. The Gatsby guy in the mansion can't pick up his white telephone and arrange to have an envelope crammed with twenties sent to the kid in the kitchen. The movie queen can't send the laundry maid round to that cold-water West Hollywood walk-up, where the sophomore bottle-blonde reddened her hands washing graying blouses in the basin.

'Hold it a second,' said George. 'If we're going to blow the fuck out of the basement, won't everyone else on the block come looking to see what's going on? Won't someone call the cops?'

'There's no one else for four blocks,' I said.

'In the industrial quarter?' George was incredulous, but I could sympathize. I'd had problems believing it could be so dead there now, but it was true.

'Earl's is the only place for four blocks still making anything,' I said. 'Unless you count a disused meatpacker's two blocks away, which continues to make flies and roaches with as much industry as before.'

They all sniggered, but this seemed crazy to me. I always thought this was the city that works, but it was starting to seem like nobody constructed anything anymore. Like those strange new towns that you saw more and more if you drove out on the turnpike – no houses, no farms, nothing except gas stations and motor inns and diners, existing for nothing except to service the traffic coming off

183

the 'pike, the same as those honky-tonk-and-cathouse places that used to spring up two centuries ago wherever rivers met. It scared the hell out of me. How could this kind of thing sustain a nation? When we just service the services? It made me wonder if we were going to stay in the twentieth century, or whether we might just find ourselves jolted back a few, to before we had slaves. We might discover, I suspected, that our kind of living was only sustainable through extraordinary and wholesale acts of inhumanity, and since we didn't fancy that anymore, we might have to get used to not fancying a whole lot else besides.

'We're some of the last guys in the world to make anything,' I said. 'We might soon be the last people on the planet who go to work and put something into the world that wasn't there before. Whatever. What we can put in doesn't seem to be wanted right now, so we're gonna take something out instead. Buddy.'

He stood up, and came around to where I was, like he was taking his place at the front of a classroom for Show & Tell.

'I have to say it,' he said. 'This is chickenshit. This is a chickenshit heist.'

I almost dropped my cigarette. I'd meant for him to talk about his part, as explosives man.

'Whadda you mean, son?' said Jack, slowly and deliberately.

'I mean,' Buddy said, caught between raised hackles and the realization, perhaps, that this wasn't such a good idea, 'that this is a no-brainer.'

I saw what he was doing at once, the little fuck.

'This is the last time anyone's gonna do such a dumb heist,' he went on. 'C'mon. Blowing safes, stealing bullion – this is grade-school stuff. We oughta be thinking ahead. There're guys out in Korea doing all kinds of twisted shit – counterintelligence, black operations – and when the war's over they're gonna come back here and go to work. And they'll be doing shit like we can't believe.

That's the kind of thing we oughta be plannin' here. Jesus, I bet even the Mob's into smarter stuff than this now.'

The others were looking like they were too polite to say it, but the general consensus seemed to be: what was I thinking of, bringing such a greenhorn little prick on the team? But Jack was old enough to maintain politeness. 'Example,' he said.

'Well I was thinking, maybe we could take a look at what money really is,' Buddy said, tentatively, like he'd waited through ten grades to have the teacher pick his upraised hand. 'Money is a figure. It's a metaphor. If we can look at how the metaphor's put together – at what the link is between what we mean by it and what it really is, then I think we could really be onta somethin'. I mean, that's where we'd make the steal. You get me? I mean, I know the idea here was that since we all spend the whole time thinkin' up ways to do new heists in stories and stuff, then we oughta be able to think up somethin' for reality. Well, what I'm sayin' is if we look a little deeper into what we do we'll come out with something really worth doing.'

That doesn't involve assisting a suicide, was what he meant. Jack's reply was measured.

'I believe this isn't your show, son. We're here to do a job because we've been asked to. It's not much of our business to be saying that the person who's giving us the work hasn't done their job properly. I think the position is, we take the work and be thankful for it; one, because we've been given it as a mark of belief in us; and two, because that's not what's on the table here. This is a matter of respect and loyalty. If you subscribe to either, then you oughta have done the work you were assigned. If you don't, and you haven't, then I guess we'll have to find a way of doing this without you. So. Did you do your work or didn't you?'

I'd had a horrible feeling it was going to be like this.

'Yeah, I did it,' Buddy said. 'But I won't have done it right if I yellow out from saying what it led me to think. I mean, really. Any of us put this in a story then we'd have a hard time pulling five bucks for it. We're gonna go in there and blow a safe? Then shoot our way out?' He didn't look at me. 'You're on drugs. Dynamite and pistols are for hoods who can't think of anything else. We can do better than that, is all I wanted to say.'

Jack drew on his coffee then twisted the tin cup a half-inch into the sand. It was just the two of them now. This was the last thing I wanted, and I took a panicky sweep of the rest – but they were all hunched over, staring at the ground, or flipped back on the dune, squinting into the sky. All I could think was that if they called on me to arbitrate, I wouldn't know what to say. I was never the kind of woman who could leap between two guys when they were facing up to each other, at a party or whatever: I was the kind of girl who gave up, and went home or somewhere else. When things weren't working, I hated it. I couldn't bear it. I traced the end of my cigarette through dry, shifting sand, losing the coal, waiting for someone to say something, wondering what the christ I'd been thinking of.

'I want you to take this how it's intended,' said Jack. 'If you think for a moment that, if I was thirty years younger, I wouldn't be thinkin' the same things you are, then you're crazy. That's one of the things God gives you youth for. But he gives you age too, and that's a sweeter gift than you can imagine. You stop looking for complication. You find a challenge in simplicity.' He took a last sip of coffee then jerked the grounds out onto the dune, pushing a heap of fresh sand over with his free hand. 'I think that's all the problem we've got here. And if that's all the problem that you've got, then I don't think we have a problem. No one's asking or expecting you to run this show. All that was asked of you was to learn how to deploy the explosive we're gonna provide you with. If you've done that, then we'd sure be interested to hear what you've found out.'

All Buddy could do was bring out his notebook.

186

'An explosive is a solid or liquid substance or mixture of substances which, on the application of a suitable stimulus to a small portion of the mass, is converted in a very short interval of time into other more stable substances, largely or entirely gaseous, with the development of heat and high pressure.' Buddy chewed the words grimly, like they were a wad of conciliatory tobacco handed him post-nuptials by a trigger-happy farmer whose daughter he'd knocked up. 'Our stuff was invented by Alfred Nobel in 1866 by mixing 92 per cent nitroglycerine with 8 per cent collodion cotton, and is still the most powerful industrial explosive. It's used primarily for excavation of shafts, tunnels, galleries and general mine workings; for excavation of railway, highway and hydro-electric diversion tunnels; for removing tree stumps and for loosening subsoil in orchard development. We, however, will be using it to blow the doors off a 1941 Siemens-Marcus safe.'

'Enough,' I said. 'We get the picture. Can you do it?'

'With eight ounces,' he said.

'LeRoy?' I raised an eyebrow at him.

'Eight ounces is cool,' he shrugged – he was tight with some radical brothers who knew where to put a hand to that kind of stuff. 'Getya twelve.'

'Just get us what we need,' I said. 'And now I hate to say it, but I need someone to take me home. I'm not feeling so good.'

I really wasn't, and for every reason you can think of.

Alice really was the living fucking end, honestly. Susan still couldn't quite believe it. She never thought she'd feel this way about someone but now she did. When she'd got the can from Smith on account of getting married, girls she used to room with would pass her in the halls with maybe just a brittle, triumphant smile to acknowledge her existence – the kind a wronged-but-rallying-round mayor's wife might wear on her way from the courtroom after her husband lost his libel action. Girls she'd used to double-date with, honestly. Susan had always wondered what could make a person turn into an asshole like that, but Alice was teaching her how. Unbelievable.

She'd never thought Alice was any kind of a brains trust, but she used to have a little class. Not much, but a little. When Susan first met her and got to talking and stuff, it'd been a relief to find out she wasn't quite the ice queen she'd conspired to seem, even if this had mostly been achieved through keeping her mouth shut, over-dressing the whole time, being supremely bored with everything, and reading magazines with her sunglasses on. This, it had turned out, was just Alice's hedge against the other girls in the chorus being more talented than her; and since they'd been more talented than Susan too, it had seemed natural that the two of them should commence to rub along together. Susan was taken aback a little when Alice'd first mentioned working for Earl, but took it in the spirit she'd thought it was suggested, as kind of a hoot – like, look at these dumb guys, they're so hot for us they'll give us all kinds of dough, and all we have to do is be as sexy as we are. But looking back, it seemed to Susan that Alice had been losing it ever since she got to Chicago, and now she was just getting embarrassing.

Susan hadn't seen her a while because there was way trouble at the House of Whacks. She couldn't help feeling part of it was her fault for baiting the asshole cop who pulled them all the last time, but she hadn't been able to help it. It'd been much too good to pass up, and besides, those coppers had deserved it. The only thing worrying them back then was a creeping suspicion that the tax-free cigarettes and unstamped crates of whiskey passing through the place weren't, in fact, Giotto's primary business, so their kickbacks weren't going to be up to the cut they expected.

But this was something they seemed to be sure of now. They'd shut down Earl's accounts with the mail-carriers, without which he couldn't do business, and charged him with postal obscenity. The trial started at the end of the week and Susan had to go give evidence the Thursday after. She wasn't worried – it was a monkey trial – but she felt sorry for Earl, who, even though Giotto was underwriting him, had the Feds right up his ass; and what with the McCarthy thing still crazy insane back west, there was a real possibility that they were going to fix him up good just for being a nuisance. It was a shame, because the only reason for the trial seemed to be to try and irritate Giotto into upping his payments to the cops. The assholes didn't, however, understand that their suspicions weren't in the same neighborhood as what Giotto really did, or that they weren't even on the same subway line. The fact was, as Susan knew, Giotto didn't even do anything illegal any-more, except the dumb smuggling and stuff that was intended to keep the cops happy that he was. This town, she swore.

So there wasn't any modeling for her and Alice anymore. She'd black-and-whited her last, at least in the current configuration. So – and mostly because the free time she had was too free and too much – she'd been doing hostessing for Giotto for the last few weeks: going out in fleets of limos with out-of-town investors to inspect

wnlands, then back to private suites at the Bismarck to
m drinks, laugh musically at whatever they said, and schlep
und trays of hors-d'oeuvres. It was only a day or two every other
week, but it wasn't a problem because Ben'd been taking care of
her rent just lately, saying that Giotto had an interest in her
building, though Susan suspected he didn't. She hadn't heard a
whisper from Alice for almost a month, so she figured Joey must be
doing the same for her – especially since they were getting married
and all. So when Susan went down to the deli one day to pick up
some lox and cream cheese, and saw Alice with a high-school kid,
coming out of the bank on the corner, she figured it must be some
kind of nephew or cousin or whatever, in town on a visit.

She wasn't even about to cross the street to say hey, because
Alice'd been a royal pain in the ass lately, but there were a couple of
things that made her stop, and sneak another look. It was only a
little after three but Alice was practically in stage make-up – high-
rouge and pancake – with her hair piled up, and wearing the kind
of cocktail dress that's a little too trashy for anywhere you'd want to
be taking too many cocktails – it was more the kind of thing you'd
wear on your husband's birthday if you were staying home.

And the kid she was with didn't look too electrified to be seeing
the sights, it had to be said, even if Alice didn't have his shoulder in
a vise-like grip – Susan could see her knuckles pearling from across
the street. She was kind of bored stupid anyways – she'd had
nothing to do all day and didn't have much in her schedule till it
was time to wash up and change for dinner with Ben – so she'd
hey'd and waved from across the street – but Alice just put her head
down and continued marching the kid along. Susan was like, this
was too cool – haughty Alice so mortified about something she
couldn't even admit to her own existence – so she'd followed them
five blocks, Alice tripping along all the while on five-inch heels that
were perfect for one of Earl's sessions but hardly the thing for a hike
across downtown. And then they went into another bank.

Susan ducked into a dinette across the street, but before she even got her ice-water, Alice was out of there and getting in a cab, leaving the kid looking lost on the sidewalk. So Susan scattered a dime and some pennies on the table, got out the door and across the street, and caught the kid just as he turned to trail back the way he'd come.

'Excuse me?' she tagged him, and he spun around like he was on a hair-trigger. 'Didn't I just see you with Alice?' He looked blank. 'I knew it!' Susan declared, before he had time to object. 'I was just passing in a cab and I saw the two of you so I thought to myself, Dolores, why dontcha hop on out and shanghai her? You see, I haven't been in the city since I married Mitch, and Alice and I used to take a dance class together over to Columbia, and the friends you make when you study are the ones – well, listen to me, I'm sure you're not even in college yet, but let me tell you, when you are you just hang on to the friends you make, okay? Will you do that, honey? Because they're the ones who shared something with you so they're the ones you'll miss most. But listen to me.' She placed a flat palm on her breastbone, and tossed her head back with a tinselly laugh. 'Here I am telling you what a sweet lady your aunt is when you oughta know yourself – I mean, not every boy has an aunt to take 'em out to lunch in the city, huh? So do you live here, honey? Or are you just here on a visit? Because what I'd love for you to do is to give me old Alice's number so we girls can catch up on the last few years. So is she married, sweetheart? Are you from her side or her husband's?'

But the kid was backing off, looking at Susan like she was crazy and/or going to eat him for breakfast, and when she put a hand on his arm he actually flinched. So she figured something was really up, dropped the crap and gave him some hey, no one's going to hurt you here honey and stuff; but then he burst into tears, and this was becoming the most interesting afternoon Susan'd had in weeks.

It took two chocolate egg creams back at the dinette, along with a Winston that he didn't really know how to smoke and an assurance from Susan that she was after Alice because she was a store detective from Carson, Pirie, Scott, before the kid started to sing. It turned out he snuck out with a couple of buddies from some Catholic-type weasel-pit of a preppy-prison out in Glenview or someplace – they'd come out to the city to try and get their hands on some whiskey, sneak into a burlesque show, kind of thing. Susan got the impression that his buddies had been kind of more up for it than he was. Anyway, they'd persuaded themselves into some sweaty-guy dive called the Lava Lounge – because it's hot Hot HOT – which was the kind of place you'd go if you're a hayseed out on your farm-subsidy check, all dick and no sense. The kind with a floorshow of old witches, where a glass of warm Connecticut champagne cost five bucks a pop, and if you didn't want to drink it, they took you in back and beat the crap out of you.

But because it was afternoon, there'd been no one around to do the beating; and since Alice was the one who'd huckstered them in off the street to begin with, it had been her fault. So she'd been the one who had to make the only kid who'd admit to having a bank book go all around town, emptying his account over and over at different branches until he came up with the hundred and twenty bucks Alice's bosses claimed the boys had run up by this time. The other kids had done a fade, and the rest Susan knew about. Unbelievable.

But the real moral of the story was just how bad things had gotten between Bellini and Giotto. Alice must only have been working at the Lava Lounge because Joey was so much Bellini's nigger now that he wouldn't have her do anything even indirectly connected to Giotto. Susan would've thought that, for all Volante's swagger, he might've been able to afford for her not to work at all, especially not as some species of half-assed hooker. But that seemed to be the way it went among the *paisans*: all show and no dough, simply because there were so many of them. Really. Ben'd pointed out a few of the gimp-joints the footsoldiers used, and Susan had been noticing them everytime she went by since; dozens of wiseguys, all trying to look like they were money, like they were waiting for the next call to come in, when really all they were was a bunch of assholes with nothing better to do than hang round commode-type diners all day, driving the owners' wives crazy.

Giotto's trying to break away didn't seem so weird now. The real money wasn't in gangster shit, but business. Or rather, the latter was so much more efficiently criminal than the former that there were few real criminals left. Just a bunch of dorks in cheap trousers sitting around drinking grappas. So what was running through her mind when she came home from the market a few days later and found Ben, white-faced and loose-tied, in her TV room, drinking whiskey and telling her Giotto had been hit, was how like a dream it had all been. Not a moon-in-June kind of thing, but more the way that everything in a dream can happen just because it's a dream and you know you're going to wake up. It had all been too weird – Ben, money, Giotto, future – and she understood that she'd known all along it was going to end.

She didn't tell this to Ben because he was busy telling her how Giotto had taken four big ones in the back at eight that morning, and was now in Lakeshore, getting pumped and jumped upside his head just to maintain vital functions. And Ben was dying even worse. He'd gone straight over to the hospital when he saw the lunchtime news-stands, but'd been shooed away like an eighth-grader by G-men, by knuckleheads, by goons and creeps and wiseguys swarming everywhere; the worst thing was that they weren't even local meat, but from Detroit or Philly, and therefore only in Chicago already because they must've known this was going to happen. And all of Giotto's soldiers renewing their contracts elsewhere, it seemed. Susan guessed that they were for hire like anybody else and, in a competing market, went where they were most comfortable; which was the old way, which was

193

what they knew, which was Bellini. So, at Susan's apartment, he sat in one chair with his head in his hands, while she was tipped back in another, smoking cigarette after cigarette at the ceiling and thinking how like a dream it'd been.

It'd been like a dream; everything'd seemed like it had a frame, was finite, and was finishing soon. They'd gone to shows, they'd gone to restaurants, they'd gone to bed. It hadn't been so difficult once it had a chance to get started. After a while there'd been no frost or fire, but just stuff instead: fun and comfort and rubbing along; the things that dreams are made of. Susan always figured, after her fruit-fly marriage, that anyone else, if ever there was, would have to carry the weight of that tinny disaster along with the weight of her: would have to be careful as Mary's midwife with her achin' breakin' heart, with she who had been wronged. She looked over at him now, face between his fists, frowning down at the whiskey-wash icemelt in the tumbler on the floor. She'd imagined him veering between seeing her as damaged goods, as leftover, as used-and-found-faulty; and being, himself, alternately strafed with vengeful wrath or crippled by jealousy of the Wronger. He could never have been just a guy in love, because that'd been spoiled; instead, he was forever the one who must pick up the pieces. She'd thought it would give her an easy, difficult ride, as eternally shifting victim, poor girl; as done-to, never doer, broken girl; so that when he left her, she could slap another stripe on her arm, stick another decal on the fuselage.

That hadn't happened. It'd just been easy. Part of her, a lot of her, was outraged. Because this was something that happened! Something bad! She'd felt it – even on the night she came home and found her husband, car and money gone – with the relief of a hypochondriac reading $103°$ on an undoctored thermometer. Okay, maybe it was something she may or may not have gone looking for; but it was, nonetheless, something she hadn't made up, and there was real, documentary evidence. She'd told Ben, early on, in a scene she'd rehearsed with grievous anticipation, expecting the skies to turn dark and the curtain in the temple to be rent asunder. But he'd just kind of shrugged, expressed the opinion that her ex sounded kind of an asshole, and told her a story about a couple of other assholes, one at Yale, one in the joint; then before she'd known it she'd found herself telling her best stories, the saved-up ones, about when she was a kid raising hell in the orphanage; and they'd both eaten their dinners and snickered a lot, then laughed so hard at something he'd said about a Sunday school picnic that he'd had to come around the table and pound her on the back.

Not at all what she'd expected. Afterward, she found herself wondering whether that was all there was to it, something to be passed between them – *here it is, okay? This is the worst of me* – and forgotten; then decided it couldn't possibly be because that's most of all she was anymore, or all she'd let herself become. So she'd continued with compensating for it by focussing so much on his work life, she suspected now, even to the extent of wanting to be a bigger part of it than he was. Which was what she'd been doing since she met him.

Still staring at the floor over there. She crushed her smoke, went to say something, then stopped. Things were too different now. Being left the last time was almost a relief. It was like, here's what you get for putting on airs, and here you go, back to life; back to normality, because everything's screwed. By marrying someone who was going to leave her, she'd loused everything up forever. No more school, no career. It had meant choices were easier to make, because suddenly there were a lot less of them – like, do this or starve, pretty much. It was going to be even worse this time. And now that the last phase was underway, all she could think about was when it wasn't; all the days she'd spent reading in that chair the last couple of months, that window she glanced over at whenever a noise in the street distracted her. It framed a pair of windows across the way, on either side of a drainpipe where two buildings met. The one on the left was in some kind of rooming house, and belonged to a guy about her age who looked like a student; the window on the right was the kitchenette of a woman maybe ten years older, who must've worked nights somewhere because she was always around during the day. Susan saw them both all the time: the geek liked to hit the books at a table flush with the dividing wall, and the woman's sink was just below the window, so she was always getting a glass of water from the faucet, or doing the dishes, or making a cheese dream in the eye-level grill. So many times Susan had looked up, and there they both were; but neither with any idea that there was someone else there, only a couple of feet away sometimes; yet they wouldn't know it if they sat opposite each other on the subway. This, Susan felt now, was how she and Ben had been before they met. All those years when things were bad and worse and not-so-good, and they could have passed each other in the street and not known it. She wasn't going back to it, and that was the end.

In the cab to the courthouse next morning Susan frowned over the newspapers. It didn't seem to make sense. Why now? Why hit Giotto the day before Earl's trial was due to wind up? It was almost like the papers were behind the hit: in addition to the trial giving them the opportunity to reprint, copyright-free, photographs from *Eyeful* that were usually only available to paying subscribers, they were also splashing on the shooting of Giotto. He'd been operated on the night before, and the front pages were having a turkey shoot: like, this old guy lying on the sidewalk is the sinister Mr Big who's been running things these last few years, and this fat guy being hustled into the courthouse has been running one of his more revolting enterprises in this city of ours. So here's frontier justice for one and city hall comeuppance for the other – it would've made her puke if it hadn't made her so sick. It was exactly like whoever did it – Bellini – was trying to maximize the coverage. Why would he want to do that? She didn't get it.

There wasn't any time to chew it over because she was called to give evidence almost immediately. Though she'd been preparing for it for weeks, it didn't seem such a big deal anymore: there was no especial heat on Susan herself, and given what was going down outside, it seemed almost like light relief. She treated the room to a little shimmy on the steps before she sat down on the stand, crossing her legs and shaking her hair out over her shoulders as the questioning started.

The DA was a dick, more concerned with running for senator next fall than with anything in the courtroom, and she dispatched his preliminary questioning almost on automatic. After establishing that she had a name, a body and a mailing address, he began by playing her as a poor, ill-used waif pressed into service by the evil Earl – who, across the courtroom, was falling slightly short of the mad Marquis in a sweat-ringed shirt and the kind of fat guys' trousers that fasten just under the breastbone.

So Susan pointed out that modeling for magazines was an informed career choice for a budding actress; and when the DA intimated that she was a good-time girl down on her luck, she raised a murmur from the press benches by making pointed reference to her education at Smith. She almost wished Ben was here to see it – she had the guy riled and running.

But then the DA suggested she tell the court about the circumstances under which she left Smith College four years ago. Her defense attorney, who hadn't even bothered to brief her, didn't make an objection; on the contrary, he looked like he was quite interested to hear this himself.

'I don't see that my private life could be of any import to this courtroom,' she said, putting some Southern into her vowels. 'And if you were a gentleman, you wouldn't pry, sir.'

197

The hacks in the gallery perked up. Susan gave the DA a Gillette glare, wondering how the hell he'd dug that shit up.

'May I remind you that you're under oath, *Miss* de Souza?'

What the hell was he getting at? So while she tried to think, she gave them the edited highlights of her academic and matrimonial careers – the scholarship board she'd sat for at Hull House, the yearly endowment she'd won, how she'd met Mack and married him, and how he'd hightailed it out of the tri-state area with her bursary checks and Chevy – answering each impertinence from the DA with what she hoped were witheringly dignified affronts.

'So you were left with no means of support, once you'd violated the conditions of your scholarship by marrying?'

Jumped-up little fuck.

'Will you answer the question, Miss de Souza? Were you left with no means of support?'

Fuck you. 'I was left, sir, with what every woman has.'

'Hmmm,' he said, and pushed his glasses up on his nose.

Even though the hacks were lapping this up now, Susan just wanted to get out of there. She could see what the bastard was doing, and she didn't want to be part of it. He'd been reported as aiming to bump up the women's vote, and his tone with Susan was concerned, sympathetic, really fucking irritating; tricking her out as a victim whom he could save by closing down the House of Whacks was clearly going to be another feather in his campaign hat.

And then she finally got it. All her life she'd had people tell her that guys were all the same, but she'd never been able to agree: in her experience, they were all uniquely fucked up. But now she saw the truth of it: it wasn't that guys *were* the same, it was that they all worked the same way. So, just as the DA was using the press coverage of this trial to get himself re-elected, Bellini was using it too – and that was the reason for the coincidental clipping of Giotto. By timing the trial with the election campaign, the DA was getting big sexy splashes in the papers at a time when he'd otherwise have been pushed to make the gardening column. By timing the hit with the trial, Bellini was having it broadcast that – since Giotto was in hospital, and the apparent cornerstone of his operation was up in front of the DA – the lawless days were over; so that now the Mob had been seen to be so publicly vanquished, the mob under Bellini could carry on much as before.

Susan did the rest almost on automatic, because this was the fucking tin lid. All this sleazebag asshole was doing to her – poor girl, broken girl – was what she did to herself, and had done, forever. If this two-shit sonofabitch used those kind of tactics, then she'd be damned if she was going to use them on herself anymore. It was time to begin the begin. It was time to get out, and start again with Ben. But first she had to get out of there.

'Tell me, Miss de Souza,' the DA tossed down his papers and took off his glasses, to show this was from the heart, 'how do you feel about the defendant's . . . operation? How did you feel – as a *woman* – when you were being trussed up, and photographed? Just what is your *opinion* of those whips, those handcuffs, those *shoes*?'

'Why, senator, honey' – with one hand flattened on her bosom – 'I think they're *cute*.'

And the house came down. She blew a kiss at the DA, now colored to his ears, tossed Earl a wink, and strutted offstage, down the centre aisle, hips swinging in time with her purse. She knew what needed to be done now. She was almost where she wanted to be, and she'd never felt so ready in her life.

First she had to sort Ben out, because she needed him, and if she didn't do it then no one else was going to. When she'd left that morning he was practically catatonic. All she could get out of him was that he needed to see Giotto, but Susan couldn't see the point. Giotto'd been operated on through the night, the papers said; so it wasn't like the old man was in any position to tell Ben where the keys to the magic kingdom were. It wasn't even that simple; there wasn't just a stash of money somewhere, and Ben's dollar-drip had been yanked out of his arm.

All of Giotto's money was tied up in leverage for Ben's dumb ideas: the safe town for the city's colored, the research facility which was proving how cigarettes cause cancer, the recording studio in Memphis full of fat Southern boys making a ruckus that Ben'd got it into his head that high-school kids could be persuaded to buy, along with magazines, fake i.d.'s and some stinking herb they were growing out in Washington State that he'd mixed up with tobacco and tried to incite Susan to smoke a month or so ago. Left to his own devices, he was a putzer: he was her guy and stuff, but he and Giotto'd had their heads up each other's asses while morons on the Volante model had been putting together a coup d'état – and now they were either pitching up for a war, or the war was already won. Ben and Giotto had allowed it to happen, because they'd thought people were more interested in money than being assholes; but it seemed that anyone who was into big money was an asshole almost by definition. Which was the worst thing. If this meant Joey Volante and Alice were the new belles of the ball, then she was through with this shit. Really. Forget about it. She barked at the cab-driver to take his foot out of his ass and put it on the pedal, and sat back imperiously.

But within four hours the wind had been knocked out of her, and her sails besides. Giotto was dead. Giotto's daughter was now in his bed. She'd gone to see her father: the goons had found her holding his hand and weeping, and tumbled who she was; so they took her up a back alley and took turns with her – maybe a dozen of them – then left her for dead. The kid from the party, that kid with cuffed bluejeans and a fading phone number inked on the back of her hand, had hemorrhaged so much from her ruined little sex that her blood ran twenty yards out onto the street. The doctors who admitted her thought she was a teen pregnancy who'd maybe

200

miscarried, till they clocked the bruises on her upper arms, the dislocated shoulder, the fractured wrist. Even if it had only been meant as the ultimate disrespect, she was unlikely to make it to the next day. It had killed the old man, anyway.

They weren't at her apartment because they couldn't be in the city anymore. They were holed up at a motor inn on the lake, two hours north of the city. When she got back to her building there'd been flowers waiting with the doorman, with a note tucked in saying, You need to tip the blushing maid – don't be like me – Peter Pan, in Ben's handwriting. She got the last bit – Peter Pan wanted to sew on his shadow, so if she didn't want to be like him, she needed to avoid being followed – but it took her the best part of a half-hour in a tourist horse-and-buggy along the lakeshore to figure out where it was she had to go. She couldn't get the blushing maid part: first, all she could think about were the kind of maids who keep their lamps untrimmed and stuff, blushing chaste and virginal; and then she was like, old maids, the orphanage, what? And then she thought maybe he meant that hotel downtown where she and Alice had done some dorky French maid stuff for one of the private shoots; she was pretty sure Ben hadn't known about that, but thinking about other hotels dropped the penny. They'd been up at a place on the lake one weekend and Saturday night they took turns fooling around, tying each other's wrists with a pair of her nylons. Trouble was, they'd woken up next morning and gone over to the diner for breakfast, calling out a cheery good morning to the maid, a blue-eyed Wisconsin farmgirl, as they passed her a couple of doors down. They'd been a little mystified when she'd looked away, coloring, but when they unlocked the door to their bungalow, the maid had done out the room and the stockings were still knotted around the bedposts. It made Susan blush all over to remember it, even now. So she'd taken a cab from the lakeshore, and found him here, and he'd told her about Giotto, and about Giotto's daughter.

'You can't go back,' Susan said.

'Things will revert. There's too much money involved.'

'It's over.'

'I'm telling you it isn't. Bellini's nothing compared to our investors.'

'It never occur to you that your investors have rivals too? Who might want things to stay just as they are? Who might be behind Bellini?'

It hadn't occurred to Susan either until she said it. Jesus, what were Ben and Giotto thinking of? Didn't it occur to them that, say, the tobacco corporations might have a problem with a couple of Chicago chancers trying to get them outlawed? That the cigarette barons might hire a little muscle of their own? She expressed this to him.

'Of course it did,' he said. 'We had them balls to the wall. Once Congress outlaws tobacco, they're going to have to let us do their marketing. It won't take much of a shift for them to do it.'

'But wouldn't it have been easier for them to hook up with Giotto's rivals and keep things as they are?'

'We made a new way of doing business. No one got hurt and everyone was happy.'

Susan took a deep one. Where did guys spend their time? Why didn't they ever know shit? It ought to have amazed her, but it didn't. They just had pretty sheltered lives, she suspected. If you're an average kind of woman and you take the tiniest interest in the way you're turned out, you can walk into any party and know you could have eight out of ten of the men there, just by smiling; if you're a guy, you'd have a chance at maybe one woman in ten, and you'd have to make an almost superhuman effort for even that.

'But most guys aren't *like* you, honey,' she said, putting her hand on his arm. 'Believe me, because I know. You think I don't? I hate to break it to you, but I've looked like this for ten years now. There's a certain type of guy thinks he can try it on with me,

202

anytime, anyplace, anyhow: they're everywhere, and they're the same kind of guy who's always going to think you owe him a living too. I look like candy to them; what you do looks like candy to them too.'

'Hey, don't tell me about guys,' he said, pacing the hell around, doing things with his hands that he must've picked up from the knuckleheads. 'I was in the joint six years, remember? In prison people get stabbed in the *eyes*. Blades are kind of thin on the ground, but any asshole can get hold of a Crayola. Ah, jesus.' He flopped down in a chair, covered his eyes with a limp hand. Susan sat down on the arm of the chair, dropped an arm over his shoulders.

'I know, baby. But there's so much *money* lying around Giotto's stuff. Money appeals to assholes like horseshit appeals to flies. For every one you pay off, there's a hundred polishing their barrels behind him. You're never about to turn this into something else. It's the *Mob*, baby. The best thing you're ever going to make it into is a flophouse with a gilt elevator.'

'Don't look down on me,' he said. 'I never looked down on you.'

She let that one slide, put her hand on his hair. 'Do you want me? Huh?' It came out a little trembly, maybe a little needy – certainly more than she meant it to – but it seemed okay. He turned his face up to her, so wide-eyed with disbelief that she could doubt it, that she nearly lost it right there, and could've just bawled and taken him to bed. But instead, she said it again, but slowly. 'For fucking ever, Ben? This is no jerking around anymore.'

And she was thinking about blond guys, guys with nice eyes, guys with necks thicker than her thigh, and guys she'd had crushes on since she was so high.

'I think there are two of you,' he said, and he'd blown it. A moment ago he looked so sweet, and he'd realized it, so now he needed to square his jaw like a dork. 'The girl who kids herself she

203

doesn't want all the things she never had – and the other one's real, and I mean to have her.'

Jesus. Must've heard that in some dumb movie. Didn't matter. Susan knew what needed to be done now.

'Then we need to get away.'

'No.' And he was on his feet again.

'Giotto's fucking *dead*, sweetheart.'

'I can't.'

'*We* can.'

It took a moment to get through.

'Where to? *What* to?'

'Whatever. You're dead if you don't. Me too, if I'm with you, and I mean to be. They got the boss, and you're going to be next.'

This ought to have been obvious. The knuckleheads, the hoi polloi, the Mob – they could work for anybody; but the right-hand man, the godson, the prince – he was always going to be ancien régime.

They both bit their lips for a moment, and though Susan sat quietly, he was all over the show; now pacing, now glaring, now sprawling himself down, now tautly bouncing up. She could tell he was caught: drawn half by inertia, by the slower-swinging bell's sentimental love of silence, by what was, and what should be again; and half by what might be, by possibility, by the potentially ever-new in this vast and most fertile of nations. Susan saw, in the too-sudden, ephemeral way that these things offer themselves – the widow's dark room glimpsed behind breeze-flickered curtains, the dull jewels of the shore disclosed in momentary hollows amongst the rockpools – she saw how she'd changed, and would change again.

'It's not even if, Ben. Just when and how,' she said.

'When?'

She shrugged. 'Soon as we can.'

'How?'

204

She thought for a moment before she spoke.

'We used to go to summer camp, a whole bunch of us from the home. Way out in the woods – the leaders used to scare the shit out of us. Bears, wolves, whatever. And even if you were just playing, there were all kinds of shit you don't get in the city – sumac, poison oak, hornets, whatever. The first thing they told us was, if you get stung and it comes up bad, look around where you are and you'll find what you need to take it down again. Where there are nettles, you'll find dock leaves. The poison always grows next to the cure.'

He was still looking kind of blank, but she was on a roll. Everything she'd ever seen, heard or read told her that once you've found him, you never let him go. Everything she did and believed now was going to be to remove the threat, regardless of what it left her with.

'The cure is next to the poison, honey. All we need is money. All we have to do is steal the future back from whoever's taken it away.'

Lucky and Lucy drove east to Chicago, into the desert, under the big sky, into the void. Soon they were so far gone that they'd lose the radio signal for days at a time, the dial delivering nothing but hiss from end to end; while, cast to each side of the endless asphalt, the roadkill seemed to get larger and larger, until it seemed a critical mass might soon be reached and they'd start passing broken-backed cars rather than wrecked animals. The sky got bigger and the sun boiled over, and Lucky, though fearful of the days between gas stations, jammed the pedal to the metal in the evenings, lest the swell behind catch up and engulf them.

Lucy had never seen him like this. From almost the moment they met, they'd been an enclave, a principality, a nation of two; now he seemed to have annexed himself. As if everything else weren't quite enough. It was almost as bad as the cheesy horror pictures he used to write, where the Good Kid, perky and preppy and with a wonderful future ahead of him, gets bitten by the monster and turns into one himself – but as the story peaks, a few tears from either his mother or his prom date make his face change back almost, and for a moment you see a flicker of the miserable, terrified kid inside the monster. Every now and then she'd see the old Lucky beyond this zoned-out shell running on empty, and that was why she went along with it. Like a woman taking holy hell from a newly unemployed husband, she didn't walk out because she knew he was in there somewhere.

So she sat, sometimes lay, on the bench seat next to Lucky,

sometimes just pissed at the heat and discomfort, sometimes forgetting everything and resting her head on his shoulder, as if it were the old days. Sometimes, too, his arm would creep up around her shoulders, and sometimes they'd haul the car off the road and make what passed for love these days, with sweat and silence, somewhere in the desert. But mostly they just drove and drove, and drove some more, past desert, past forest, and past sites of outstanding national interest that they'd read about, in happier times, on the back of matchbooks.

Lucky pushed on, less refusing to discuss with Lucy why they were making straight for Mantegna's lair in Chicago, than not noticing that she might require explanation. Truth was, he was still working on it. In the old days he could've come up with a dozen scenarios in a morning, culled and spliced from the arsenal of heist-stories he'd assimilated from twenty years of inhaling B-pictures: now, he felt a disinclination toward them. He couldn't explain why; couldn't have articulated, even to himself, why the stock-in-trade of a lifetime seemed redundant now. He could see Lucy wheeling herself up to the door of Mantegna's new building, and barking at the goon that she was his wife from LA (who'd got her legs fucked up in a loused-up car-bomb hit on Mantegna), and that she wanted to see him *now*: but beyond that he couldn't see anything. He just felt a pull, and was as helpless to resist it as a character in one of his own scripts; all that he knew was an instinct that, if they presented themselves at Mantegna's place of business, then the situation would resolve itself. In the meantime they drove, out of the dead lands, away from the rock formations and canyons, and testing sites and Trinitite, away from the desert and toward the lakes, to where Chicago shimmered like the emerald city between the water and the sky.

They used Alice to get to Susan. They were smart. They knew she and Ben must both be hiding out somewhere, that Ben would have covered his tracks, and that there was no way he was going to show his face in the city in the immediate future, if ever.

Alice and Susan used to read the Lonely Hearts for yuks when they were waiting around for Earl to get the lighting right, or whatever: used to try and pair off the guys with the girls, first off how they ought to be, and then how they'd end up, if either of Susan or Alice's histories were anything to go by. It was an old game that Susan used to do in movie-house queues, firstly to see who she ought to be with rather than her date, and then for whoever else. Common girl-strategy when she was at college was that if you went out with every guy who asked you and treated them like a king, the word'd get around among the guys about what a good-value date you were, and eventually, after kissing an awful lot of frogs, you'd start to get the ones you wanted. So when Susan was waiting on line for the movies or wherever, she always saw the wrong girl with the wrong guy, and it turned into a game. Like, you with the blonde bangs and earrings – you could do way better than him, why don't you go with the quarterback over there; and you, mousey little thing with your dirndl and eyeglasses, you go with Mr Books-for-breakfast-lunch-and-dinner over here; then his date, Mlle Mayflower, can share her milk duds with Pencey Prep by the door. But it was more fun with the Lonely Hearts page because there was the hooey-factor to take into account also – like, oh sure you trained in classical dance, you lard-ass little tramp, kind of thing – and the habit stuck. So that was how Joey used Alice to get to Susan. Even though they were walking into her trap, not she into theirs, she had to hand it to them.

They had to do it, Ben explained. He'd finally come to his senses a few days after Giotto was planted. Bellini had to flush Ben out because no one except Ben and Giotto had any idea how far their influence currently spread. In a business where you don't make a point of advertising your scheming and scamming, your allegiances and alliances, then for all Bellini knew, Ben might be calling down the might of Giotto's combined underwriters to restore things to before and ensure the return on their investment. Ben would've been only too happy to do this, but Giotto didn't have any who were committed enough to get their hands dirty; as far as Susan could get it out of him, the deals were all leveraged by Giotto, cash on delivery. So Bellini had to coax Ben out and kill him: Bellini would use bait to facilitate this; and the trick for Ben was, like Jerry mouse, to steal the cheese off the trap and get back into a hole that was too small for Tom to follow. And if you could smack him round the chops with a frying pan meanwhile, then all the better.

So in the Lonely Heart column last week – '*Happy-go-lucky* [which meant 'doormat' in the game Susan and Alice used to play], *vivacious* [drunk], *gregarious* [tramp], *sporty* [stupid] *ex-cheerleader* [speaks for itself], *seeks debonair* [rich], *kind* [profligate], *sensitive* [blackmailable], *mature* [sheets turned down on the deathbed] *gentleman* [patsy] *for marriage* [better get yourself a slick attorney while you can still afford it, bub]. *All Letters In Confidence, Etc*'. A-L-I-C-E, see? So Susan sent a note to the box number saying just, bar at Grand Pacific hotel, noon Wednesday, and went herself.

But she was smart. She broke out her stage-school make-up box, and put twenty years, rhinestone glasses and a gray schoolmistress wig on herself; and combed flour through Ben's black hair, gave him some lines, liver spots and an olive tan, and installed him in the reading room four hours early. She had a bad moment when she couldn't recall what old ladies ordered to drink, but settled for coffee and a table by the window.

By twelve-fifteen the room was beginning to fill up with business guys from the Chamber of Commerce across the street, ordering heavy glasses of Scotch-rocks, sending up a fug of cigar-smoke and talking too loud and all at once; they reminded Susan of this one girl at Smith whose father was some kind of hotshot banker, got scurvy and nearly died because all he ate was steaks and Scotch. There was no sign of Alice but, although Susan's newspaper was up in front of her face, she couldn't help the feeling of being watched. Every time she flipped the paper down there was no one, but she could almost feel a pair of eyes tracing hot little trails all over her from somewhere. By twenty of one she was fit to be tied, but she figured nothing was going to happen: the ad must have been a coincidence, and she walked on over to have the barkeep call her a cab.

It took a second for her eyes to adjust because there he was – Joey Volante, in white apron and black waistcoat, polishing martini glasses with a white cloth.

Susan was good – nothing could throw her, though it almost did. Keeping her composure, she walked on out to the lobby, scribbled the name of a diner on a dollar bill, then took out another, gave it to a bellboy and told him to get her a cab, and to give the scribbled bill to the barkeep when she was gone. He did as he was told, and Susan was out of there, leaving a message for Ben to follow with the desk clerk.

At the diner she ordered the blue plate special and waited. This wasn't quite how she'd planned, but that's what Ben was for – to follow whoever was there to meet her, make sure they were alone, and shoot them in the legs before they got to her if they weren't. This wouldn't have been an ideal conclusion to events, since it would mean that they'd both have to get out of the city, and probably the country, with only the few thousand dollars Ben could lay his hands on; but they were, however, dealing with murderous assholes now; the *paisans* had come to get theirs, and they weren't jerking around.

But once a *paisan*, always a *paisan*.

'Of course it's a trap,' said Ben, back at the hideout. 'All we have to do is turn it around.' He wiped the make-up off his face with his handkerchief, and Susan proffered a pot of cold-cream.

'Use this. And put soap on your hair before you wet it, or the flour's gonna turn to glue.' She was on the bed, in a silk wrap with wet hair, smoking cigarettes and feeling pretty pleased with herself. It was so good that even he could see what'd got to be done.

Joey had offered them both a heist. He started off trying to be an asshole about where Ben was, but when Susan explained to him it was her or nothing – and that trying to follow her when she left would mean everything was off – he gave her the gravy. If he hadn't been so convincing, she would've thought Alice had been giving him acting lessons; as it was, he must've been going to the Strasbergs.

His shtick was that Bellini had been as thrown by this as Ben was; that Giotto had been whacked by Detroit-Pittsburgh wiseguys, who'd heard things were going soft and saw their chance to muscle in. Susan knew straightaway everything he was going to tell her was hooey because Ben had said those guys were getting into the same stuff as Giotto once they saw how the money could roll in if they opened up the picture, paid off the assholes and ceased with the smalltime. So she sat back and let Joey shoot the shit, nodding wide-eyed while he got off some good ones about Bellini being holed up too with a price on his head, and how the only way out for all of them was to use what they knew about this 'hood while they still could.

So here was the hooey. The Motor City crew had taken over all of Giotto's turf, including the House of Whacks. Because coups

211

only ever change the generals and not the grunts, Joey was still getting the skinny from the guys on the ground, and this was where, he claimed, he got the whisper. A federal-standard bank vault was being installed, lickety-split, under Earl's old basement studio, ready to take a shipment, in ten days, of Nazi bullion. The gold had come to New York via Switzerland during the war, but had to be moved because the Israeli secret service was almost on top of it. The ingots were only going to be in Chicago for two days, stored at the House of Whacks while they were melted down in batches at the steelyards – then the resulting sovereigns could go out on mailtrains all over the Union, to be deposited in hayseed banks wherever.

Naturally there'd be wiseguys out the wazoo, guarding the stuff while it was here. But, as Joey reminded her, one thing that always happened since the knuckleheads had been around Earl's place was that, whenever Earl was doing a shoot, they'd all drop what they were doing and come over to watch. So Joey's idea was, since he'd heard the Detroit outfit had been talking to Earl about keeping up his business, though strictly underground now, the three of them could fake up a camera and a set. Since it wasn't going to be real, Joey's little brother could stand in for Earl (who was in his first month of a nine-stretch in County), and he'd orchestrate the action while Susan got dolled up and tied up, and then Volante and Ben would hit the place while the Detroit knuckleheads were wide-eyed and fat-crotched.

Even before she got away from Joey, Susan could see that this would work. There was always something strange about how the footsoldiers would come over and gawp, something in the way they'd stop talking but just hotbox cigarette after cigarette, not standing too close to each other like they were suddenly weird about their personal space. There was none of the cat-calling and back-slapping you'd expect. They'd stop acting like they were part of a gang and turn into dead-eyed sleepwalkers. Susan, for one, couldn't see a better method of catching them with their pants down.

Except this wasn't the way it was gonna be.

'Motor City my ass,' said Ben, spreading out the plans Joey had given her to pass on. 'Those are going to be Bellini's guys in there. It's gonna be a turkey shoot the moment I show up. Look,' and he showed her how, with Volante coming in one way and him the other, he'd be caught in a triangulation cross-fire between Joey on the one side, Joey's little brother on the camera, and the knuckle-heads gathered at the end of the room around the stage-set.

'But you'll be carrying, won't you?' Susan pointed out. 'Joey said that's how you're gonna do the raid. That's what's gonna be your security too. Think about it. If he's telling the truth, then you two drop in while the assholes are gawping at me, and stick them up from behind, with Joey's bro' in front. They all have to drop everything, and you have them unload the gold into your van at gunpoint, then lock them all in the vault afterward. Joey knows that if you get the smallest bit antsy about anything you can just pull your piece and pop him. He's not going to risk it.'

'Huh,' he said. He really hated being wrong, but this wasn't any time to spare his feelings. This could be the only chance Susan had to come out of this featuring money and a future, and if she couldn't figure what was going on here and how to turn it around, then she may as well have been gone already. She said,

'If he really wants to lure you there to whack you, he's going to need to be smarter than that. Think about it. He's totally prepared not to meet you beforehand because he knows you're in too weak a position to allow it. He's going out of his way to get you there, to where you're both going to have your asses hanging out as far as each other. There must be something else there that'll give him the edge over you, otherwise he wouldn't be doing it. All we gotta do is figure out what that is.'

213

'Thirty heavies with .38s,' he said obstinately, like any stubborn asshole of a guy would, but, still, she let it slide.

'If they turn on you, you turn on him. C'mon, sweetheart. Think us out of this.'

'I can't.'

'Yes you can. You're the brains trust. C'mon, baby. What about that heist you told me about when we first met, huh? The one you planned when you were the boy wonder? The one you went to the joint for?'

'I went to the joint for it.'

'That wasn't your fault. It was brilliant, and it was a million-to-one accident that loused it up. You said so yourself. C'mon, hon. You had it then and you've got it now. If anybody can think of a way out of this, it ought to be you.'

'How can I? If I go there I'm dead; if I don't, I'm as good as. I'm a fucking dead man.'

'You will be if you don't think.'

'Think, she says.' He appealed to the window, waving his arms about. 'Think! Easy for you to say. It's not your ass that's going to get shot at.'

Then he stopped dead, the color draining out of his face.

'Christ.'

'What?' Susan was worried he'd had some kind of apoplexy.

'You are.' Staring at her.

'Huh?' Susan almost went to look behind her. 'I'm what?'

'You're right. It is your ass that gets shot at.' He clapped his hands and hooted. 'Yes! You're the hostage. *You're* the one who's going to get shot!'

'Hey,' she said, but kidding. 'You're tired of my action, just dump me, huh? I won't call you up all the time. You don't need to get me shot, buster.' But she was just glad he finally got it.

'You see?' he said. 'You're the weak point. He gets a gun on you

214

to make me drop mine. Then he pops me and probably you besides. All we gotta do is figure out how we can stop that.'

'How?' Susan said – but the only how she was worried about was how she was going to kid him into believing it was his own idea.

Letter from Danny, at the end of his contract. He was going to stay out there till the studio decided whether to pick up its option on the next series, so he'd got time on his hands. And weighing heavy, I could tell: four single-space pages out of the six he sent me were agonizing over the decisions he took over the last eight months, heading up the story unit. What informs the choices you make, he wanted me to tell him. Why pick one strand over another – why make a character lean one way rather than the other? I wasn't going to reply to this. I'd send him the goodbye note I was always going to send, and post it the night before the heist. 'By the time you're reading this . . .' But he'd got me thinking, picking at a long-dried scab, and damn him because now I couldn't stop.

If there's a big What If in everyone's life, then mine was about what would've happened if I hadn't thrown in the towel – if I hadn't packed in scriptwriting, twentysomething years ago, when I moved from production to supervision. It was stupid, but it seemed like every page I turned in a magazine lately, there was a clip-out coupon for some mail-order painting course or short story class, promising success in business and family if I'd only unleash the creativity within. The glowing testimonials were enough to put me off – *'Since signing up for your correspondence story workshop I've found a whole new attitude, that's gotten me two raises at work and helped me relate to my children like my own father never could – JF, Terre Haute, Ind.'* – because, quite aside from what they suggested about the proprietor's own creative skills, I always thought that the desirable effect was the opposite; it ought to make you less the functioning citizen than a desk-bound wretch with the midnight disease, wincing at birdsong and shunning the distraction of friends and family. But while I couldn't buy this self-help crap wholesale, it occurred to me now that everything commenced getting weird on me the moment I made the switch; so, that morning, I was suspecting there might be something to it.

I had to think about this because I found, on the day I died, that I would have been happier if I could've played the last scene like it really was a scene: like, if I'd ever put it in a script I'd probably've chickened out and gone for the condemned man routine. She wakes, on her last morning, showers up with the Chicago Bears, and eats a breakfast of chicken-fried steak, brandy alexanders and chocolate malts, then goes out on the roof to smoke cigars in her good silk underwear. Trust me, I almost tried it, but nothing had gone right. The plan was to raise some hell on my last night, but I knew how it would be: a miserable, lonely debauch, drinking champagne cocktails in my sharpest tailoring at the bar of the slickest pick-up joint I could remember; with no one looking at me twice. Everyone, I knew, would have dates, wives or mistresses, looking satisfied, successful and secure, with themselves and each other. So I would've split, before the bartender could look at me like I was a hooker, hit the sleaziest meat-rack I could remember, and there it'd be again: smart, slicked up, and not a solitary single save me. It'd be the same everywhere I wove my way to: smug, self-satisfied couples; where there ought to've been racks of men, smooth-skinned and eager as the guys who laid me down twenty years ago. I knew just how it'd go. Even if I got down so far as to try and come on to my cab drivers, the only ones I'd get talking would just want to show me the backyard photographs in their wallets.

I didn't need to find out I was an anachronism. So instead I went to *The Seagull* at the Opera House. It was weird. I never saw it with him, but one thing about marrying Walt was that I thought he'd be the guy I'd go to plays over and over with. Shakespeare and stuff.

The only time we ever went to the theater together was *Lear*, just after we were married. I thought, this is the first time we'll see this together, and we'll probably see a dozen more productions of it in our life. That was the only one, however.

So, this *Seagull*. I'd forgotten there was so much about writers in it. 'Women can forgive anything except failure,' one actor said. Okay. In the row in front a guy took off his girl's watch and put it in his pocket. It was one of those gilt-type evening jobs, the kind you get for your eighteenth birthday, the kind that can't help but look like they came out of a cracker however costly they were. It was probably just that the ticking was too loud, with her chin propped on her fist like that – it was the kind of watch you'd keep in a jewelry box, so you wouldn't ever have noticed, in the dead of night, how loud it was – but I could've put a thousand loving spins on it: I spent the whole rest of the play thinking them up. I take your watch off because: my time with you is outside time, so I'm opening up a parenthesis in its passing; I take your chronology and put it inside me, set my heart beating to yours; that kind of stuff. I didn't drink anything, couldn't smoke a cigarette, was in bed by eleven, and awake, feeling sick with health, by the sunrise.

So this morning the condemned woman did not eat a hearty breakfast, wiping chicken fat from her fingers onto oyster-colored silk, and letting globs of ice-cream slub between her breasts because she'd never done it before. Instead, I poured half my cup of coffee down the sink and squeezed some oranges instead. I had to stub my cigarette almost as soon as I lit it, surprised even through the nausea by the unfamiliarity of the gesture; I think I must've last done that when I was maybe fifteen, smoking in my attic room and hearing footsteps on the stairs. I felt like I wanted to go hike in the country, go swim in the lake, haul down clean blasts of air and feel the good blood wash through my body. It was terrible. I really should've gone and got loaded the night before. I should've cut loose and spread myself thinner'n the skin around my eyes. I should've had one last mad letting go, and then I could've kept it tight today.

Instead, I was all over the show. It wasn't my fault. Buddy's latest stunt was to wheel Walt on. I don't know for sure it was his doing, but I wouldn't put anything past the little fucker. Yesterday morning, Walt was on my porch, looking tan and tired. He pushed some flowers at me.

'I heard,' he said. 'Wanted to see you.'

It was kind of a shock, though it wasn't totally unprepared for. I had, it has to be said, thought about going out to see him one last time, or posting off a letter; putting some kind of a lid on whatever might still be open. Whether there had been – or was – unfinished business, I wasn't so sure; it was more a feeling that I ought to set my affairs in order and that he, more than anyone, ought to be at the top of the list, simply because he'd been around me more than anyone: he did, after all, wake up with me for most of a dozen years, and stayed up with me, filling hot water bottles, the one bad night a month when I had cramps; went on holiday with Nicky and me, plaid-shorted, rowing on lakes, leaving wet footprints on sun-shriveled boards; supervised Christmas, birthdays, anniversaries; shopped and cooked all the time I was working late. I felt, soon after I was diagnosed (and was surprised by how strongly), that there ought to be some kind of emotional payback claimable from him – some sort of resolution. But now he was there on my doorstep, I wasn't sure what to do with him.

Though I wasn't so sure what to do with myself at the time, either. Since I stopped working the days had gotten kind of nameless, drifting up against each other, and spilling over at the edges. Every so often there'd be a week of mad activity – driving up to North Dakota with Jack to negotiate with the guy who was going to buy whatever we could steal, going on marksman training with George (if he was going to shoot me, I wanted to make sure

219

he'd do it good) – but mostly there was just mooching around my place, reading the newspaper slowly, going to the store for gourmet stuff to cook, then long afternoons waiting to do it. I'd thought that I'd find significance, in those last days, that they'd acquire some kind of form and weight; but I didn't suppose they knew they were the last, and I didn't have the heart to tell them. So quite apart from anything else, a big part of the problem, with Walt there in my parlor, was just that I hadn't had anyone over for so long that I didn't really know what to do with him.

'I don't have anything for you to drink,' I muttered, 'let me run out for some whiskey.'

'It's okay,' he said.

'Just down to the corner,' I said, looking for my purse. I was a little self-conscious about what a mess the place was in, but only because I used to whale on him the whole time about how he could be eating a sandwich or whichever and then, halfway through, think of something better to do and forget all about it. It appeared that I did this myself these days, I noticed for the first time.

'I don't keep anything around the place,' I said, feeling stupid for saying it as soon as it was out, like I was trying to deny being a lush or something, when actually I really couldn't have kept booze here – I was far too nauseous most of the time now to even think about it. I said,

'But you can buy whiskey down on the corner. We can make highballs. I have some ice.'

'Let me go,' he said, looking concerned, 'I shoulda brought some.'

So I let him, just so we didn't start some stupid allow me/no, allow me kind of crap and wound up not getting any Scotch at all. I felt that I wanted some if we were going to get through this in one afternoon.

Because there was no question of just telling him to get lost. In some twisted kind of way I had wanted to see him one last time, though I ought to've known how it would go. The problem with marrying Walt was that I did it because I wanted some kind of buddy; just to have someone around while I drank my coffee, or to call up and tell when I had to work late, kind of thing. I think I'd suspected that was what I wanted all along: I think we all did, when we were the first women in Hollywood, when we were the first women to be someplace no woman had been before. We all cut loose a little: some a lot; but even the girls who were really helling it up never put a ring on their third finger to show the world that all that horse's ass had nothing to do with us – we, the devil take the hindmost sisters, who wore rings on all our other fingers and spent all of our free time proving we could do what the hell we liked. Maybe we didn't want a ring there cramping our style; not that it would've put many of the guys off, though maybe it would've encouraged some of them to repeat the process, and complete the transaction, and take us away from whoever forever (guys are like that, however new they seem each time; step back a little and all you see is a chain of pain, a rope of dopes). Maybe we didn't want to queer it for the rest, whom we came from and might yet go back to. Or maybe we knew all along that this was just an intermission, and that we'd have, someday, to sell while we still could if we didn't want to die alone.

By the time I got to Walt I wanted some stability: I'd tried everything else in my life, it seemed. But – and I don't know whether it was something he'd decided or whether it was something he couldn't help – he wasn't up for having a marriage like that. He was going to have the first love of the world, or nothing; some kind of high-maintenance hothouse where we'd both spin faster under the influence of each other's energy fields, pushing each other and ourselves until we exploded in brilliance and life and almost farcical degrees of success. When all I really wanted was someone to split the newspaper sections with on Sundays. We really ought to've talked about it more.

So once he'd been out and come back and the whiskies were in our hands, we couldn't have had any kind of a regular conversation because we never used to. This had been fine when we were dating, because I'd think, wow, this guy's so intense, I'm never going to run out of things to say with him, and I was clapping my hands and not believing my luck. But then you put a couple of years on the clock, and you want to be having the kind of conversations that regular people have – the kind that don't go too far beyond which relations you ought to go visit over the holidays, which schools we wanted Nicky to go to, that kind of thing. I mean, those aren't the most fantastic examples because neither of us were exactly breaking our necks to see too many of our relations again, and Nicky was always going to go to the same school as everyone else in our bracket of studio employee; but do you see what I mean? And then, when it became clear that he couldn't shake being so in my face the whole damn time, it was – I don't know – like he was a book that you read one summer, that seemed to make everything you were come alive that one time; then you pick it up again, two years down the line, and it means nothing to you. So I'd commenced to kid myself that he was maybe the kind of book that you give up on first time you read it, but then pick off the shelf a few years later when you're grippey and it's raining out, and then you can't believe you didn't get it the first time. It worked for a while. Whatever. It was over now, or ought to've been.

'So how'dya hear?'

'Just did,' he said.

'Okay,' I said, 'fine.'

'What?'

'Why don't you want to tell me who told you?'

'Does it matter?' he said. 'I just heard, okay? Bunch of people started saying, sorry to hear about Misty.'

'Who?'

'Jesus. Mottie Schulman. Tommy Van Dries.'

'I don't know who they are.'

'Sure you do. Mottie? At Canyon?'

I shrugged. Mottie Schulman my ass; he retired in the war, and bet my fur if Walt hadn't seen him since. Buddy had told him, somehow, and I wanted to hear him admit it. But instead he said,

'Had the office two doors along from you in what, '32?'

'Don't recall.'

'Okay. No biggy.' But in this maddening conciliatory tone.

'What's that supposed to mean?' I said.

'Let's not, huh?'

'No, I'm interested. What's with this you-gotta-walk-on-egg-shells routine?'

He took a drink from his glass, put it back on the coffee table.

'Nothing. Gimme a break. I heard you're sick, I came to see you.'

'You heard from who?'

'I told you. Jesus, don't you think that hurt? That I had to hear from people you can't even remember?' I didn't say anything to this. I could kind of see it. 'Couldn't you have let me know?'

'What would've been the point?' I said. I mean, I had thought about this. Obviously I had. 'I left a letter with my attorney to be sent on afterward.' It occurred to me that if he hadn't come then he would've been reading it inside a week.

'Don't you think I might've wanted to see you again?'

'Don't you think I might not have wanted to see anyone? C'mon. Give me a break. I'm dying, here. Fast. It's not supposed to make you feel good. It doesn't turn you into the best company. C'mon. See what I'm seeing.'

He didn't say anything.

'Would you've let me know, if it was you?' I tried.

'Yes,' he said, but too fast. He didn't think about it at all, and that was everything that was wrong with him. Walt's problem was that he always assumed that, since he was such a deep guy, he was going to have the perfect set of emotional responses to fit every new situation; it didn't seem to occur to him that this didn't quite key with everything else he said and did.

I saw fit to inform him of this, mostly because I was feeling lousier by the second; he told me not to start with him. I pointed out that I'd already finished with him and who the hell asked him to come around here anyways, and there we were, off again. Gorgeous, how you can slip straight back into it. The worst thing was that, straightaway, however much I knew I was riling him deliberately, I still wanted to be helping him, helping us, making this easy. I swear, it was just like when we were married. About ten minutes into it, I was saying, 'Look, I tried with you, really I did. I didn't want for everything to go straight to hell again. You think I did? After my damn family and everything? Huh?'

Bringing up the horrors of my home life which, I'm afraid, I had embellished on occasion, was never really fair, but was always kind of useful, it has to be said.

'So why'd you fuck Dan Merrickson, huh?' he said, and gave me – thanks Walt – another chance to see how a face you love can be twisted up with loathing because of you. He was talking about the first time he found out about me and someone else, after we were married.

'You know why.' A girlfriend of mine had told me that, after a woman has a baby with someone, she can't enjoy sex again until she does it with someone else. At the time, I'd thought it worth a try. 'We went through this enough times twenty years ago. Do you want to do it again, huh? Is that what you came here for?'

'No,' he said, exasperated – realizing, I guess, what we were doing as much as I was. I walked to the window and looked over the street a moment, trying to think of the best way out of this. Then I started thinking that I'd better say something before he did, in case he got in first and took it somewhere I didn't want to go. I turned around.

'You know I tried with you, don't you?' He dropped his head, sighed. 'C'mon, Walt. You told me about Isabella and Pearl, and I hated them. You see? I didn't want to be like them. I didn't *want* to be just another asshole that whoever you ended up with next could hate for screwing up so bad. For messing you up so bad. You see? You say you didn't like picking up the pieces – *I* didn't like picking up any pieces.'

'Why do you do this?' he said, with that old expression of genuine scientific inquiry that used to irritate the pants off me. 'Huh? Where do you get off on this crap? Making out like it was all my problem and not yours?' And he got up, reached for his hat.

'What're you doing?'

'I'm going,' he said, waving the hat at me. 'It was dumb of me to expect you to be any different.'

Which was totally unfair, because he knew that was the worst thing anyone could do to me. I just flip out when I'm left. I can't stand it, and I can't do anything about it. I had an aunt who was in charge of me when I was a kid, used to lock me up in a bare attic room if I started to cry; made me stay in there till I stopped. If there's leaving to be done, ever since, then I have to do it. So just as he knew I would, I flipped right off the handle.

'Oh yeah, g'wan then, leave. That's what you're good at. Just walk the fuck out. What d'you think this was gonna be if you came over? Some kind of fucking picnic, huh? Or d'ja come here to make sure you were finally gonna be shot of me?' The trouble with screaming matches, in my experience, is that the moment you start fighting dirty, you feel guilty if the other one doesn't come straight back with something outrageous. Of course, often their keeping quiet is just as dirty as anything they could say, so it would be good to establish a few ground rules before you begin. Like, if I go in below the belt, you're not allowed to grab the high ground by keeping quiet. But we hadn't. So,

'Okay,' I said, 'you've seen. You can fuck off again now, same as you always do.'

225

He threw his hat down, color rushing into his face.

'How can you say that? *I* leave, do I? Is that the way it was? Because, y'know, I must be going crazy. I must've really flipped out, because all I can remember is you not coming home. Me sitting up with Nicky and *you* putting it all around town.'

'Damn you. Damn *you*. How can you bring that up?' I really didn't need this. He was talking about the time Nicky broke his arm at school, and I didn't know, till I came home to an empty house, because I was in a motel room all afternoon with some loser named Mack McKinsey. Our marriage was pretty much over, and the only bad thing about what I did was that I didn't leave a number at my office, so the school couldn't get hold of me and Nicky had to be at the hospital on his own. Walt knew where I was, but I never admitted it to him.

'Well?'

'Okay, yes I was. All *over* fucking town, buddy. I was with some loser in some shitty motel outside Burbank. Okay? That make you feel better? It ought to, asshole, because you drove me to it.'

'Oh, I did, huh?'

'Yes, Walt, you did.'

His eyes were bright with animosity, and I couldn't bear it; him all bunched up, breathing hard, fists clenched at his thighs. He used to be so damn placid – used to drive me crazy – but when I made him like this, it made me feel even worse. Suddenly all the fight was out of me, and I started to cry, and just kind of folded up into the chair, and then he was on the floor in front of me, hugging my knees.

'You did,' I sobbed out, 'I'm sorry, Walt, but you did. Do you know how hard it was to come home to you? When you'd got the house and Nicky and all so perfect? And then I tryta ask after what you wrote that day, to try and make you feel like a man, and you'd just grunt?'

'I'm sorry,' he said, sorry but sulky, drawing away from me a little.

226

'So you made me feel like I was stopping you working because I was out all day. *And* you made me feel like the biggest slack Alice because apparently I wan't good enough to talk about writing anymore.'

He looked at the floor.

'I'm dying, Walt,' I said, trying to get my breath regular. 'I'll be dead before fall. There's no use in letting this go on, buddy. If we don't talk now we're never gonna.'

'I don't know what you want me to say,' he said.

'I want to know why everything got fucked up,' I said. 'I want to know why my life didn't work out.'

'What's the use?' he said. 'Even if I could tell you, you couldn't send it back to when it could make any difference.'

'I need to make an end,' I said, simply. 'I need to wrap this.'

He reached for his cigarettes, lit one for us both. 'Okay,' he said.

'Then take me back twenty years,' I said. 'We were okay till I made the switch. We were both fine when we worked at home. Then it went to hell. We didn't work together anymore. You stopped talking to me.'

'Ah c'mon, you oughta know how it goes,' he said, fast. 'You have maybe one day in fifty when there's something worth talking about. You're in the house all day. You don't see anyone. Most of the time you're going over something you're sick of the sight of. Don't you remember? Wasn't it like that with you before you quit?'

'That's not the point,' I said. 'I quit. I took a straighter job so that we could be a family – not just a couple of writers with a kid caught between them and no idea where the rent was coming from.'

'Misty, c'mon,' he complained. 'That was nothing like we were. You always made double what I did, even at the start. If anyone oughta have stopped writing and gotten a straighter job it was me.'

This was news to me. I always assumed that because he was the guy, his writing was sacred. 'So why didn't you?' I said, incredulous.

227

'You did it first,' he shrugged. 'You didn't even talk about it, you just did it.'

Christ, what a mess. I'd thought I was stepping down, giving him his head; he'd thought, it seemed, that I was going over to the other side, making me the getter and him the stay-home.

'Is that what you thought?' I said. 'I stopped because I figured I was too good for it?'

'Naw, c'mon,' he said, sitting back into a hunker, but I interrupted him.

'I stopped because of my damn family,' I said. 'All the time they could think I was a writer they could picture me like Jane fucking Austen, sitting in the parlor with a pad on my lap. Just like the studio sold us – they swallowed it the same as the rest of the civilians. Fuck that. If I was a businesswoman they'd have to recognize who I really was. They'd hate it, but they'd have to see it. That's what it was. Every rung up the ladder meant I was another step away from my fucking family.' This wasn't the truth, but it seemed like it might fit. I hadn't had any time to prepare anything else.

Only fifteen years, anyway.

'That's crazy,' he murmured. 'You can't kill guilt just by doing what you were made to feel guilty about. Pushing yourself beyond where you wanted to go wasn't gonna cancel out eighteen years of not being allowed to go anyplace.'

'Oh Walt.' He never mentioned his own damn family, and they didn't even have money. I took his face in my hands, and he let his shoulders drop forward, so his forehead was on my knee. I stroked his bald old head and said, 'I wanted to be a woman, Walt. I didn't want to be one of the boys. I didn't want to wind up some mannish old broad with a bottle of bourbon next to my Remington and permanent ash-streaks down my front from typing with my face screwed up round a cigarette. I wanted to wear pressed suits and lipstick, and varnish my nails. I wanted to see people. I wanted them to come to my office, not me go to theirs. I wanted to go to meetings every day, not twice a year. And then I wanted to come home to a family. I wanted to be a woman.'

'Woman my ass,' Walt said. 'You're a writer, Misty.'

This was hard. The weirdest thing about the cancer was how it had made me aware of my own body, for the first time in twenty years. For the first time since I was pregnant with Nicky. It made me feel like things were happening in me again.

'I'm not a writer,' I said, smoothing my hand over the top of his head, where the part in his hair used to be. 'I had it once, but I lost it.'

He seemed to concede this. 'You changed when we were married. Your stuff changed.'

I didn't know what to say to this, though I'd given it a lot of time when I was thinking about quitting writing. Do you put your life into it? Does it help you work things out, somehow? I used to watch Nicky with the neighborhood kids sometimes, and wonder if the stuff they got up to outside wasn't holding some kind of mirror to what went on in their homes. Are the stories a person comes up with the same? I couldn't bear Walt on the floor anymore. 'C'mon,' I said. 'Up.' I helped him till he sat sideways on my lap, his arms around my neck and his face in my hair.

'After I met you, what came from inside me wasn't anyone else's business anymore,' I said. 'It was just for you, and then it was for you and Nicky. I wasn't going to put any of me into stories anymore.'

'But you should've,' he said. 'We were you too. We were new parts of you. You coulda kept writing and stayed loyal to yourself.'

'I did,' I went to say, but he cut in on me.

'But you didn't want to go it alone anymore. You didn't want to be loyal just to yourself. When you moved to supervision you spread your loyalties over a whole bunch of people. When you started the magazine you just made it clearer. Taking a little strain from each of a bunch of people was easier than taking it all from yourself.'

'So what's wrong with that? That was why I married you. That was why . . .'

'That was why you never left home,' he said.

'Fuck you I did.' I made to draw away, but he wouldn't let me. 'I wasn't born in California, buddy. I went West when I was eighteen and it was damn hard.'

'Sure you did,' he said. His eyes were bright, but his arms were still around my neck. 'Sure, you turned yourself around, and you went it alone, and then there was enough of you to try with me and Nicky for a little while. But you needed to be pulled a dozen ways by a dozen people too much. You couldn't take responsibility when it was focused instead of broadcast. You gave up on the new life you'd carved out for yourself and went back. You came back here. Ah, shit on it,' he said, swivelling his ass round on my thighs, so he could put his elbows on his knees and face away from me. 'I didn't come here to tell you this.'

He rubbed his face and exhaled. I leaned forward onto his back, put my arms around his shoulders. Maybe this new weirdness – this probably misplaced allegiance to my elite gang of conspirators, my ultimate-heist perpetrators, my losers' club – maybe this was all to do with what I did. Like, things got too complicated on me when I stopped, so I wasn't going to let them quit, ever. If this worked, if we could in fact get in and out of there and then fence the proceeds, I was just sentencing them all to more of the same. There'd be no danger of them having to go out and be changed, because they wouldn't need to. They'd be able to do what I couldn't. I didn't want to think about them ending up like me.

But I couldn't tell Walt about it. If Buddy told him about me, then he probably knew anyway. He stroked my hair in the silence, while I tried to think of how a person might go about putting a lid on things that don't want to be closed up, but I found myself

230

looking at his shoes instead – don't know if this was a reflex reaction from being rich, from being out west, when you were supposed to signify your success on your days off, not with your uniform Sea Island cotton but with your leather, with your shoes and your watch. He was wearing a pair of beat-up wingtips that looked as though they cost plenty when he bought them. Even so, they couldn't be more than a few years old, and it made me feel strange that he'd been out buying shoes without me to see them when they were shiny and new. Regret flushed through me like orgasm.

'There's no use in letting this go on, buddy. I'm here. You have to be too. Be here now.'

It was quiet in there. The sun fell in a bright, window-shaped square on the floor.

'Shit on it,' he said again, rubbed his forehead across my ear. 'I didn't mean that. I didn't know what went wrong with us then and I don't know now. Maybe we're just different, and I couldn't stand that we were. I thought it was going to be enough just that I found you.'

'I know,' I said. 'I thought it was gonna be enough too.'

'I'm sorry,' he said.

'I miss Nicky,' I said, out of nowhere. It's what I say when I'm feeling bad about something – out it pops. Stupid, because what was really on my mind was why I always have to make things so difficult. All I really wanted to do, quite literally, was crawl into a corner and die, stuffed to the gills with all the diamorphine the doctors weren't going to give me. But instead I had to make everything so public. I needed to have fifty guys, fifty strangers, looking at me when I die.

'I miss him too,' said Walt.

I found myself thinking about Buddy a moment – about the first time I met him, after I read the story he mailed me and demanded he meet me for coffee downtown. I'd waved the typescript at him,

231

grinning like a retard. *This is the story I always wanted to write,* I said. *I don't want you to think of me as an editor but as a writer.* Jeez.

'Is it any use getting older?' I asked Walt, finally. 'Is there any use understanding things better now?'

He kissed my ear, and said, 'You can't send it back.'

And so I understood what I had to do. I figured, if you're going to screw up, you might as well take Texas with you.

'How long're you in town for?' I said. 'Don't you have to go back?'

'I said I had to take a powder,' he said, tracing his fingers down the back of my neck. 'I said I was going to see you. Everyone remembers you. I said I'd be gone for as long as it took.'

'You could stay a day or two?' I said. I was testing to see how much Buddy told him.

'If you'll put me up.'

'Hmm,' I said, like I was changing the subject. 'You still know how to write heists?'

'Sure,' he said, looking like I'd strayed from the point. 'I mean, I've been doing creature features the last couple years, but I guess. They don't change.'

'Don't change, huh?' I said, breaking my old face into a grin.

'Naw,' he said. 'You know it. Write one and you've written them all. Why?'

'I might need a refresher course,' I said. 'And maybe I'll teach you something you've forgotten in return. Come here.'

When Susan had convinced Ben, she took him to the Art Institute. They'd spent the last week driving like madmen all around the plains, getting as irrationally far from each last motel as they possibly could. It was a weird intermission, an endless touring weekend; neither was up to talking much, so there was little else to do but sit back and look at the scenery, like a couple of tourists.

It seemed like every place they came to was an attraction: every pissant little burg they passed through was 'home of' something. Susan's high school class had been encouraged to write to soldiers during the war, and she'd wound up with a guy named Hap, who was stationed in Yorkshire, England through '44. He used to write her about how you couldn't take a leak without noticing in mid-flow that you were copiously defiling some pagan slaughter-stone or medieval torture-tablet. They were so damn brazen about it over there; but here, after crossing half of the Union, it seemed to Susan that there was a great deal less to divert and enlighten the roadside relief-seeker. Sure, every thousand miles or so a guy could take a rest-stop up the side of a cave into which native women and children had once been herded before ravenous dogs were tossed in and the entrance sealed up; and she sampled with her own rear end the restrooms at concessions on the edges of national parks where you could get your picture taken with genuine, sickly, pissed-off Cherokees. It was just, unless you knew the history, there was nothing to tell you about it; while, over in Europe, you couldn't unbutton your pants without seeing a sign saying, Gruesome Site of Whatever – slave-ship X sailed from here, clan Y butchered there,

233

King Z red-hot-pokered-up-the-ass here (ice creams, lunches, and souvenirs). But it seemed to her, after a few days of passing signs that said things like Lindberg: home of Happy Hank's Hemorrhoid Heal-All, that a country with plenty of history you could frighten the kids with had settled for commercial nostalgia instead.

If Ben had been half his usual self this would have got him off on one, but after a whole week he still wasn't even pointing out the newest shaving cream billboards: the kind with a few words of jingle spaced every eighty yards or so on the highway – Don't take this curve/At sixty per/We hate to lose/A customer/BURMA-SHAVE. Ordinarily this kind of stuff would have elicited an excitable spiel from Ben – given a reason to do it, he'd put Interflora ads inside golf holes, the addresses of local cathouses in the bottoms of beer glasses, ads for high-fiber cereal in the pans of motel johns – but he didn't talk about anything much these days. He played the radio in the car, and didn't even gurgle on about his music-for-teenage-kids plan, and how easy it would be for radio or TV stations to start charging record companies to play their records or feature their artists in best-album-of-the-year competitions. His continued silence was worrying to Susan, but she guessed she wasn't the one with a price on her head.

It was a little crazy for them both to break cover and go into the city – not to mention tiring, bookended as it was by two punishing overnight drives – but the libraries and bookstores of the Great Plains only seemed to have artbooks featuring rural scenes, if they had any at all, and she needed to look at pictures of men and women. So they came in through the south, slipped along Lake-shore and parked in back, and she dragged him round the galleries, pointing out differences in whispers as they went, more so as not to incur the censure of the attendants than for reasons of conspiracy.

She stopped him, for example, in front of a pair of civil war plantation owners, dressed up like money and surrounded by stuff you can buy or cheat for.

'See how the guy is bolt upright, even though he's sitting down? Men in portraits are always flush with the frame. But look at his wife here – see how she's leaning? See how she's still kind of vulnerable, even when they're both supposed to be looking all prosperous and fuck-you in their finery? And look at where their eyes are: she looks at him, he looks at the world. Women don't look guys in the eye too much – they look down demurely, or busy themselves with stuff. I saw some dumb mad-scientist brain-switch movie last year, but the actress in it was really good; even with the guy's brain in this blonde bombshell body, he still talked, walked, sat and stood like a guy. And see in this one' – *Beata Beatrix* – 'see the way her back's diagonal to the frame? And Dante and Love are flush?' And so on. It'd always felt like goofing off when Susan came here before – she always suspected that if she wanted to do something cultural and useful she ought to go to a movie, which would at least show her something about people's lives – but it'd turned out kind of useful after all. While they were in the city they dropped by Carson, Pirie, Scott to pick up a big boned corset, and then returned to the theatrical costumiers on West Randolph and Houston who, since they'd often provided useful stuff for the latest phase of Susan's career, she figured might help in her current one. She wasn't wrong.

She didn't have any doubt anymore. It wasn't even a question of getting out. Giotto had been an experiment, she thought now – the Outfit had let him have his head for a while, to see if the kind of things he and Ben came up with could work. Maybe they had worked, maybe they hadn't. Now the Mob who controlled the unions in The City That Works had called time, and time it was; but Susan and Ben had been inside once, and knew where the boss hid the cashbox. This was the only asset they had left in the world: either they used it, she figured, or it had all been for nothing. They could go away with nothing or they could go away with everything. It was as plain as that.

You have to dress for success. You've gotta be clean to be mean. You've gotta be fly or know why – gotta keep it tight. You've gotta have flair to be there, you need spiel for the deal, you need the schtick to be slick, you've got to keep it tight. If you're gonna be alright. Tonite.

Listen to me.

You have to take full responsibility for who you are, accept the obligation to make something of yourself, and believe that success or failure is largely of your own creation. The worth of your life should be judged by what you do: life is about doing, not being, so time and resources must be exploited. There is no level of achievement that justifies giving up on trying to do still more: the horizon must be forever retreating. Life is a serious business, and I don't use the word lightly. You need to be good value to everyone around you; you must be certain of being good and deserving, and you need to maintain friendships, and service them. If you find yourself feeling emotions that don't fit, then you just need a spiritual overhaul, or to work harder at your leisure time. You've got to keep it tight. Listen to me. This is the last testament of a desperate woman. I'm dying here.

I spread the plans over the table one last time and checked them over. We'd meet in an hour, drive downtown, and stake out the place from dawn with Jack and George on the roof of an abattoir two buildings along; from there they could see the entrances and exits, and talk to me via my shortwave radio, which the rest of us will be sitting round in the armored van parked two blocks away.

They'd see the changeover of the guard at eight a.m. – about a dozen, if it was the same as what I counted yesterday – and see the studio lights go on for the photo-shoot. This could be anytime during the day – we don't know when they do it, so we've gotta be ready until they do.

When we saw the arc-lights at the windows, Buddy was just going to walk through the door and down to the vault in the basement. This was the one weak point. This was where I worried we're crazy, but the others were quite sure that all eyes would be on the broad. If we were wrong and he did get challenged, Buddy would just show them the explosive strapped around him and point out that, if they shoot, they're all gonna go sky-high together.

If Buddy made it okay, he'd prime the explosive and go back up the stairs almost to the top, to protect him from the blastwave. Then he'd detonate, and in the confusion generated by the explosion I come in through the window, looking like I expect my cavalry straight behind me. The goons think that too, and when my back-up isn't immediately forthcoming, they grab hold of me; then the rest of my gang come through the door, and the show-down begins. My guys all draw guns, but the mobsters will only need one, on me, the hostage. The wiseguys tell my guys to drop it, but my guys shoot me instead. This blows the knuckleheads away enough to give my crew the upper hand; and they make the wiseguys toss their pieces on the floor, and load the gold into the van with a dozen nine-millimetres locked and loaded on their asses. Then they herd the bad guys into the basement, lock them in, and drive to North Dakota to offload the stuff.

It was only then that the most important thing occurred to me. I didn't want to be left there when I was dead. Hadn't thought about it before; been kind of preoccupied with the thought of getting shot in the head. But now I went out to my potting shed, got a couple of tarps they could wrap me in, and a shovel so they could bury me out on the plains somewhere. And then it didn't matter if I was ready or not, because it was time.

It wasn't till we were parked in the stake-out spot that I began to feel even vaguely panicky about my final business today. It almost surprised me; not because I'd known that things were going to go, more or less, this way for such a long time now, but because everything'd been too busy, too complicated, for me to think any. I'd assumed that things would kind of slow down as I got closer to it – as the gramophone playing the syncopated soundtrack to my life began to wind down – getting lower in tone, thereby assuming a more solemn and monumental air. It hadn't, however, and things had been as crazy as ever. Whether this perpetual distraction had been good or necessary, I didn't know. It'd just been, and for weeks now.

The worst part was when that monkey-trial with Earl was all over the papers and they sent him to County and we thought the whole thing was off. We spent three whole weeks trying to figure a way to do it without being given the distraction of a photo-session at the site, but there wasn't any. So we figured if we were going to do this at all we'd have to find a new target, find a new plan; which meant months of new work, by which time I'd probably be incapacitated, in hospital and in agony, and it would all have been for nothing. But then, four days ago, purely through forlorn chance, Jack heard from Donnie Hood, the *Eyeful* artist, that there was going to be one last shoot. Something extra weird, for extra big money. He'd said that the goons on security detail at that place were all talking about it, looking forward to it like Christmas. And so we were back in business. But when that was back on keel and I could've had some time to myself, Walt came; and I spent the last few days flipped out, and then here we were. No time.

I would've preferred it if things had got grave on me, because now I didn't know how to be. We were all crammed in the van, everyone was nervous so they were all kind of kidding around, we were all smoking up a storm, and I was like, yeah, okay. Okay. It just seemed unlikely today. I looked out the window at a pale blue sky and it was madness that I wasn't going to see it turn orange in the west that night. I scanned the funnies in the paper, and it was crazy that I wasn't going to know how Dick Malone got out of the abandoned mineshaft he just fell into. It got quieter from time to time, and we had to crank down the windows a little to let some of the smoke out, and I tried to look out at one thing alone so that I'd think. And when I could and I did I was thinking about my big brother, and all his friends who went off to the war when I was a kid, and the way all the ones I liked – the ones who didn't use to either ignore me for being a kid or else put a move on me – all those ones died and only the assholes came back, and some dumb line came back to me from something about those who care little for life live long, and those who care lots die, and I was wondering, have I cared? And I was thinking about all these guys behind me and about what my final empire amounted to, and whether I left the movies just so I could get more control and be a bigger fish in a smaller pond or whether there was no meaning to it at all and that things just happen and you can get fucked up along the way, and it seemed to me for a moment that if you're fucked up a little then things in the world are going to fuck you up worse and I knew for a moment, really *knew*, that this was all crazy and it was just the illness getting the worse of a very foolish, fond old woman, but then someone behind started talking about the job, and all I knew was that it was all hooey. We stopped at some lights on the way here, and I saw a little girl with a lollipop in her mouth, but when she pulled it out there was just a frayed white stick. This was going to be the last thing I thought of.

The corset fit over the rubber, and the rubber fit over everything. Cinched in tight, it threw the curves above and below into sharper relief. The black latex hood, contour-stretched over the skull, chin and cheekbones, was only open at the eyes, so false lashes were necessary to pick them out. Susan had never worn them before – no need – and she had to practice applying them a few times before she got it right. The shoes she'd bought were the highest she'd ever seen, but she figured they had to be, to make the feet look smaller, and the body as taut as the rubber stretched over it. A few lessons were necessary to facilitate walking, but, as she pointed out, since cuffed-restraints were going to be a big feature of the shoot, it wasn't going to be too necessary to be note-perfect. As long as the posture and demeanor remained womanly through the obscenely slick latex, she figured the boys would have plenty to keep them happy.

And neither was she wrong. The knuckleheads around the place probably didn't know what to expect – all they'd heard was that there was going to be one final shoot, extreme enough to make the risk worthwhile. They probably could have been forgiven for thinking that this would involve more rather than less nakedness; if they did, then their anticipation of shock was made complete by the insect-shiny form in front of them, tied to an X-shaped rack by bull-hide whips around the wrists and ankles. The ass swelled under the rubber in a grotesque come-on, pushed up and out by the seven-inch heels, and the arch of the spine thus forced accentuated even further the serpentine curve in front.

Even before the action started, every asshole in the room was transfixed. But when the camera was ready to roll, and Joey's brother stood up to explain the morning's work to the gathered mob, the BVM herself could've come through the door in a sequined hootchie-kootchie skirt, and none of the good Catholic boys assembled would've looked away from the rubber and the rack for a second.

'This is one single reel, and we've got to get it right first time. It's going to be called *Let Her Have It*. I need four volunteers. The first guy will go over to the rack, untie the whip from one wrist, then step back and whip her a couple times. Then the second guy unties one of the whips from around her ankle and does the same. Then the third guy and the fourth guy. The kink of the flick is that, even though she's gradually being untied, she stays where she is because she wants it.'

This was something that Ben was really worried about – the pain of the whipping and whether it was necessary. Susan argued that it had to be as extreme as possible, to keep them watching. She didn't tell him, but the idea kind of appealed to her a little, she had to admit.

'Okay?' said Joey's brother. 'Then you, you, you and you. Any questions? Huh? Four strokes each. Hard enough to make a good swish; not hard enough to break the rubber. Maybe the lady'll join you for a cocktail afterward if you manage not to flay her alive. Keep your backs to the camera as much as possible. Put on these eyemasks. Yeah, just like Zorro. Okay, no more kidding around. Let's go.'

And then our guys on the roof saw the girl go in, tottering out of the cab in her heels under the raincoat, and then there was no time for anything anymore. The guys in the van quietened down as Buddy opened the steel trunks, lifted out the explosive, and commenced cinching the webbing around him. Nobody could watch him do it, and, when he was done, we all put on our balaclavas, except for him. He couldn't have anything impairing his sight or hearing, and this somehow made it worse. He wouldn't look at me as he endured the last back-slaps and slipped out of the van. And then there was nothing to do, except maybe to wait for him to come backing out with a dozen guns on him and his finger on the detonator; and if that didn't happen inside the duration of a cigarette, then I'd have ten minutes to live.

*It didn't. Instead, a '38 Chevrolet woody pulled up on the other side of the block, and a gray-faced guy got out, checked the street numbers against a folded-open copy of* Variety, *pulled a fold-up wheelchair out of the trunk, and set it up on the sidewalk by the passenger door.*

*Meanwhile, the whips were going in hard. It was like it must've been in the alley behind the hospital: twenty guys with their eyes bulging, whooping and yelling encouragement at four guys hunched around a writhing, twisting form. Joey Volante, watching from a high window, couldn't help noticing the similarity, having himself participated in a number of gang-bangs, either for business — as a disciplinary measure — or for fun. Giotto's daughter, in back of the hospital, had been both. With a sigh of regret at having to bust up*

242

*such sport, he knotted the rope once around the window frame and fed it through the fireman's winch-belt round his waist. And then he saw the shadow arrive at the opposite window, and then it was time.*

As I opened the door, two windows burst at the far end, and two overalled figures hung suspended on ropes above the racked figure, both with big black .45s in each hand. It threw me as much as the knuckleheads on the floor. Both were wearing gas masks, and both had one gun trained on the mob, and one on each other.

'Everyone face down!' screamed one of the spidermen, and the assholes hit the deck. But the other insect, the bigger of the two, shifted both of his guns to the shiny black figure at the rack.

'Drop the weapons, Kahane, or your bitch takes both barrels.' His voice was flat and firm, and as he hung in the air it seemed that, although the Smith & Wessons were pointed below, his whole consciousness was trained on the figure hanging opposite, waiting for the wrong move.

But the movement came from beneath. The rubber-girl pulled a coiled whip from a belt-hook, and with one swift crack had both the executioner's hands pinioned together; one sharp tug, and the guns fell to the floor. The second spiderman tossed down a gun to the whip-girl, and they both trained them on the disarmed figure. And then the guy in the air with the gun pulled off the gas mask and shook out her long black tresses, and then the rubber-girl pulled off the hood and ran a hand over his short black hair. And then the world gave one mighty shiver, and then the knuckleheads disappeared.

The last ten seconds had been surreal enough for me to believe, for a moment, that the twenty or so cowering gangsters had been the subjects of a vanishing act, and that the girl and the guy hanging on the ropes were about to start doing the flying trapeze. But then my ears popped back out with the shockwave, and I heard the tumult

243

below; and then the dust rose, hugely, and I fell to my knees in sudden, choking darkness.

*'What the fuck?' said Lucy, and Lucky stopped the wheelchair. 'What was that? Gunshot?'*

*'Maybe someone's done me a favor and blown Mantegna to hell,' he said.*

*'How're you planning to bleed him if he's dead,' snapped Lucy, at the end of her tether; and then they both shut up as they watched what looked like a scuba diver crawl out of a skylight and commence hauling on a rope.*

*'Asshole!' Susan screamed, as Ben tore off his spike heels. 'Those weren't fucking Volante's guys! They were out-of-town, like Joey said all along!'*

*'How come they all just got wasted then, huh?'*

*'Wasted my ass,' she spat. 'It was self-defense. There was one of them standing at the door all along, I saw him. Must've pulled a switch. Shit, they blow out the floor and the gold's safe till the bulldozers come. Asshole!' And she went to slap him, but he caught her hand, and then she was crying too hard to do anything.*

Hands locked under my armpits, and wrenched me out into the street. When I could see well enough, through the tearing in my eyes, there was Buddy's blackened face peering anxiously down at me.

'You were only supposed to blow the bloody doors off,' I croaked. But he just hooped his arms under mine again, started dragging me up the street, and then the world really did fall in.

*The gang of crack writers, spilling out of the armored van, had heard the first explosion, but it was nothing compared to what came now. They saw it before they heard it. In one swift instant the warehouse was in front of them; and then it was heaving and surging outward. The walls seemed to flex, grotesquely; but then spoke the thunder, and the walls opened asunder in fifty places, collapsed, and fell. Deafened by the noise, stifled, choked, and blinded by the dust, the writers hid their faces behind their forearms, while the very pavement seemed to roll beneath them. The dust cloud surged between the street and the sky, but some whirlpool effect made it part for a moment, revealing the building's central chimneys, left standing alone like a tower in a whirlwind; but then they too rocked, broke, and hurled themselves down, as though every last brick in the building was intent on burying the gold beneath it deeper.*

The fires were already licking at the rubble by the time I came around. There were a ring of balaclavas bent over me but I couldn't see my explosives expert.

'Where's Buddy?' I said. 'Where is that little shit?'

'She's coming round,' said one, waving his gun at the others. 'Go get the van and let's get the fuck out of here.' The rest ran off, but the guy who'd spoken stayed with me.

'Where's Buddy?' I demanded again, though I couldn't speak too well.

'Fuck knows,' said the guy holding my head.

'Little fuck blew out the floor supports.' It was only then that I registered he'd blown out a lot more besides. 'Ah, shiiiiiit,' I moaned. 'Shit on it.'

'I can still do it,' he said, weighing the gun in his hand. 'Or . . .'

'Or what?' I said, and pushed up my mask.

'Or you can come back west with me,' said Walt, peeling back his mask too.

*The blast hit hardest at street level. The shockwave threw Lucky against a car: since he'd only had two feet to accelerate in, he didn't hit it so hard, but stayed pinned against it for a good ten seconds. Lucy wasn't so lucky. The blast swept up under her wheelchair, threw them both in a high arc across the street. In the moment before she hit the storefront opposite, the tornado sequence from Dorothy's dream flashed through her mind, and she almost laughed out loud.*

★   ★   ★

Up in the air, it was the padding that saved Ben and Susan – his false ass and bosom, her quarterback's shoulders and breastplate. Since they were on top of the roof, they fell rather than were fallen on; so when the second blast came, and the building disappeared from under them, they just dropped thirty feet, and landed on the foam and rubber strapped around them.

No one could agree about the details afterward, but they reached a consensus on the basics. When the writers were all piled back into the van, Jack gunned the engine and spun the wheels as he U-turned, heading back up the street toward the fallen editor. But as the van raced up to the House of Whacks, a heavy figure in a black suit stepped nonchalantly into its path, hands in the pockets of his pants. The only thing Jack could do was wrench on the wheel, and the van tipped up onto two wheels a moment as it shrieked through ninety degrees. But then it righted itself, as its momentum carried it down an alley between two meat-packing warehouses – so when the second blast came and a black flower bloomed in the sky, they were shielded and safe. They screeched to a halt, and sat, too shaken for a moment to talk. But then the moment passed, and they spent a good few minutes arguing about what the guy had looked like, before someone pointed out that they ought to go back and look for their boss. The only thing they could agree on was that he'd had a very fat ass, as though he'd spent most of his life sitting on it in front of a desk.

Lucy knew who it was straightaway. She'd read Dark Hour stories as long as she could remember, and, in her freshman year at high school, had cut out Isadore van Doren's cover mugshot to go with the dozens of others inside her locker. She'd wondered why he never seemed to age in the two decades she'd been reading him, and when she saw him picking his way across the debris now he was the same as he'd ever been.

'Hi,' she croaked.

He turned his head.

Lucky scrambled over the debris, crying out her name. Moans drifted toward him from the rubble and he started toward where the building had been, but *the wind fanned the flames beneath and beat him back. He sat down on the torn-up sidewalk, put his head in his hands and howled. The sound of the wheelchair being clattered across broken stone didn't register until it was almost upon him. He looked up, and saw Lucy standing over him – grimacing, gripping the arm of the chair, her legs sagging beneath her – but standing.*

*'Lucy?' he whispered.*

*'I fell on the same part again,' she said, and then collapsed into his arms.*


*Susan lay on the rubble until she felt the heat underneath and understood that there was fire below. She crawled away then, and Ben crawled after; and then when it was sure enough to stand, they helped each other up and staggered far enough away to collapse in a doorway, and turn to watch the flames. She didn't say anything, because there was nothing much to say. He'd been wrong, and he was an asshole – they both could've died in there, and they'd still come out with nothing. She closed her eyes and let the dark ripples of concussion lap up to the edge of her consciousness.*

'What in hell . . . ?' said Ben.

*Susan lifted her head a little, but the movement drove spikes of pain into her temples. But even as the world faded and she fell back, the smoke seemed to part for a moment, and she caught a glimpse of two guys ambling arm in arm over the rubble toward them.*

*One was young, twenty maybe, but so coated with dust it was hard to tell for sure; the other was twice his age, easily, but as spick as if he were taking a stroll through a park rather than this bomb-crater. The younger was leaning hard on the older man, but though the latter was hardly the picture of health – he had, in addition to a generally untrim aspect, an unconscionably fat ass – they seemed almost to glide over the wreckage.*

*As they drew closer, Susan could hear that they were deep in talk; but just at the point when they were near enough for her to make out what they were saying, they seemed to pause a moment, and then all there was was the wafting roar of the fire. The older one drew a handkerchief from his pocket, and seemed to shake something from it that was carried toward her, floating on the rising heat. Then the smoke billowed up again, and they were gone.*

*The fire was far below, but you didn't have to see it to know it was there. The heat above ground would soon be sufficient to disperse all the remaining players, but underneath it grew intense enough to turn stone back into the stuff it came from. The gold, stacked up in slimy yellow bars, melted long before that; and, bubbling white-hot, ran down through the sewer to the creek under the city, where it boiled off the water, and hissed down to the river; there, it dripped from a storm drain onto the fast-flow below, the cooling droplets urged along by the tide to the lake as they sank. Only then, as the current met the stillness, did the gold reach the bottom, dispersing into the sand where no one could ever steal it again; and then it was lost forever.*

*Ben started up after the disappearing figures, but Susan couldn't summon the energy to tell him it was useless. She lay still, wondering if he'd ever come back, and found that she was easy either way. You do your necessary discoveries when you're alone, she decided; and thought of Alice, who hadn't been without a guy for more than a week since she was in junior high. She was never going to know anything about herself. She'd wake up, early one morning in 1970 or so, and not be able to go back to sleep because she'd think, I don't know who I am. This was going to be her own fault. Susan had always thought she was just going to come upon something – and she'd deserve it, she'd waited forever – and that it would solve and satisfy, and then the rest of her life would start. The only tough part was to find it: the person who could let her be a spy, or a hitman, or a movie star, or a mother. Now, it seemed that she knew something that she'd known for a long time: that it wasn't enough just to find. No one else was going to do what she wanted for her life; she had to do it herself. For the first time in ever she knew that what she was looking for – what she'd wanted all along – wasn't something you found, but something you had to make. When Ben put his arms around her, she put her head on his shoulder and wept.*

\*     \*     \*

And I wept on Walt's shoulder because he'd come to take me away from home, and I was ready to leave now. Finally I was ready to go.

If the shoulder had belonged to someone else, they would've said something smart, and we could've gone out on a laugh. They could've improved on reality. But it wasn't anyone else's shoulder, it was Walt's: the guy who could hold me and make it go away, because he did it every night for ten years. He didn't say anything, but I knew it was time to call in my loyalty. It was time to see where it got me.

So it was that I found that an end – like a start – isn't something you find, but something you have to make. So I made a start, and so I make an end; and so I was brought to life twice, and both times in Chicago.

## A NOTE ON THE AUTHOR

Matthew Branton wrote *The House of Whacks* in Sheffield and London between the ages of 27 and 28. He is also the author of *The Love Parade*.